HOLDING OUT FOR A HERO

Also by Ana Leigh

One Night with a Sweet-talking Man
His Boots Under Her Bed
The Lawman Said "I Do"
The Frasers: Clay

HOLDING OUT FOR A HERO

ANA LEIGH

Pocket Books
New York   London   Toronto   Sydney

Pocket Books
A Division of Simon & Schuster, Inc.
1230 Avenue of the Americas
New York, NY 10020

For information about special discounts for bulk purchases, please contact Simon & Schuster Special Sales at 1-866-506-1949 or business@simonandschuster.com.

The Simon & Schuster Speakers Bureau can bring authors to your live event. For more information or to book an event contact the Simon & Schuster Speakers Bureau at 1-866-248-3049

Cover design by Anna Dorfman; illustration by Aleta Rafton

Manufactured in the United States of America

ISBN-13: 978-1-61523-178-2

I dedicate this book to Don and the celebration of our fifty-sixth wedding anniversary this May.

"—and if God choose,
I shall but love thee better after death."

HOLDING
OUT FOR
A HERO

1

Arizona
1874

As Rico Fraser stuffed extra boxes of cartridges into his saddlebags, he studied Captain Don Masters and the two women who were engaged in conversation nearby. He felt a heated tug at his groin as he focused on the young woman dressed in a yellow gown. A wide-brim white hat restrained the auburn hair that hung past her shoulders, and against the austere background of the fort she looked like a brilliant statue.

A sudden breeze grabbed her hat and sent it soaring, and he smiled as the lilt of her laughter carried to his ears. The sound brought to mind the pleasing tinkle of the vesper chime at the mission where he grew up. Then the warmth in his velvety brown eyes faded, clouded by the memory of his last visit to the mission: the death of Father Chavez, his beloved uncle. He lowered his gaze and tied the strings of his saddlebags.

Masters scurried after the hat as it fluttered along the ground and lodged against Rico's legs. Rico bent down and recovered the hat before it could take flight again, then smacked it across his thigh a couple of times to get rid of the dust.

Grinning, he handed it to the captain. "Best tie it down, Captain, or she'll lose it for sure."

The officer laughed and the men shook hands as the two women joined them. "Rico, these lovely ladies are Miss Andrea Burke and her niece, Miss Jennifer Burke."

Rico doffed his hat. "My pleasure, ladies."

"Rico is our civilian scout," Masters said.

Andrea Burke smiled graciously. "How do you do, Mr. Fraser. Were you raised in this area?"

Rico returned the friendly smile of the pleasant-looking blond woman. "No, ma'am. I was raised in California."

He swung his gaze to the younger woman, meeting her green-eyed stare. *My God, she's gorgeous.* She acknowledged the introduction with a nod but said nothing.

"Where are you off to, Rico?" Masters asked.

"Colonel Hardy's sending me out to find Private Hanson."

"Is the poor soul lost?" Andrea asked.

Masters shook his head. "No, Andrea, Private Hanson abandoned his post and deserted."

"So you're going out to track him down and bring him back for punishment, I suppose." The reprimand had come from Jennifer Burke.

Rico turned his head and encountered her look of disapproval. "I *suppose* so, ma'am."

"But why? You're not army, Mr. Fraser."

"That's what I'm paid to do, Miss Burke."

Their stares remained locked: hers emerald with disgust, his guarded in reflection.

Masters spoke up quickly. "Jenny, if a man deserts his post, it can start an epidemic among the others. We can't let that happen."

Ignoring the captain's explanation, Jennifer said, "So in truth, Mr. Fraser, you're nothing better than a bounty hunter."

The hostile look in her eyes challenged him to refute it. "I wouldn't say that, ma'am. I'm much better at the task than most of them." Rico tipped a finger to his hat. His smirk was a subtle teasing. "Pleasure meeting you ladies."

He nodded to Masters, mounted his horse, and rode away. He didn't look back, but he could feel her green-eyed stare boring into his back right between his shoulder blades.

"Well, Mr. Fraser put you in your place, Jenny," Andrea said.

"Rude and arrogant, isn't he?"

Andrea shook her head. "Honey, I'd say you were the rude one."

Jenny shrugged. "I suppose so, but I can't blame anyone for wanting to get away from this place. I dream of the day I'm old enough to do so without my father sending a bounty hunter after me to bring me back."

"Jennifer Burke, you know that isn't so. Mr. Miles was not a bounty hunter, he was a Pinkerton detective."

"In my eyes, that's no different. He was being paid by my father to bring me back against my will, wasn't he?"

"You were only eighteen years old, Jenny. I don't blame your father; I was as concerned for your welfare as he was."

"I was only trying to find a job to earn the money to go to college. If my father was that concerned about my welfare, why wouldn't he give me the money to do so?"

"Dear, I'm sure Don's not interested in listening to us air our dirty laundry,"

Jenny blushed. "Forgive me, Don. It's impolite of me. But even if Mr. Fraser isn't a bounty hunter, he still appeared to be very arrogant."

"Perhaps with good cause," Don Masters said. "Colonel Hardy claims Rico's the best scout he's ever known."

Andrea's eyes glowed with admiration. "Well, he's certainly the best-*looking* one I've ever seen. Tall, handsome, and did you notice his gorgeous brown eyes, Jenny?"

How could I not? They were warm enough to melt an iceberg, Jenny reflected. "I didn't notice. But I did notice his complexion looked too olive to be Indian, and he was taller and more broad-shouldered than any of the Mexicans I've seen."

Andrea was too wise to swallow her niece's act. Amused, she said, "You noticed all *that,* but not those brown eyes. Or that dark hair, I suppose."

"His mother was Spanish," Don Masters said. "He speaks the language fluently."

"The name Fraser doesn't sound Spanish," Andrea remarked.

"If I remember, Rico said his father was a Virginian who came west shortly after the gold rush." Don clutched a hand dramatically to his heart. "But I'm crushed, Andrea. I had hopes you'd prefer a man with light hair."

Andrea blushed. "And I do. Especially men in the army. Blond hair is so handsome with their blue uniforms. I'm simply looking out for my niece's prospects."

"Your niece can look out for her own prospects, Aunt Andrea," Jenny scoffed. "And it won't be an arrogant bounty hunter." Her gaze swung to where Rico Fraser was just riding out of the gate. Then she opened her parasol and strolled casually away.

Rico dismounted and hunched down to examine the spoor. The hot sun had dried practically all the moisture out of the horse manure, but it sure hadn't diminished the odor. He stood up and stretched the tired muscles of his tall frame.

"This is where he stopped before crossing, Bucep. He can't be more than a few hours ahead of us."

As if to respond, the black stallion flicked its tail.

Rico's gaze swept the distant mesas and canyons of the mountain range, and he shook his head. "The damn fool's riding straight into the Apache stronghold, Bucep, and I'm a bigger fool for following him. But I need the money, and I'm too close on Hanson's heels to stop now."

Remounting, he worked his way down to the riverbank, then reined up when he found what he was looking for in the moist silt: the hoofprints of a horse.

"Looks like this is where he crossed." He patted the horse's neck. "A cool swim should make us both feel better."

His gaze once again swept the mountainous terrain, laden with ponderosa pine, juniper, and piñon. Rays of bright sunlight transformed the rocky ridges and crags into ever-changing colors. Cinnamon became red, red became orange, and orange became gold.

"It sure is a might pretty sight, Bucep, isn't it?" He goaded the horse into the water.

An hour later, driven by the rumble of distant thunder, dark clouds drifted across the sky, shrouding it in gray. Large drops started to splatter down and Rico pulled a poncho from his saddlebag. If the downpour forced Hanson to halt, this might be the break he was looking for.

Within minutes the rain became a torrent, making the granite slopes slippery and treacherous. At nightfall he finally pulled up. He'd get an early start in the morning.

Rico stretched out under the protection of an overhanging ledge, confident that by this time tomorrow he'd be headed back to the fort with Private Hanson. As he chewed on a piece of jerky, he thought about the green eyes of the feisty gal in the yellow dress and how the bright colors matched her spirit.

The next morning, circling buzzards led him to his quarry—whom the Apaches had reached sooner. A dozen arrows protruded from Hanson's slumped body bound to a tree.

Rico shook his head sadly as he cut off the arrows. "Looks like they used the poor fool for target practice, Bucep." After wrapping the body in a blanket, he tied it to the back of his saddle. "Let's get out of here."

Bone-tired, Rico arrived at the fort two days later and faced an angry Colonel Hardy across a desk.

"I'm not paying for any damn blanket you bloodied up. Why in hell didn't you just bury him instead of toting him back here?" Hardy took several puffs from his cigar, then rolled it expertly back to the corner of his mouth.

"You told me to bring him back, sir. Nothing was said about dead or alive."

"The man deserted his post and stole a horse belonging to the United States Army," Hardy declared. "I wish you'd brought the horse back, instead. I've got no sympathy for a man who deserts his post in hostile territory."

"At least he'll have a decent burial now."

"Just the same, I ought to cut this figure in half," Hardy grumbled as he signed the voucher. "Turn this in to Sergeant Levens to get your money."

When Rico got up to leave, Hardy said, "I haven't dismissed you."

"I'll remind you *again* that I don't take orders from you, Colonel Hardy. I'm a civilian scout, not part of your army. And as soon as I cash in this voucher, I'll no longer even be that."

Hardy broke into laughter. "Civilian or not, everyone within the walls of this fort takes orders from me, and you damn well know it. But that's what I like about you, Rico. That doesn't intimidate you." He grinned and picked up his cigar case and offered one to Rico.

"Sit down, son, and relax." He leaned across his desk and lit Rico's cigar, then opened a bottom drawer of his desk and pulled out a bottle of whiskey and two shot glasses.

"We're going to miss you, Rico. You're the best at what you do."

"Thank you, sir. But I think Jake Bedford will do just as good a job for you."

"So where are you headed?"

"I'm going back to California for a short visit with my family. But first, since I've only had about eight hours of sleep in the past four days, I'm going to spend five bucks of this fifty I just earned and soak the trail dust off me, eat the largest steak Maude Evans can dredge up, and then sleep the clock around. Then it's good-bye to Fort Redemption."

Rico swallowed the shot, which hit his empty stomach with a stinging punch. He stood up and set the glass on the desk. "Thanks for the whiskey and smoke, sir."

After cashing in the voucher, Rico led his horse to the stable. "I bet you're as tired as I am, aren't you, Bucep?" he murmured as he rubbed down the horse. After feeding and watering him, he put the horse in a clean stall. "Have a good rest, pal. You've earned it."

He went to the town bathhouse located outside of the gates, and it was all he could do to stay awake as he soaked in a hot tub. Too sleepy to shave, he headed back toward his quarters in the fort and encountered Andrea and Jennifer Burke.

"Good afternoon, ladies."

"What a pleasant surprise. Good afternoon, Mr. Fraser," Andrea said. Jennifer nodded.

"What brings you to town?"

"Actually, we're just on the verge of leaving," Andrea said.

"Andrea, will you come here for a moment?" a man called from a nearby carriage. Rico recognized him as Frank Burke.

"Excuse me." Andrea hurried over to him.

An awkward silence developed between Rico and Jennifer Burke. He was about to excuse himself when she said, "So, Mr. Fraser, did you bring back that soldier you were chasing after?"

"Yes, I did."

"I can't help but feel sorry for him. It seems to me that if he hated it here enough to desert, why not just let him go? What will they do to him now? A public flogging in front of the regiment, or send him to a federal prison for the rest of his life?"

"Actually, they've probably buried him by now, Miss Burke."

Jennifer paled. "You mean you killed him?"

"No, he was dead when I found him. All I did was cut off the dozen Apache arrows in him."

Her shock was evident and left her momentarily speechless. Then she said, "I suppose I owe you an apology, Mr. Fraser."

"Not to me, Miss Burke. To the army, for jumping to conclusions on matters that don't concern you and that you don't understand."

"How rude of you, Mr. Fraser."

Rico's patience snapped. "Fine talk, from a spoiled brat with a nasty tongue."

Her rising anger returned the color to her cheeks. "Now who is jumping to conclusions? You know nothing about me, sir."

"And I have no desire to know more." He tipped his hat. "Good day, Miss Burke."

Andrea returned as he walked away. "Your father said he still has some business in town and won't be returning to the ranch until tomorrow."

"And I'm sure that *business* is Maude Evans," Jenny remarked, still seething over her conversation with Rico Fraser.

"I don't understand why my brother doesn't marry the woman, instead of pretending they're just friends," Andrea said.

"Marry a woman who runs a saloon? You know how much of a snob my father is—or should I say hypocrite? He sees nothing wrong with sneaking around and spending the night with her. But marry her? Heaven forbid. Yet the whole town knows what he's up to."

"He loved your mother very much, honey," Andrea said, in defense of her brother.

"I'm sure he did, but my mother's been dead for twenty years. And Mr. Evans died fifteen years ago. Since then, the two of them have been carrying on this relationship."

Andrea smiled kindly. "A man has needs, honey."

Amused, Jenny replied, "Apparently so does a woman."

Andrea linked an arm through Jenny's. "Well, do you want to remain in town or go home? Stumpy and Charlie are ready to leave."

"So am I." Jenny sighed. "This town is getting too small for my taste."

Andrea gave her a perceptive look. "I gather you and Mr. Fraser crossed swords again."

"*Touché*, Aunt Andrea. Haven't you noticed I'm dripping blood?"

2

An insistent knocking awoke Rico. Drowsily, he staggered to the door and opened it, then stared in surprise at the caller.

"What in hell do you want?" Rico walked back to the bed, sat down, and cradled his head in his hands.

Colonel Hardy stepped in and closed the door, then lit the dim lamp.

"What time is it?" Rico mumbled.

"Six o'clock," Hardy said.

"Dammit, Colonel, I told you I intended to sleep around the clock."

"Rico, I need help."

"You've got the wrong room. Bedford's is next door."

"Rico, have you met Frank Burke?"

Damn, did I have an outraged father to contend with now?

"Not actually. He's the big gun who has that spread north of here on Gila Basin, right?"

"Yes and Burke's ranch was hit at daybreak this morning," Hardy said grimly.

"Apaches! I didn't think they came this close to the fort."

"Not Apaches. Four white men. Burke was in town, and his hands are on a cattle drive to the railroad in Albuquerque. The gang killed Charlie Wells and Stumpy Burton." Hardy shook his head sadly. "Poor old Stumpy. Used to be one of the troopers here at the fort until he got shot in the hip and couldn't ride anymore. Frank gave him a job when the army kicked him out. Stumpy made it into town and told us of the attack before he died."

"What about Burke's daughter and sister?"

"Snatched. If Burke wants to see the women alive again, he'll have to pay, according to the ransom note."

For an instant, the thought punched the breath out of Rico as a vision of Jennifer Burke filled his mind.

"I need you, Rico. You can follow a trail better than anyone I know. Captain Masters is preparing to take a patrol out in pursuit."

Rico shook his head. "You don't need me. Jake Bedford knows what he's doing."

"He does, but he's not the scout you are. I want *you* with them."

"Sorry, sir. I've made other plans."

"I thought you'd be interested in knowing it was the Slatter gang that hit the ranch."

Rico jerked his head up. "What?" He'd been pursuing that gang for years. "How can you be sure?"

"Before Stumpy died he recognized Ben Slatter from the wanted poster, and also heard one of the men call him by name. I know you're trailing the gang, and with the help of the army this is an opportunity to see them captured, tried in a proper court, and hung for their crimes."

Rico snorted derisively. "I knew a sheriff who believed the same as you. He died from a bullet in the back when Slatter's gang escaped from his jail, waiting for that proper court to dole out that justice. Those bastards have left a bloody trail from California to here. Now if you'll excuse me, I have to pack up and get out of here."

Hardy smiled with relief. "I knew I could count on you, Rico."

"I'm not riding out with your patrol, Colonel. I travel alone. And if you intend for a *proper court* to bring Slatter to justice, you better hope your patrol finds them before I do."

"Rico, this is personal to me, too. Burke's a close friend. My wife and I are Jenny's godparents."

"Then you'd better face reality, Colonel. Those two women will be raped and killed before any damn patrol gets near them." Rico went to the door and opened it. "Sorry, I don't have time for any more talk."

Rico quickly dressed. A knock on the door interrupted him as he packed his few belongings into his saddlebags. Rico recognized the caller at once.

Although he had never been introduced to Frank Burke, the rancher was a legend. Burke had moved from Wisconsin to the area twenty-five years earlier, before the fort had been erected, and had succeeded in building the biggest cattle ranch in the area while fighting off Apaches and drifters.

Now, the hard life showed in the gray at his temples and the lines chiseled by wind and sand on his face. But his steel gaze confirmed that he could still hold his own in any fight.

"You Rico Fraser?" the man asked.

"I am, Mr. Burke."

"Then you know what I'm about to ask."

"Afraid so, sir. You have my sympathy, but my answer is the same."

"Tom Hardy claims you could track an ant in a sandstorm. Name your price, Fraser. I'll give it to you if you bring my daughter and sister back."

"I'll tell you what I told Colonel Hardy, sir. I travel alone. And if it's any consolation to you, I intend to kill that murdering bastard, Ben Slatter, when I catch up with him. But I'll be frank, sir: all I can promise you is revenge—it's too late to help your daughter or sister."

Rico felt sorry for the man, but there was no sense in giving him false hope. The women were probably dead already.

Anguish softened the steel gray of Burke's eyes. "You aren't telling me anything I haven't heard before. But I have to find that out for myself. Will you at least let me come with you?"

"I'm doing you a favor and saying no, Mr. Burke. Good-bye, sir."

Rico finished packing up his few belongings. The gang wouldn't be more than half a day ahead of him. This was the closest he had been on their trail in the past three years. This time he would finally catch up with them, and once he got his revenge, he would go back to Fraser Keep in California and join his cousins.

Rico was cleaning his rifle and pistol when another knock on the door interrupted him. "It's unlocked," he shouted, then stared with annoyance at the man who entered.

"I'm going to start selling tickets to this room. And the answer is no, Masters," Rico declared before the captain could say a word. "I travel alone."

"Use some common sense, Rico. You can't take on that whole gang alone," Don Masters said.

"I have a personal issue to settle with Ben Slatter, and I don't intend to let army rules and regulations interfere."

"For God's sake, man, can't you put aside your personal issues to save those women's lives?"

Once again, the thought of Jennifer Burke at the mercilessness of Ben Slatter flashed through Rico's mind. Frustrated, he shouted, "Save their lives! When will you people face reality? Those two women have been raped and killed by now! Do you think that gang would slow themselves down with prisoners?"

"Then why the ransom note?"

"They obviously need money, and know that Burke's got some."

Don pressed on with his argument. "But if they're riding far enough until they feel it's safe to stop, the women might still be alive."

"All the more reason for me to ride alone. The dust a patrol raises is as good as blowing a bugle to announce its arrival."

"But what if only two men go?" Don questioned. "I just had a talk with Colonel Hardy, and he gave me permission to accompany you out of uniform. One man can't take out the entire gang before one of them would have a chance to kill the women. But two men could."

Rico began loading his weapons. The whole damn situation was wearing on his nerves. He took a deep breath and tried to maintain his composure. "Captain Masters, I know that gang; I've been trailing them for three years. Didn't Colonel Hardy tell you that?"

"He only told me you have a grievance against them."

Rico jerked up his head. "Grievance? Yeah, I guess you might say that. They beat me bloody, and then tried to hang me."

"I gave you credit for more intelligence, Rico. You've wasted three years of your life looking for revenge for *that*?"

Frustration had pushed Rico to the limit. He shoved back his chair and bolted to his feet. "Is raping and murdering my mother enough of a grievance?"

For a long moment the captain stared speechless at him. "Oh my God, Rico. I'm sorry. I had no idea."

"I'd appreciate if you'd keep it between us. Only my family knows my motive."

"If that's what you want, I'll respect your wishes. But I think Colonel Hardy would be more sympathetic to your refusal to cooperate if he knew the truth."

Rico's face curved in a wry smile. "Or attempt to stop me."

He looked thoughtfully at Masters. The captain was a good officer, and could prove to be helpful when he caught up with Slatter. But Masters was army, and his hands would be tied by army rules.

"Captain Masters, I'm sure you'd be a big help in any fight, but I have no intention of taking prisoners or returning to this fort."

"What about the reward you'd be entitled to?"

"I'm not interested in the reward—I've told you my reason for hunting them down. What's your motive, Masters? Those were civilians killed, not army. This is a case for the law to handle."

"It's as personal for me as it is for you. I'm in love with Andrea Burke. I intended to ask her to marry me."

The poor bastard. "Believe me, Masters, I'm sorry for you, and it would be better for your sake if you don't go. I'm certain those women are dead by now."

"I won't believe it until I see it for myself. You, of all people, should understand why I must do this. I'll resign from the army if I have to, but I won't stop looking for Andrea until I know for certain she's not alive." He opened the door to leave. "I'll follow you if I have to."

Rico knew if he were in Masters's boots, he'd do the same thing.

"I'm traveling light and I'm not turning back for any reason, Masters. You go at your own risk. I'm not stopping for anything."

"I don't expect you to."

"And if you're wounded or lost, you'll be on your own."

"I understand."

A short time later, Rico reined up in front of Colonel Hardy's office. Don Masters was dressed in civilian clothes and the two men were engaged in conversation.

"Enjoyed doing business with you, Colonel Hardy," Rico said.

"Good luck, Rico." Hardy reached up and shook his hand. "And take care, son," he said to Don. "Those men are merciless."

"I will, sir."

As Hardy watched the two men ride away, a worried Frank Burke came over and joined him.

"You think Fraser can pick up that trail?" Frank asked.

The colonel patted Burke on the shoulder. "If anyone can, Frank, Rico Fraser will."

3

The sun blazed down on them relentlessly. Jenny's throat was parched from thirst and perspiration pooled between her breasts. The rope that tied her hands was rubbing against her wrists, and she tried to no avail to ease the strain on her aching back. She wished she could walk; her legs were numb from gripping the horse to keep from falling off. Yet she feared that once they stopped, Lord only knew what these heartless killers would do to them. Her heart leapt to her throat when she thought about Charlie and Stumpy. She had seen them fall. Had they perished in the attack? She prayed they had survived.

And what of her and Andrea's fate? Her hopes had risen when she'd overheard one of the men tell Slatter that an army patrol was pursuing them. She prayed it reached them before it was too late.

Slatter had forced her to write a ransom note, but there was no denying the lustful gleam in his eyes when he looked at her. If the gang truly intended to hold them for ransom, perhaps their lives would be spared. Or would these madmen ravage and then kill them? The thought of what might lie ahead was horrifying.

Jenny glanced ahead at her aunt, who looked as uncomfortable as she was. As if sensing her stare, her aunt turned her head and looked back at her. Even now, Andrea sent her a game smile. That always had been her aunt's way; she bore aches and pains and any misfortunes with an optimistic spirit.

Jenny tried to smile back, but tears rolled down her cheeks. She wanted to scream aloud, but it would only result in another cuff on the cheek from the leader of these cutthroats.

She closed her eyes and prayed for deliverance.

Jenny suddenly hit the ground, and she lay in a stupor for several seconds before Slatter rode up to her and dismounted.

"What in hell are ya tryin' to do?"

She tried not to cower under his black glare. "I guess I must have fallen asleep."

He yanked her to her feet. "It'll be a long sleep, sister, if ya try that trick again."

"It wasn't a trick. I dozed off and slipped off the horse. I've never been a good rider, and with my hands tied behind my back I'm even worse."

The numbness was wearing off, and it felt like a

thousand needles stabbing her legs and feet. She sank to her knees.

Slatter jerked her upright. "Quit stallin' and get back on that horse." He slapped her on the rear end when she attempted to mount the horse, and she cried out in pain.

"It's gonna hurt a lot more before we're through with ya. Right, boys?" he taunted with a malevolent laugh. Picking her up, he shoved her onto the saddle. "Maybe ya'd like me to kiss it to make it feel better?"

Her emerald eyes seethed with contempt. "Over my dead body."

The men broke into laughter. "Need any help, boss? I'll be glad to give ya a hand," the one called Eddie yelled.

Slatter snorted. "The day ain't dawned when I need a boy to help me with a man's work. Let's get movin'."

"Jenny, are you okay?" Andrea called out.

"Shut your mouth, bitch," Slatter shouted. "I told ya no talkin' to each other."

"May I please have a drink of water?" Jenny asked.

"You'll get one when we stop." Slatter gazed skyward. "The sun'll soon set. I remember a water hole close by. We'll take a chance and pull up there. The horses need the rest."

"A pity you can't manifest some of that sympathy for a human being, Mr. Slatter," Jenny declared.

"What does that mean?" Slatter asked.

"It means you're a merciless animal, sir. Not fit for the human race."

"I'll show ya how fit I am," he roared. She screamed when he jerked her off the horse and dragged her across the ground, heedless of the rocks and rubble. Her skirt snagged on a fallen branch that ripped a hole in the skirt and gashed a bloody scrape to her knee.

"You've been askin' for this, sister. Now you're gonna get it."

Eddie came over to them. "I'm next, boss?" he said, licking his lips when Slatter started to loosen his gun belt.

"You boys hold the bitch's shoulders down," Slatter ordered when Jenny tried to squirm away.

"Are you crazy? We ain't got time for this!" Curly yelled. "There's a goddamn posse on our tail."

"Yeah, you're right." Slatter straightened up and rebuckled his belt. "You ain't gonna be so lucky next time, sister."

Jenny managed to sit up to examine her leg. "My knee is bleeding badly. Will you free my hands so I can clean it?"

Slatter grabbed her by the back of the neck and forced her head down to her bended knee. "Lick it." She tried to turn her head away, but his fingers were like a vise on her neck, pressing her mouth against the wound. She tried to clench her mouth shut, but it was impossible. Laughing, he rubbed her mouth back and forth across the torn flesh. "Don't like the taste? Maybe that'll teach ya to keep your mouth shut." He released her and stomped away. "Put her back on the horse, boys, and let's get movin'."

As the two men lifted her back onto the saddle,

Jenny glanced at Andrea. She knew the tears running down her aunt's cheeks were for her. She realized that she had taken her aunt's lifelong devotion to her for granted, and had not shown enough appreciation for it. She'd never told her she loved her not only as an aunt, but as a friend. Her *only* friend. Somehow, some way, she would tell her before these animals harmed them. Murdered them.

The patrol was their only hope. Was that cocky scout with them? "I'm much better at the task than most." *Now would be the time to prove it, Rico Fraser.*

The sun had set by the time the fleeing gang reached the water hole. Slatter lifted Jenny off her horse and pulled her over to the shade of a tree. "You ain't lookin' so good, sister."

Jenny was so thirsty, her throat felt swollen and she could barely speak. "Please, Mr. Slatter, may I have a drink of water?"

"Hey, Curly, fill a canteen and bring it over here," he ordered. "And take care of the other bitch. We don't want these ladies dyin' of thirst, do we, boys?"

"Her name is Andrea," Jenny declared defiantly.

Slatter shoved her to the ground. "Sit down and keep your mouth shut. Eddie, you see to waterin' the horses. We'll rest here for a few minutes and then get movin'."

Putting her mind toward a way of escaping, Jenny glanced across the clearing to where Andrea was sitting under a tree. Hands tied, kept separated so they couldn't talk to each other, how could they ever plan an escape?

Sighing, she checked her throbbing knee. It had stopped bleeding, but it needed to be cleansed and bandaged. Closing her eyes, she leaned back against the tree.

Where is that patrol? A vision of the tanned face, thick dark hair, and brown velvet of the scout's eyes flashed through her mind more often than she wanted to admit. *Where are you, Rico Fraser?*

Curly handed Slatter the canteen, and after he drank his fill, he held it to her mouth. She couldn't swallow it fast enough and began to choke, which only produced a laugh from the bully. "Thought ya was thirsty," he said.

The water helped to soothe her throat, but no sooner had she begun to feel better than Slatter announced it was time to move on. Wearily, she got to her feet.

Before they could mount up, Kansas arrived on the scene. "I think we lost that patrol, boss. 'Pears we ain't bein' followed no more."

"Ya better be damn sure of that, 'cause if them soldier boys show up here, I'll shoot ya myself."

"I'm tellin' you, Ben, we've lost them. There ain't been a sign of dust behind us for hours. I need a drink."

"Sit yerself back down, sister." Slatter ordered. He and Kansas walked away and joined the Carson brothers.

Despondently, Jenny sank back down and tried to hear what the men were saying as they talked among themselves. If what Kansas said was true, there was no hope for a patrol rescuing them.

Slatter retrieved a bottle of whiskey from his saddlebag, and Jenny watched worriedly as he drank from it as the men argued. Time and again, she heard Curly raise his voice in anger to declare they should keep moving until they reached the town. Kansas agreed. It sounded as if Slatter and Eddie wanted to camp at the water hole.

"Who's runnin' this gang?" Slatter finally shouted. "We stay here for the night."

Jenny braced for the worst when he trudged back with his saddlebags in one hand and the whiskey bottle in the other. Dropping the saddlebags, he sat down and dug out a stick of jerky and began to chew on it.

"You hungry, sister?"

Food was the furthest thing from her mind, but she attempted to stall him. "A little."

He held the jerky to her mouth. "Take a bite of this."

She wanted to gag, but did as he said.

"Tastes better when you wash it down with this." He shoved the whiskey bottle to her mouth, and she had no choice but to swallow. The scalding liquid burned her throat and she started to cough.

Slatter laughed. "Ya ain't much of a drinker, are you, sister?"

"No, I don't drink alcohol."

"Bet a proper lady like you never tasted it before." He took another deep swallow.

"That's not true. If I dislike something, it's because I've tried it before."

" 'Zat right. Ever tried killing a man?"

"Of course not."

"Then how d'ya know if you'd like doin' it or not?"

"If you untie my hands and give me your gun, I'll find out."

He threw back his head in laughter. "I like your spunk. Too bad I'm gonna hafta kill ya when we're through with ya. Wouldn't mind keepin' ya around for a while."

"If you intended to kill us, why did you leave a ransom note?"

"The pickins have been slim lately, and we need some cash. Yer papa's a rich man."

"Then you don't intend to return us to him?"

His chilling laugh sent a shiver down her spine. "No, but once we get the money, I'll let him know where he can find your bodies."

His eyelids were starting to droop from the whiskey. If she could just keep him talking, maybe she could delay the inevitable.

"Would you untie my hands, Mr. Slatter? My wrists are rubbed raw, and my knee needs to be cleansed."

He shifted over and shoved up her skirt. She forced herself not to shudder when his fingers curled around her calf as he examined the cut.

"Reckon it could use a cleaning." He poured some water from the canteen over it.

"Thank you," she said.

"You see, old Ben ain't so bad after all."

"Will you free my wrists?"

Uncertain of his intent, she held her breath when he pulled the knife out of the top of his boot. He reeked of whiskey and body odor, and she turned her head when he leaned across her to cut the rope binding her wrists.

Relieved, she stretched out her arms in front of her. "Oh, thank you."

His cold eyes followed every move as she wet the hem of her skirt and dabbed at her knee. "Waste of time, sister. Ya won't be around much longer, so it ain't gonna matter. Ya shouldn't have made me lose my temper. I didn't want to hurt ya, but I don't take no sass from a woman—'specially in front of my men." He took another deep swallow from the bottle. "They depend on me to look after them."

She pretended to believe him. "I can see that."

"I didn't pick this life," he continued. "I had a nice little spread in California, 'til the bank took it away from me 'cause I couldn't keep up the payments."

"Is that when you turned to a life of crime?"

"Reckon you could say that. My wife died and I lost interest in the place."

"That's unfortunate. What did she die from?" *Revulsion, no doubt.*

Slatter drank from the bottle again. "She stumbled and hit her head against the fireplace."

Stumbled, indeed. More than likely she was shoved, or he banged her head against that fireplace. "How tragic. Do you have any children, Mr. Slatter?"

"No. The woman weren't no good at producin' offspring." The corner of his mouth curled in a salacious smirk. "Bet a gal like you is made for birthin' kids. Havin' you for a wife would drive a man to spend more time in bed then out of it."

She cringed when he reached out and groped her breast. "Yep, these tits of yours are made for a baby— or a man—to be suckin' and lickin'."

She wanted to throw up. She had to change his train of thought, or he'd be on her like the animal he was. "You know, Mr. Slatter, my father won't give you a cent if he has no proof Andrea and I are alive. Now, I could convince him to give you more cash than you asked for."

He tossed the empty bottle away. "Ya must think I'm dumb, sister. Ya think I'm gonna ride up to the front door with ya? He'd have a whole troop of cavalry waitin' for me."

"Then keep me with you, and send a note back with Andrea for him to bring you the money alone. As long as I'm your hostage, my father couldn't call in the cavalry, knowing you'd kill me."

"Yeah, but once he has ya back, the whole United States Cavalry would show up."

"I don't think he'd risk my life trying that trick. And even if he did, you escaped from them before, didn't you? I can't believe you couldn't do it again. Surely the fortune you would get from him would be worth more to you than the satisfaction of raping and killing us."

"That's for sure. There's plenty of bitches in the world for a man to screw. Now you, sweetheart, have got a lot of spunk and fight in ya. I like a woman to fight me when I take her. I figure that aunt of yours is already dead from the neck down. She ain't fought or spoke up since we grabbed ya."

"Of course not. You've threatened her if she did."

Slatter yawned as the whiskey finally took effect. "I threatened you, too, but ya don't pay it no mind." Slatter's words slurred and his eyelids drooped. "Sure ain't shut ya up at all," he mumbled, just before he fell back in a drunken stupor.

For a long moment, Jenny held her breath. Had he really passed out? In the moonlight, she saw that two of the others were stretched out, but Kansas got up and headed over to them. She quickly put her hands behind her back as if they were still bound, and closed her eyes.

"Ben, what do—"

Jenny opened her eyes. "He's asleep. I think he passed out from the whiskey."

Kansas listened to the snores emanating from the drunken sleeper. "Yeah, he drinks himself to sleep every night. When he wakes up, he's meaner than a rattler in the sun."

"Is Andrea all right?" she asked.

"For now. None us dare touch her 'til Ben has her first." He walked away.

For the first time since their abduction, Jenny felt some hope. As soon as Kansas fell asleep, she would free Andrea and they'd try to escape. Even if the attempt failed, they were doomed regardless.

Pretending to sleep, Jenny forced herself not to move.

Patience, Jenny. Just be patient.

4

Don Masters folded his arms across his chest and leaned against a tree as he watched Rico examining a couple of crushed leaves on the ground.

"This is their trail, all right." Rico stood up and gazed thoughtfully toward the west.

"What makes you think a few crushed leaves is their trail?" Don asked. "A wild animal could have crushed those leaves."

"Could have, but didn't." Rico climbed on Bucephalus and rode away.

Don scurried to mount up and follow. "Dammit, Rico, I'm not a child," Masters said when he caught up with him. "Do you mind telling me why you're so certain this is their trail?"

"Those leaves were pressed into the ground. That would take a heavy weight," Rico said.

"Like a horse and rider—is that what you're think-ing?" When Rico nodded, Masters added, "There are some big cats in this area, you know."

Rico shook his head. "A cat is light-footed; it would never disturb those leaves like that. But a shod horse would."

"So would a lumbering bear," Masters argued.

Rico's patience was dwindling quickly. He was used to traveling alone and not explaining his actions to any-one except his horse. "A bear would have eaten the eggs in the quail nest that was nearby, Captain Masters."

"I didn't see any nest."

"Why doesn't that surprise me?" Disgusted, Rico goaded his horse to a faster gait.

"Don't you think we should slow up a little?" Don warned. "At the rate we're traveling, we could thunder into their camp before we even realize it."

"If that's your worry, *you* can slow down. I know what I'm doing."

"I'm sure you do, but logically, this doesn't make sense. It's slower heading higher into the mountains than taking the quicker route to the border. They must know they'd be better off there, because the pa-trol is forbidden to cross into Mexico."

Rico snorted. "Maybe they figured the army would lose the trail in the mountains."

"They had no way of knowing the patrol would lose the trail, so your sarcasm isn't necessary, Rico. I may not be as knowledgeable at following a trail as you, but I do know horses. You'll run them to death if you keep up this pace."

Rico glared at him. "That bastard's not escaping from me this time."

"Then why don't you take the time to think this through thoroughly and weigh *all* the possible options, instead of racing off in a gallop?"

"I'm racing against the sun, Captain. If we can reach them tonight, we might be in time to save the women."

"Then you *do* feel there's hope for them?"

"From dying? Maybe. From being raped? I doubt it."

"At least answer me this," Don said. "At this rate of speed, isn't there the danger of losing the trail?"

"I've figured out they're headed for Perdition."

"From what I've heard of them, I'm sure of it. They deserve to burn in hell."

"I'm referring to the town, Masters."

"I didn't know there was such a town. We never patrol this particular area, and I've never seen it on a map."

Rico slowed the pace. "That's because decent folks don't go near it. It's just a few scattered buildings, no law, and a haven for every outlaw and cutthroat in the territory. Until he gets the ransom, I figure he might hole up there."

"If this town is as bad as you say, Slatter might have more men waiting there."

"I suppose he could, but he never has before. Slatter, the Carson brothers, and Kansas Brody have been riding together for at least the past three years."

"Have you been to Perdition before?"

"Once. I trailed a deserter to it, but he'd already gotten into a fight with one of the locals and died from a knife to his gut. I didn't hang around to claim his corpse." Rico grinned at him. "You still want to continue on, Masters?"

Don's jaw hardened in determination. "More than ever. They've had to keep moving as fast as we have, so I believe the women are still alive or we'd have discovered their bodies."

"Maybe you're catching on after all, Captain Masters."

Perdition was nothing more than a cluster of small terra-cotta–roofed structures and mud huts. Darkness had descended when they reached it. The few people on the street appeared to be Mexican and regarded them with curiosity as they rode into the town.

Spanish was a second language to Rico, but when he'd asked about Slatter, he received only head shakes or shrugs. Nobody claimed to have seen him.

They dismounted in front of the cantina and tied their horses to the hitching post.

"If they're in town, I'd think we'd find a couple of them here," Rico said.

"Do you think you'd recognize any of that gang if you saw them?" Don asked.

"I never forget a face, *amigo*. Especially that of someone who tried to hang me."

"What if they recognize you?" Don asked.

"I doubt they would. It was three years ago, and I wore a mustache down to my chin back then." He rubbed a hand across the dark stubble on his jaw. "I haven't shaved for the past five days, so that helps, too. Remember, I'll do the talking," Rico said, pulling his rifle from the sling.

"You figure on doing it with that Winchester?"

"If I'm lucky enough to find them here."

Rico shoved open the swinging doors and looked around through the haze of tobacco smoke. Five men were playing cards at one of the tables. A half dozen other men were at scattered tables and two more were standing at the bar.

The occupants all glanced up and regarded them with the same curiosity, before returning to their drinks or their card game.

"See any of them?" Don whispered.

Rico gave him a disgruntled glance. "Keep your mouth shut." He moved to the bar and tossed down a gold piece. "Couple beers."

"Whiskey only," the bartender said. He filled a shot glass for each of them, then regarded them through narrowed eyes set closely in a blotched face. "Don't recall seeing you boys before."

"Slatter around?" Rico asked.

"Don't recall the name," the bartender said.

"He's expecting us," Rico said calmly. "Told us to meet him here. We'll wait. And send over a couple plates of steak and potatoes." He picked up the bottle and glasses and moved to a table.

"What do you have in mind now?" Don asked quietly. "Are we going to sit here all night waiting for Slatter to show up?"

"Be quiet and let me think," Rico said. "Just eat fast so we can get out of here."

As soon as they finished their meal, the bartender came over to collect their plates. "Where can we get a room for the night?" Rico asked.

"I've got one upstairs that's open."

"We'll take it. When Slatter shows up, tell him where he can find us. You got a livery in this town?"

"End of the street," the bartender said.

"Any whores around?"

"My wife. She works the rooms when she ain't frying steaks in the kitchen. She'll take you both on at the same time."

Rico wanted to punch the salacious smirk off the bastard's face. "Sure about that? We both like it rough."

"She likes it any way she can get it, boys."

"If she's half as good as she is at cooking, I figure we're all in for a good time. Right, pal?" Rico poked an elbow into Don's ribs. "We'll be back as soon as we take care of our horses."

Outside, Rico started to lead his horse toward the livery, and grinned when the swinging door on the cantina squeaked as they walked away. "Don't turn around, but I think my plan is working. A man at the next table was listening to our conversation. I think we're about to find out where Slatter is."

They entered the deserted livery. A moment later, a lone man slipped through the door.

Rico recognized him as the man who had been in the cantina. "You in charge here?"

"Yeah. I heard you asking about Ben Slatter."

Rico exchanged a quick glance with Masters. "What about him?"

"He ain't coming to town tonight."

"How do you know?"

"I passed his camp earlier. Him and his gang were bedded down for the night."

"Two women with them?" Don asked.

"Looked to be. I only got a quick look. As soon as I saw it was the Slatter gang, I hightailed it out of there as fast as I could. You don't fool around with them boys."

"Where were they?"

"At a water hole about five miles from here."

"Will you take us to it?"

The man snorted. "Not on your life. Them fellas are mean, and they'd kill me for sure if they found out I told you. I've seen Slatter when he was drunk gut a man for just bumping into him. And I've heard what they do to women before they kill them is worse than what a Indian would do."

"We'll pay you if you take us to them," Rico said.

"Money don't do a dead man no good. Are you lawmen?"

"No. We're trying to rescue the women with them," Don interjected.

"I can't help you. I just thought I'd let you know they wouldn't be in town tonight."

Rico burned with desperation. This could be the culmination of his three-year search, and he wasn't going to let it slip through his fingers!

When the stranger turned to leave, Rico grabbed him by the shirt front and slammed him up against the wall.

"Listen, you yellow-belly coward. You're going to show me where to find them or I'll kill you myself."

"All right I'll take you there!" the man cried out.

Rico released him. "Let's go. We're wasting time."

Rico's excitement grew with every heartbeat as they moved through the night. After three years of endless pursuit, he was about to confront the men who raped and murdered his mother.

Finally, he'd be able to resume a normal life. He could return to his cousins in California whom he loved dearly, and most important, he could commit himself to loving a woman and raising a family.

They reined up when they heard a woman scream, and swiftly dismounted. "Get out of here," Rico ordered their guide. He didn't have to tell the man twice; he wheeled his horse and pounded away. Rifles in hand, Rico and Masters approached on foot.

The minutes had passed like hours as Jenny waited to make sure Kansas had fallen asleep before she made an attempt to escape. Without a campfire, the figures on the ground were hard to distinguish, but she knew where Andrea was lying. Slatter's snores continued and her hand was trembling as she leaned over him and cautiously removed the knife from the top of his boot. Then squatting, she stole across the clearing to Andrea and put a hand across the mouth of her sleeping aunt to keep her from crying out in alarm.

Startled, Andrea's eyes popped open. Jenny motioned for her to be silent and quickly cut the rope binding Andrea's hands. Then Andrea's cry of warning came too late.

Slatter grabbed Jenny by the hair and pulled her to her feet. Cursing, he backhanded her with a slap that knocked her to the ground. Andrea leaped at Slatter to pull him away, but the powerful man grabbed her by the throat and started to choke her.

Clutching the knife, Jenny got to her feet and drove it into Slatter's shoulder. His enraged bellow woke the others and they came to his rescue. Releasing Andrea, Slatter reached back and pulled the knife out and then turned his full wrath on Jenny.

She tried to run away, but hands reached out to restrain her as Slatter approached her, knife in hand.

"You treacherous bitch. You're gonna pay for this. Hold her down, boys." Eddie and Curly stretched her out spread-eagled on the ground.

Slatter's eyes gleamed with evil and madness. "You wanted to play with knives, sister, you'll find out what fun it can be. Your daddy's gonna get your parts back in a bag."

"No-o-o!" Andrea screamed, horrified. She tried to come to Jenny's rescue, but Kansas grabbed her.

The sound of a rifle shot split the night, and they all jerked up their heads. Eddie pitched forward, blood flowing from his temple. Slatter and Kansas dove for the nearest cover, but Curly scrambled over to Eddie's body.

"He's dead. My brother's dead!" he shouted, then

keeled over when the shot that followed struck him in the heart.

"It's that damn patrol," Slatter snarled at Kansas. "I oughta shoot you on the spot."

"It ain't the army—they'd have ridden in! It must be bandits after our horses and supplies."

With Kansas and Slatter hunched down behind the protection of a boulder, the two women remained flattened on the ground. Since the two men couldn't reach them or shoot them without exposing themselves, Jenny crawled over to Andrea.

"Were you hit?" she whispered.

"No. Are you okay?" Andrea asked.

"Yes. Now's our chance to escape. Kansas said it's bandits attacking, and they're probably just as bad as Slatter's gang. Let's get out of here and hope they kill each other," Jenny said as bullets continued to fly. "Stay down and follow me."

They crawled away and disappeared into the darkness of the surrounding trees.

5

"Dammit!" Rico swore when he moved into the clearing. If Eddie Carson hadn't been blocking his view, he could have taken out Slatter with his first shot. Masters's shot had killed Curly, but Slatter and Kansas had returned his fire. Now everyone was gone.

Masters had gone after the two women when he saw them crawl away. What condition they were in was hard to tell from a distance, but there hadn't been time to move any closer, because Slatter was about to use a knife on the Burke girl.

He bent down and picked up the knife Slatter had dropped at the outbreak of the fight. There were traces of blood on the blade.

The slight snap of a twig caused him to spin around and he made out the faint outline of an approaching figure, then lowered his rifle.

"Dammit, Masters, I could have shot you. Did you even think of calling out to me?"

"How was I to know it was you until I got closer?" Don asked.

"Any sign of the women?"

"No. It's pitch-black in those trees; I couldn't see a thing. Are Slatter and Kansas dead?"

"No, they got away."

"My God, those animals could stumble on Andrea and Jenny! They'd kill them for sure, now. We've got to find the women before Slatter does."

"You go right ahead, Masters. There's not much that can be done until daylight," Rico said. "Then I'm going after Slatter."

"And the women?"

"Are your problem now."

"But they're probably lost, could even be hurt! Lord knows what those killers might have done to them before we arrived—or will do if they find them."

"You don't need me to get them back to the fort."

"Rico, I need your help right now. There are other dangers out here besides Slatter. Finding them as quickly as possible is critical."

Rico sighed. Deep inside, he'd known his conscience would never let him walk away from the plight of the two women.

"All right. But there's nothing more we can do until daylight, so let's get some sleep. It'll be light in a couple of hours."

*   *   *

After an hour, breathless from their hurried escape through the darkness, Jenny and Andrea paused and leaned against one of the huge boulders that lined the path.

"How does your ankle feel?" Jenny asked.

Andrea slumped to the ground. "It hurts, but I can still walk on it. I'm sorry for twisting it, Jenny. I know I'm slowing us up."

"I think we should try to find a safe place to conceal ourselves until the sun comes up. Then we can take a better look at it," Jenny said.

"Do you have any idea where we are?"

Jenny shook her head and sat down beside her. "I'm just trying to get as far away from that water hole as we can."

"But how can you be sure we're even going in the right direction?"

"Have you ever known me to lose my way? When we reached that water hole, the direction we came from was directly to my back. I never moved from that spot until I crawled over to you." She pointed skyward. "See that shiny star up there? That's the polestar—the North Star. I'm using that as a guide. Once the sun rises, we'll head east."

"We could still miss the fort by miles."

"But once out of these mountains, we're sure to stumble on a ranch or town."

"I hope so," Andrea said. "Then let's find a safe place to hide until morning."

"I guess this is as good a place as any. We'll squeeze in between a couple of these boulders. That will rest your ankle and maybe we can get some sleep."

They managed to wedge in between two of them and cuddled together to stay warm.

Andrea continued to be plagued with doubts. "Jenny, what if that was actually Captain Masters's patrol attacking?"

"I think there would have been more shots fired. I suppose it might have been the scout, Rico Fraser. More than likely he would have been alone." Jenny thought for a long moment, then said, "No, I think it was another bandit gang."

She closed her eyes and was on the verge of drifting to sleep when Andrea said, "If it was Mr. Fraser, do you think he survived the battle? It would have been four against one."

"I don't know. I wasn't about to raise my head to watch what was happening. All I could think of was getting us out of there."

Andrea's voice trembled when she asked, "What if Slatter's still alive and is trailing us?"

"I doubt he'd head back toward the fort. He'd be riding into overwhelming odds against him. Of course, he's insane enough to ignore that."

Andrea shuddered. "Well, if it was Mr. Fraser, I pray he survived."

"I don't think that bounty hunter is easy to kill, or someone would have done so by now." Jenny finally slipped into slumber.

*   *   *

A light sprinkle woke Jenny and Andrea at daylight. "Oh dear, your ankle is badly swollen!" Jenny exclaimed.

"I'm sure I can walk on it." Wincing with pain, Andrea tried to take a few steps.

"You can't travel with that foot. We'll have to stay here until some of that swelling goes down. I'll help you back into the rocks, then I'll try to find us someplace more comfortable. If I'm lucky, maybe I'll find another water hole."

"You aren't going far, are you?"

"No. I'm sure I'll find something nearby, now that it's daylight. Stay concealed until I get back."

"Be careful, Jenny," Andrea said.

"I will. Just stay there and rest your ankle. I'll be back shortly."

Don awoke to discover there had been a mild sprinkle during the night and the ground and leaves on the trees were wet. There was no sign of Rico or his horse, and his first thought was that the scout had left in pursuit of Slatter. He felt overwhelmed with hopelessness. Rico had given him his word that he would help him find the girls, and would have staked his life that the scout would honor it.

He knew his limitations. He was no scout, and his only certainty was that the fort was northeast. Would Andrea and Jenny figure the same and head toward the rising sun? he wondered as he saddled his horse. Perhaps, if he was lucky, he'd find some sign of them.

Damn Rico! Don reflected as he mounted his horse

and headed north, where the women had crawled. How could he desert these two helpless women?

Not even certain of what he was looking for, Don rode along slowly, studying the ground. He dismounted when he saw the faint outline of a footprint in the damp earth. A closer examination proved it was too small to belong to a man. And it had to be fresh or the rain would have washed it away. Now confident he was on the right track, he continued on.

He paused and dismounted in front of some large boulders where the ground showed signs of scuffled prints. The girls must have spent the night here.

"Andrea, Jenny," he called out.

"Don!" a voice cried joyously. Andrea slipped out from between the rocks and, sobbing, she threw her arms around his neck and clung to him. His arms closed around her protectively.

"Where's Jenny?" he asked when her tears subsided.

"She's looking for water and a better place for us to conceal ourselves. I twisted my ankle and can't walk on it."

He sat her down and checked her ankle, "There's no doubt you'll have to stay off that ankle for a couple of days," he said as he got his canteen from the saddle. "As soon as Jenny returns, we'll get out of here. The two of you can ride double on my horse."

"Your horse? Where's your patrol?"

"There is no patrol. I'm alone."

"Then it was you who attacked that gang last night? We thought it was bandits, that's why we ran away."

He grinned. "At least you ran in the right direction.

But I have no idea where we are other than that."

"You mean you're lost, too?" Her disappointment was evident.

"I came with Rico Fraser, the scout I introduced you to last week. But he was gone when I woke up this morning. I assume he went after Slatter and Kansas Brody. They got away last night." Don glanced around nervously. "How long has Jenny been gone?"

"I guess about thirty minutes or so. Do you think Slatter might have followed us?"

"I don't know. I'm not an experienced scout, so I can't read trail signs too well."

"Dear God, what if they find Jenny?"

"I think they'd have headed out of this area. And the sooner we get out of here, too, the better."

"Do you know the way back to the fort?"

"I'm pretty sure I can get us there. If we continue east, we should cross the path—"

The sudden sound of a rifle shot startled them as a bullet shaved a strip of bark off a tree nearest Don. Spooked, his horse bolted away. "Stay down," Don shouted and they crawled toward the cover of the rocks.

"I don't know who you are, mister," a voice called out, "but I want that woman with you."

"That's Slatter," Andrea said. "I'd recognize his voice anywhere."

"Damn! My rifle's on my horse, and a pistol's useless at this distance."

"Did you hear me?" Slatter called out.

"I'm Captain Donald Masters, United States Cavalry," Don shouted. "Lay down your weapon and come out with your hands in the air. My patrol is nearby and your shot will attract their attention."

"You ain't no soldier boy—I seen ya, and you ain't wearin' no uniform. And there ain't no army patrol in this area or I'd of seen it. So hightail it out of here, 'cause I ain't tellin' you again."

Don slipped Andrea his Colt. "As soon as I get up, get back into those rocks and shoot anyone who comes in after you."

"He'll kill you the minute you stand up," she said.

"Andrea, do as I say. Now get going."

"Time's up," Slatter shouted. Several shots whizzed past their heads.

"Okay, okay," Don yelled. "I'll get out of here. How do I know you won't shoot me when I stand up?"

Slatter stepped out in the open and laid his rifle on the ground. "I'm a man of my word, mister."

"This woman said you have partners."

"They're all dead. You got ten seconds to get on your way."

Don stood up and Slatter shouted, "Have a good trip, sucker. And tell the devil Ben Slatter sends his regards."

Kansas's shot from concealment hit Don. He fell to the ground after the second shot.

Andrea crawled over to his fallen body. She emptied the pistol at them, but her shots went wild. Sobbing, she laid her head against Don's chest as Slatter and Kansas approached.

6

Jenny felt a rising panic. Not only had she failed to find food or water, but she had lost her sense of direction.

She took a deep breath as she looked around for the dozenth time. *Don't panic.* She would have sworn she was on the right path; now everything looked alike to her. The trees, the rocks. . . . Why hadn't she paid closer attention to where she was going?

She sank down to the ground. *Think, Jenny. You haven't come that far, so you must be near the spot.*

When she left Andrea she had walked downhill, so she had to go uphill to return. She had already done that. Had she turned right or left?

She jumped to her feet. *Right! I turned right when I reached some dying piñon trees! Find that copse of trees, Jenny. It has to be around here somewhere. And this time mark where you're going.*

Jenny struggled up a bluff that overlooked the immediate area and located the dead trees. Upon reaching them, she found a broken branch, then picked up a rock and drove the stick into the ground. Gathering up some pebbles, she formed an arrow pointing in the direction she was heading, and stuffed several handfuls of them in her pocket for whenever she changed direction. This time she would make certain she wasn't going in circles. With a determined stride she started out again to find Andrea's location.

After about half a mile, certain she was on the wrong track, she reversed her steps to get back to the marker.

She screamed in alarm when a figure stepped out from behind a tree.

"You out for a stroll, Miss Burke?"

"Oh, thank God," she managed to gasp when she recognized Rico Fraser.

"May I ask what you're doing here, ma'am?"

"Looking for some food and water."

"Stay where you are. I'll be right back," he said.

Relieved, she slumped down on the ground and waited for him to return.

She couldn't even find the spot she was looking for in a small area, yet he had succeeded in following their trail all the way from the ranch.

After a few minutes, she began to feel uneasy that he hadn't returned. Surely she would have heard some commotion if he'd been attacked. Should she remain here, or try to find him? She started to rise to her feet when he returned leading his horse, and she sank back down in relief.

"Thank you," she said, when he handed her his canteen. The water was warm, but it felt good going down her throat.

"You'd be wise to sip it slowly," he advised. "Especially on an empty stomach." He handed her a stick of jerky.

"Where's the army patrol?" she asked as she chewed on the jerky.

"There's no patrol."

Jenny stared at him in disbelief. "Then it *was* another gang that attacked us last night."

"No. It was me and Captain Masters."

"Oh, no—was he killed in the gunfight?"

"No. Both of the Carson brothers were killed, but Slatter and Kansas got away. When I woke up this morning I made a quick trip back to Perdition to—"

"Perdition?"

"A nearby town Slatter and his gang had frequented. But there was no sign of them. By the time I got back to the water hole, Masters had left. He's probably out looking for you. Where's your aunt?"

"Hidden. She hurt her ankle and can't walk on it, so I've been looking for a better place for us to hide."

Jenny raised the canteen to her mouth again and Rico saw the condition of her wrists. The bruises on her face were another indication of what she had suffered as Slatter's prisoner.

"You look as if you could use some medical treatment yourself, ma'am."

"My knee could use a cleansing. It was scraped open."

"May I see it?"

She untied the torn strip from around her leg and poured some water over the ugly gash.

Rico examined the wound, then went to his saddle-bags and returned with a few medical supplies. "This is the best I can offer." He knelt down on one knee and began to treat the scrape.

His touch was gentle, and the hand gripping her calf was warm and surprisingly comforting. But surely the tingle that raced up her leg was due to the wound, not the excitement of his touch.

There was compassion in his warm eyes when he met her confused stare. "Take a deep breath, Miss Jennifer, because this is going to sting."

Jenny sucked in her breath when he applied iodine to the open wound, and bit her lip to keep from crying out.

"How did this happen?" he asked.

"I scraped it on a fallen branch," she managed to mutter through drawn gasps.

The stinging gradually subsided as he covered it with gauze, and then ripped another strip off the bottom of her torn gown and tied it around her knee.

"That should hold until you get back to the fort. Now, I suggest we get Miss Andrea and get out of here. I've trailed Slatter and Kansas to this area, and my instinct tells me Masters is somewhere around here, too. I hope to God we meet up with him before they do."

As disheartening as his information was, Jenny couldn't help but feel secure with him. Rico Fraser generated a confidence that she had to admit wasn't arrogance, as she'd once believed. This man was as comfortable in nature as any four-legged creature that roamed it, or one of the mighty pine trees reaching to the sky.

"So you think those outlaws followed us?"

"I know they did. I crossed their trail a time or two. Between their footprints, Masters's, yours, and your aunt's, I thought I was in a parade. And if I was able to find you, so can they. As clever as it was, leaving that marker and arrow in the direction you were going, it can also help *them* pick up your trail."

"I left it for myself so I wouldn't keep walking in circles. But how did you know *I* did it?"

"A man would have used a knife and marked a tree."

Considering she'd had nothing else to use, his criticism was irritating.

"How silly of me. The next time I need to escape from outlaws, I'll remember your advice and ask one of them for a knife.

"Or instead of looking for water and safe concealment, maybe I should just wait for you to come along and find me. As I recall, you said you were better than any other scout."

He chuckled. "I guess I did say that." He grinned and added apologetically, "But you weren't supposed to take me seriously."

His contrite grin soothed her bruised feelings. She

grinned back. "I didn't. I attributed the remark to your vanity, sir."

Amusement flashed in his dark eyes. "And I'll at-tribute your sharp tongue to the fact that you've been through a harrowing experience. So where did you leave your aunt?"

Pride goeth before the fall, Jenny thought woefully. "Well—there's another problem, Mr. Fraser. You see, I don't . . . ah . . . that is to say—I'm . . . lost." She al-most choked on the last word.

He shoved up his hat. "You're what?"

"I can't find where I left her." Humiliated, she lashed out defensively, "Well unlike you, sir, I'm no Daniel Boone."

The sudden sound of a rifle shot ended the discus-sion. Rico shoved her to the ground. "Stay down. I think Slatter might have just located your aunt for us."

"Dear God, do you think he shot her?"

"Either her or Captain Masters." A few more shots rang out, "They must have found Masters." He grabbed his rifle from the sling. "Stay here. I'll come back for you."

"Not on your life. I'm going with you." Jenny fol-lowed him as he raced away.

Andrea's screams led them to the spot. Masters's body lay near to where two men were struggling with her. Fixed on their intentions, the outlaws were un-aware of Rico's approach.

"Hold her arms more steady," Slatter shouted, rip-ping at Andrea's clothing. Suddenly he grabbed at his neck.

"Dammit!" Slatter shouted. "The bitch broke open my wound and it's bleedin' again." He pulled the bandanna from around his neck and started to bind his shoulder with it.

"Stay here and don't make a sound," Rico ordered Jenny. He moved closer and took careful aim. He hit Kansas in the head, and the outlaw slumped over, dead. Rico swung his rifle to take aim on Slatter, who was already running for his horse. His first shot barely missed Slatter, but as the outlaw swung himself into the saddle, Rico's next shot hit him in the leg. Slatter released Kansas's horse and slapped it on the flank and kicked his own mount into a gallop after it.

Rico had already burst from cover and pursued him on foot. He got off another shot on the run, but Slatter had disappeared into the trees. Frustrated, Rico turned back to join the others.

Jenny rushed to Andrea's side and gathered her sobbing aunt in her arms. "Don't come any closer," she called out to Rico. "Find something I can put on her. Her clothes are all ripped."

Rico took off his shirt and tossed it to her, then knelt down to examine Masters. One of the shots had caught him in the upper left shoulder, the other in the fleshy part of his left thigh. Rico put his ear to the captain's chest. "He's still breathing."

Andrea sat up. "He's alive?"

"He is right now." Rico rolled Don's body over and found an exit wound in the shoulder. "It's a clean wound. Looks like the bullet went right through him." An examination of the leg wound was even more encouraging. The bullet had only grazed the thigh, though it was bleeding heavily.

Rico pulled off his bandanna and tied it in a tourniquet around Masters's thigh.

Andrea crawled over as Rico cut away Masters's shirt and used it as a compress on the shoulder wound to slow the bleeding.

"He's lost so much blood," she said. "Do you think he'll survive?"

"Time will tell, ma'am. At least we don't have to dig any lead out of him. We can't move him right now, so I'll have to get my horse. If I'm not back in ten minutes, release that tourniquet on his leg."

"What if Slatter doubles back here while you're gone?" Jenny asked.

"I doubt he'll try. He probably thinks it's the same bandit gang again."

"And if you're wrong and he *does* double back?" Jenny pursued.

He drew his Colt and handed it to her. "You know how to fire a gun, don't you?"

"Of course." She took it from him and Rico started off on a run. "I just can't hit what I aim at," she murmured.

Andrea had been kneeling at Don's side, and she now looked up with a smile. Tears glistening in her eyes. "He's still alive, Jenny. He's still alive."

True to his word, Rico rode back on Bucephalus a short time later, leading another horse. "I found Masters's horse. It hadn't strayed too far."

He dug a flint out of his saddlebags and handed it

to Jenny. "Get a fire going while I take care of Masters. I'll need some hot water."

Jenny looked helplessly at the flint in her hand. "Don't you have any matches? I don't know what to do with this."

"Then I reckon it's time you learn," he said.

"I can do it," Andrea said. "Stumpy taught me how."

Rico pointed to the nearby trees. "I'm sure there's plenty of dry wood over there, Miss Jennifer," he said as he quickly unsaddled the horses and tossed down the saddlebags. "You'll find some jerky and coffee in these, ma'am, and also you ought to find more to wear."

"Thank you, Mr. Fraser," Andrea said.

He grinned at her. "Name's Rico, ma'am. I'd be obliged if you'd call me that."

She smiled at him. "I'd be glad to, Rico. And I'm Andrea."

By the time Jenny returned with an armful of broken branches, Rico had succeeded in reducing the blood flow to a trickle from Masters's wound, and Andrea had found a shirt and pair of jeans in the saddlebags. Andrea quickly got a fire started, and while Rico waited for the water to boil he cut her a length of rope to use as a belt.

Rico was still shirtless. A trail of dark hair tapered from his muscular chest to his flat stomach. Jenny stared with fascination at the play of muscles in his arms and broad shoulders as he lifted Masters and carried him over to the shade of a tree, where Andrea had spread out a blanket. Every motion appeared effortless.

Don still hadn't regained consciousness, and his breathing was ragged by the time Rico finished tending the wounds. He then folded a bandanna into a sling to take the pressure off Don's shoulder and keep him from trying to use his arm.

Andrea remained at Don's side the whole time. "All we can do now is hope for the best," she said when he finished.

"How much water do we have left?" Rico asked as he went to his saddlebags for a shirt.

"We've used up your canteen and Captain Masters's is about half full."

"I know where there's fresh water." He grabbed his rifle and the canteens. "I'll be back within an hour. Don't budge from this spot while I'm gone."

Jenny sighed. "I hope Slatter doesn't turn up here while Daniel Boone is gone."

"Jenny, we all owe Rico a debt of gratitude. He's saved all our lives. They shot Captain Masters; Slatter would have killed you back at that water hole; and those savages would have raped and killed me, if it weren't for him."

"Oh, Aunt Andrea, of course I'm grateful to Mr. Fraser. Immensely grateful. But from the time we met, he's rubbed me the wrong way. And I must say, I think it's much too soon for you and Mr. Fraser to be on a first-name basis. I find it exceedingly improper," she huffed.

Andrea smiled knowingly, but said only, "Don't

you think that under the circumstances, it would be ludicrous to conform to drawing-room propriety?"

"Drawing-room propriety is what keeps us from being animals," Jenny sniffed.

For the first time in days, Jenny saw a twinkle in Andrea's eyes. "Keep up that attitude, honey, and you'll end up an old maid like me."

She turned back to minister to her patient.

7

Jenny had dozed off and woke to discover that not only had Rico returned, but Don Masters had regained consciousness.

"He's so hot, Rico. I think he's running a fever," Andrea said worriedly when Don slipped back into unconsciousness.

"I figured he would, but I don't have anything to give him for it," Rico said.

"May I use some of the water and put a cool compress on his head?"

"Sure, it might make him a little more comfortable."

A short time later, Don regained consciousness again. He attempted to get up, but Rico restrained him.

"Don, please remain still or you'll start those wounds bleeding again," Andrea implored.

Barely able to talk, he said weakly to Rico, "We

should get out of here. We're putting the ladies at risk."

"His three men are dead, and Slatter's too wily to take the chance of coming back alone. Miss Jennifer wounded him with a knife and I put a couple of slugs in him with a rifle, so he's probably dug in somewhere nursing his wounds. He might even be dead."

Andrea glowed with a restored optimism, the terror and hardship of the past two days put behind her. That was so like Andrea, and Jenny envied her aunt for always having that ability to move on.

Although immensely relieved and grateful that Don had survived, she couldn't generate any enthusiasm. They were still in the middle of nowhere with no food or shelter, and dependent upon a man who was no better than a bossy bounty hunter—who was approaching her now with two dead fowl dangling from a piece of rope.

"Now that your nap is over, Miss Burke, perhaps you could dress these quail while I gather more firewood."

She refused to tell him she had barely slept last night due to keeping watch while Andrea rested. "Dress them in what, Mr. Fraser?"

His laugh was as irritating as the smirk that ended it. "Prepare them for cooking, ma'am."

"I'm not stupid, sir; I know what you meant. But we have no pots or pans, utensils or seasonings."

"Just pluck them and gut them," he said impatiently. He shoved the quail and a knife into her hands, climbed on his horse, and rode away.

Jenny stared aghast at the dangling dead birds, and Andrea hobbled over to her. "I'll do it, Jenny." Relieved, Jenny handed the fowl over to her.

The rest of the afternoon passed slowly. Despite Rico's confidence that they had seen the last of Ben Slatter, Jenny was wary that he would suddenly pop out from the trees.

It was dusk by the time Rico finally returned with two sizable stones and his horse loaded down with a pile of wood.

He handed them a handful of nuts from his saddlebags. "Here, these will take the edge off your hunger until the quail is roasted."

He shaved the bark off two of the tree limbs and whittled the ends into a point. Then he slid a bird onto each stake, placed the stones into the rim of the fire, and rested the stakes on the stones to roast the fowls.

"Perhaps you could keep turning them over to keep the meat from burning," he said to Jenny.

"Why, thank you for that advice. It might never have occurred to me," she replied sweetly.

She hadn't fooled him for a minute. "Is there something bothering you?" He appeared too amused to be riled by her attitude.

"Bothering me? Of course not. Just because I've been kidnapped and brutalized by a madman; a friend has been shot and might possibly die; I'm hungry, tired, and need a bath; I'm being pursued by a man who intends to rape and kill me; and I'm dependent upon another who treats me like an idiot . . . why should something be bothering me?"

For an instant she saw a flicker of compassion in his eyes. Or had she imagined it? Because he said, "Trust me, Miss Burke, I know what I'm doing."

"I have to; I have no other option."

He grinned. "And that's what's bothering you the most, isn't it, your ladyship?" He walked away before she could get in the last word.

"See, what did I tell you?" Jenny declared to Andrea. "Isn't he conceited?"

"He's just teasing you, dear," Andrea said.

"Teasing, indeed! Then he's very ill-mannered. I'll be glad when we're no longer under his dominance."

"Right now I'm thankful we are," Andrea said. "Just remember to keep turning those stakes, honey." Her aunt kissed her on the cheek and limped back to the side of her patient.

Deep in thought, Jenny hugged her knees to her chin as she gazed into the fire. Hopefully, if Don was strong enough to travel in the morning, by this time tomorrow they would be back at the fort. It would be too much to hope that she'd be home, where she could sit down at their table and eat a delicious meal cooked by Andrea, and take a hot bath and climb between the clean sheets of her own bed. Funny, how she'd taken such things for granted. Despite her discontentment with living on a ranch, she had to admit that her life—with the exception of never knowing her mother—had been a physically easy one. Her relationship with her father had blinded her to these blessings in her life, for the Lord knew it would be unbearable were it not for Andrea's companionship.

She glanced over to where her aunt was sitting at Don Masters's bedside. Andrea's eyes were closed. Was she sleeping or praying? The poor woman had done little of the first and a lot of the second these past couple days. Although only ten years older, her aunt was more like a mother to her. *Another thing you've always taken for granted, Jenny,* she scolded herself.

"What in hell are you doing?"

Rico rushed to the fire and yanked the burning stakes off the hot stones.

"Good Lord, woman, can't you even do a simple task!" he shouted as he stamped out the flames.

She jumped to her feet. "I'm sorry. I didn't notice the stakes were on fire."

"Of course you didn't, because you weren't paying any attention to them."

She flinched under his scathing glare. "I said I was sorry."

"You should be. Maybe if you ever tried doing something for yourself, your ladyship, you'd appreciate what others do for you."

Experience with her father had taught her well not to cower under male outbursts. She couldn't help smiling at finding herself in the same position with Rico Fraser.

"I *do* appreciate what you've done, but forgive me, Daniel Boone, if I don't find the same pleasure in tramping through the mountains in torn garments, ungroomed, chewing on a stick of jerky, and sleeping under the stars as you appear to do."

He burst into genuine laughter and rubbed his whiskered jaw. If nothing else, he was a good sport, she reflected.

"I probably could use some grooming, but thank you for the flattery, Miss Jenny. I do admire Dan'l Boone's exploits. Rumor has it he preferred his meat raw rather than burnt, too."

Fortunately, Andrea had joined them and checked the meat, and she now said, "It's not as burnt as it looks. I'm sure it's still edible."

"Hallelujah!" Jenny said. "Sorry it's not raw for you to chew on, Dan'l. But if it doesn't satisfy your hunger, try eating your words." She spun on her heel and walked away.

Rico grinned as his gaze followed her, then he turned to Andrea. "That gal's sure got a lot of spunk, hasn't she?"

Smiling, Andrea said, "Spunk and courage. You wouldn't believe how she stood up to Slatter." Her smile faded. "She paid the price for it, too."

Andrea told him briefly what had occurred, and of Slatter's and his gang's treatment of them, then went back to Don Masters.

Rico sliced off a piece of the meat, put it on a tin plate, then cut it up into bite-size pieces. Then he poured a cup of coffee and carried it all over to Jenny, who had sat down under a tree.

"Here you go. It'll taste a lot better than jerky." He

handed her a fork. "Thought you might like to use this."

Jenny accepted them gratefully. "Thank you. Ah, Rico, I'm sorry—"

"No apologies necessary, Princess. Eat it while it's hot." Then he went back to the fire.

The quail was delicious even without any seasoning to enhance it. Jenny picked up the tin cup and finished off the remaining coffee. Dark and strong, it did not have the lighter and satisfying taste of a cup of tea, but she was glad to have it just the same.

She returned to the fire and glanced over to where Andrea was trying to feed Don Masters, who had been in and out of sleep throughout the afternoon. How her aunt could look so blissful as she literally spoon-fed the man was a mystery to Jenny. She swung her gaze to Rico, who was feeding and watering the horses. She saw a smile soften his face as he patted and spoke to his horse as he fed it several handfuls of oats.

The man was a paradox. He treated his horse as if it were a child in his care, yet he could hunt down and kill a man for the bounty. Then she remembered his gentleness when he checked her knee. Remembered the compassion in his beautiful eyes when he dressed the wound. And she remembered the most disturbing thing of all—the excitement of his touch. The memory sent a warm flush through her, and she shifted back from the heat of the fire.

"You treat your horse so well," she said when he returned to the fire and sat down.

"Bucep's my best friend."

"That's an unusual name for a horse. Is it a family name?"

"No, his full name is Bucephalus. That was the name of Alexander the Great's horse. Probably the most famous horse in world history."

"So you see yourself as a world conqueror and the most heroic king of all time, Mr. Fraser?" she teased.

If her knowledge of history surprised him, he concealed it behind a smile. "Not at all, ma'am. I see Bucep as the greatest *horse*. Are you done with the cup, Miss Burke?" he asked, with a nod toward the cup she still held.

When she handed it to him their fingers brushed, and she felt a pleasant tingle from the brief contact. Glancing up in surprise, she saw that he must have felt it too. For a moment their gazes met, then he looked away and filled the cup.

What are you thinking, Rico Fraser? she wondered when he leaned back on one arm, stretched out his long legs, and stared broodingly into the fire as he sipped the coffee.

Deep in thought, Rico stared into the flames. Was Slatter dead? Was the purpose that had driven him for the past three years over? The search finally ended?

He wouldn't believe it until he saw it with his own eyes. Dammit—if only he could have pursued the bastard, he would have found him for sure. Now it would be another three or four days before he'd get back here; by that time the trail would be cold.

But he couldn't abandon the women in these mountains with only a wounded man to protect them. Whether the trail was hot or cold, he wouldn't stop until he knew Slatter was dead.

He raised his head. Andrea had moved over to the fire and was braiding Jenny's hair into a thick plait that hung past her shoulders. He watched as the fire's glow caught the auburn strands and sent shimmering coppery ripples racing up and down it. Andrea tied it with a vine to hold the braid together, then kissed Jenny on the cheek and returned to Masters's bedside.

Rico's fixed gaze swept Jenny's face. The bruises on her cheek failed to diminish her beauty. She was as beautiful as she was feisty. Although spoiled and coddled, her intelligence and spunk attracted him.

Or maybe it's because you just haven't had a woman for a while.

His pursuit of Slatter had driven any thought of a relationship with a woman out of his mind until now.

As he continued to stare at Jenny, Rico felt a rising physical need for her. Maybe once they were back at the fort, he—

What in hell are you thinking! There's no place in the life of a woman like Jennifer Burke for you, until you can put Slatter behind you once and for all.

He stretched out and closed his eyes. He was just tired, and needed to sleep.

Long after Rico fell asleep, Jenny remained huddled at the fire. An evening chill had set in, and she wasn't about to leave the fire's warmth. The men's blankets had been put to use keeping Don warm, and if she drank any more hot coffee to try to stay warm she would surely burst. Jenny threw some more wood on the fire to make certain it didn't die out. She hated to think of what kind of fit *that* would send Rico Fraser into.

Glancing across the flames, her gaze swept the length of him. Once again her thoughts drifted to the memory of his touch, and what it would feel like curled up against the heat of that long, muscular body.

A short time later Andrea came over and sat down beside her. "This fire feels good."

"How is Don doing?"

"Still feverish. He drifts in and out of sleep, but at least he's no longer unconscious."

"If you were smart, Andrea, you'd crawl under that blanket and cuddle up to him. It would be a good way of staying warm."

"I wouldn't think of doing that."

"Why not?"

"It would be improper, missy. Aren't you the one who complained of the impropriety of using first names?"

"Desperate situations call for desperate measures. What if he was shivering? Wouldn't you do it then to warm him?"

"I suppose I would, if it was a matter of life or death."

"Exactly. And one good turn deserves another. If your roles were reversed, I'm sure he would do it for you. I'm cold enough to be tempted to do it myself, just to get under a cover," Jenny said flippantly.

Andrea slipped an arm around her shoulders and hugged her. "That kind of sassy talk doesn't fool me. I've watched you grow up, and under that glib façade of yours lurks a woman yearning to fall in love. Have you and Rico reconciled your differences?"

"My dear Aunt Andrea, there aren't enough seconds in a minute, minutes in an hour, or hours in a day for us to reconcile our differences."

"I don't understand your animosity toward him. If I were your age, I'd be swooning over those dark eyes and long, thick lashes."

"Too much mystery lurks behind them," Jenny replied.

"Well, you can't deny he's a fine specimen of a man."

"He's a specimen, all right. So is an insect," Jenny teased.

"But an insect doesn't have long muscular legs, broad shoulders, a brawny chest, and rippling muscles," Andrea said with a sly glance at her niece. "Rico is downright beautiful."

"Beauty is in the eye of the beholder."

"Come, dear, surely you aren't trying to deny his face is a sculptor's fantasy. High cheekbones and—"

"A stubborn jaw," Jenny said.

"A sensuous mouth—"

"With which he uses to bark orders to everyone."

Andrea gave her niece a stern frown. "A beautiful nose that—"

"He sticks into everyone's business." Her aunt's attempt at matchmaking was so blatant.

Folding her arms across her chest, she declared, "I know what you're trying to do, Aunt Andrea, and it's not going to work. The less I have to do with Rico Fraser, the happier I'll be. And no matter how handsome he is, whenever I fall in love, it certainly won't be with Rico Fraser. I already have one tyrant in my life, and have no desire to live with another one."

"Honey, all men aren't like your father."

"If that's true, why haven't you married?"

"I regret that I haven't, and had children of my own. I guess I never met the right man until—"

"Until now? Is that what you're going to say?"

"What does it matter?" Andrea said. "It's too late now."

"How can you say that? You'd make a perfect wife and mother. You're beautiful in body and soul."

"Honey, I'm a thirty-year-old spinster. An old maid, as some would say. No handsome bachelor like Captain Masters would consider such a choice. A man wants a young woman to bear him sons and daughters. Perhaps I could attract some widower with a passel of children to raise."

"Like my father did to you."

Andrea laughed lightly. "My brother did not have a passel of children. He had one daughter, whom I've grown to cherish as if she were my own."

"And that's always been the problem. You've dedicated your life to me at the sacrifice of your own fulfillment, Aunt Andrea. I'm as much to blame as my father. I've taken the same advantage of you. I needed your love. You're the only mother I've ever known, and I love you dearly."

"I know you do, honey. And I love you more than life itself. So how can you say I've sacrificed?"

"Because now you have the chance to focus on your own happiness instead of someone else's. I've always noticed that Captain Masters is attracted to you. Can't you see that for yourself? Just once in your life, will you shed my interests and consider your own?"

"And what of your father's, Jenny? I was only ten years old when we were orphaned. Sure, he's tyrannical and set in his ways. But even though he married, your father continued to raise me. He saw that I had a home, made me a part of his family. I'm indebted to him. And when the day comes when you leave, he'll be alone—and what will become of him?"

Disgusted, Jenny declared, "You've paid that debt. You came west with him, raised his daughter when his wife died, and you've been his housekeeper and bookkeeper so that he could fulfill his dream: building the biggest ranch in Arizona. So help me, Aunt Andrea, I will *not* stand by another minute and watch you let Don Masters slip through your fingers in order to continue paying back a phantom debt to a self-absorbed man like my father, who considers no one's interests above his own."

Andrea sighed deeply. "Honey, you're exaggerating your father's weaknesses considerably. But speaking of letting an opportunity slip by, you're misjudging Rico Fraser. He's not the egotistical, strong-willed bully you accuse him of being. He's a courageous young man who has risked his life to save us. How can you condemn him?"

Jenny's brow arched in disbelief. "Have you forgotten the man is a bounty hunter? He didn't follow the Slatter gang to rescue us; he followed them for the *reward*. And my father probably offered an extra amount if he brought us back alive. When he chased after that poor soldier who deserted, his price was fifty dollars. Since there's two of us, that would be an extra hundred dollars for Mr. Bounty Hunter. And just what are you smiling about, Aunt Andrea?"

"I think *'the lady doth protest too much.'*"

Jenny threw up her hands in disgust. "And I'll tell you what *I* think, Andrea Burke. I think that pain in your ankle has traveled to your brain, and made you as feverish as Captain Masters. That's what *I* think."

Deep in reflection, Andrea nodded. "Maybe *both* of us protest too much. I think I'll take your suggestion and crawl under that blanket after all. Love you, darlin'." She kissed Jenny on the cheek and limped away.

8

The following morning, the smell of rain hung heavily in the air. The low clouds threatened to dump their burden at any moment, and Rico was impatient to move on.

Still feverish and weak from loss of blood, Don insisted that he was well enough to ride. "Just help me get on the horse."

But as soon as he got to his feet, his knees buckled and he would have fallen were it not for Rico holding him up.

Rico shook his head in exasperation. "It's too dangerous. Have you forgotten how treacherous the terrain is ahead? You don't have the strength to navigate it on horseback—and you sure as hell can't walk."

Rico lowered Don back onto the blanket, and

the two women exchanged surprised stares when he walked away without further discussion.

"I agree that Don's unable to ride, but he certainly could have been a little more gracious about it," Jenny said.

Even Andrea appeared disheartened. "I must say I am disappointed in his attitude."

"I tried to tell you how unpleasant he can be when he doesn't get his own way."

Knowing full well the reason for Rico's irritation, Don came to his defense. "Don't be too harsh on him, ladies. It's important that he catches Slatter. Having to remain with us prevents him from following the outlaw."

"Who's asking him to remain with us?" Jenny retorted. "I'm sure we can take care of ourselves."

"I doubt that," Andrea said. "And I regret my hasty criticism of the man. We're the ones exhibiting ungraciousness. We'd all have been doomed without him. There's little we can do to repay him for it other than show him our respect and cooperation."

"Frankly, I don't think he much cares what we think of him—or anybody thinks of him. He prefers the company of his horse. And right now we're a nuisance to him by preventing him from getting the reward on Slatter's head."

"I'm the one at fault," Don said. "Because I'm unable to travel, he can't leave us. Before I was wounded, we agreed I would get you women safely back to the fort so he could continue on his pursuit of Slatter."

Andrea's face softened into a tender smile. "And

why aren't you able to travel, Captain Masters? Would it be because you were shot defending me?"

"That's beside the point, Andrea. It's no wonder Rico wanted to come on this rescue without me. I made one mistake after another. I should have remained at the water hole yesterday morning until he showed up. Instead I set off on my own, believing he'd gone on in pursuit of Slatter. When I found you—which we all know Rico eventually would have done—I not only left my rifle on the horse when I dismounted, I failed to tether the horse so it couldn't run away. That's why it was able to bolt when the first shots were fired."

"Well, if we're going to point guilty fingers, I could blame myself," Andrea chided. "If I hadn't been so careless as to trip over a rock and twist my ankle, Jenny and I would have been long gone from this spot yesterday morning. Isn't that right, dear?"

Jenny shook her head. "No, not at all. As long as everyone wants to blame themselves, I guess I could say if I hadn't insisted in returning to the ranch, you and I wouldn't have been there when the Slatter gang raided it. Hence Captain Masters would not have been shot, and Daniel Boone most likely would have been off tracking some other miscreant. Isn't *that* right, my dear aunt?" Jenny offered a small smile. "This is all perception on our parts. Now take Mr. Fraser. He's a realist, so he doesn't suffer such anxieties; he's always confident that he's not at fault."

As weak as he was, Don couldn't help chuckling. "And it's been my experience that he's usually right."

"Sad but true." Jenny frowned as she saw Rico piling up fallen tree limbs and boughs that were too long for a campfire. "What is that man up to now?" She hurried away to investigate.

"What do you intend to do with all these branches you're piling up?" Jenny asked when she joined Rico.

"What would *you* do with them?"

"I have no idea. We don't have an ax to chop them up for firewood."

"Really?"

"Sorry I asked, Mr. Know-It-All." She spun on her heel to leave.

"Wait, Jenny. I'm sorry. And I could use your help. Will you bring me that coil of rope hanging on my saddle?" He started to sort through the pile and by the time she returned with the rope, he had cut four narrow tree limbs into poles of equal lengths. Picking up a heavy rock, he drove one of the poles into the ground. Then he stepped off a few feet and drove another one into the ground. By the time he finished anchoring all four poles, they formed a rectangle.

"Now go over and bring back the blanket that Masters is lying on."

"The blanket?" Then it dawned on her what he was doing. "You're building a cot!"

Rico drew in a deep breath. "The blanket, Jenny. Please?"

She strode across the clearing to Andrea.

"Daniel Boone wants the blanket Don is lying on."

"You mean this minute?"

"You better hope so, Aunt Andrea."

"But Don's sleeping. I hate to wake him."

"I'm awake," Don murmured.

"I think Rico's building you a cot," Jenny said.

"He doesn't have to do that. The ground is good enough."

"I'm afraid you'll have to tell him that yourself, because if I go back with that message, he'll kill the messenger."

Laughing, Andrea started to roll Don over carefully. "We can't have that, can we?"

Devilishness danced in Jenny's eyes when they finished extracting the blanket from under Don. "I'm afraid if Rico succeeds in building this cot, it won't hold the both of you tonight." Chuckling, she left them.

As soon as she gave the blanket to Rico, he slit a hole in each corner, looped a hank of rope through each hole, pulled them taut, and tied them to the stakes. When he finished, he climbed on the cot and stretched out. "Jenny, come here and lie down."

She came over and stood at the side of the cot. "It's not wide enough for both of us."

"I'm not testing the width. I want to see how much weight it will hold. Masters has a few pounds on me."

She threw back her head with mockery. "Do you actually believe I would lie down on top of you?"

His eyes challenged her. "Not even for Don's sake? I can't believe this wouldn't be better for him than the cold ground."

"Very well, I'll *sit* down on top of you."

"As you wish," he said, amused.

When Jenny tried to step over his prone body and straddle him, her foot got caught in her gown and she started to fall forward. Rico caught her, preventing the fall, and for the instant of a drawn breath they stared startled into each other's eyes.

Embarrassed, she murmured, "Oh, I'm so sorry."

There was no amusement in his eyes when he whispered, "I'm not, Princess."

He flattened her against the length of his body. Sliding his arms down her back, he looped them lightly across her hips. The contact provoked an excitement she'd never felt before. Pressed against his solid chest, the sensation escalated.

Their gazes locked again, and he recognized the blend of fright and excitement in her emerald eyes. Raw lust surged through him and he tightened his hold on her. Her gasp of shock when he swelled against her excited him more.

"Are you going to release me?"

The breathlessness in the question became more of an inducement than a rejection. He slid a hand to the nape of her neck and drew her head down and covered her mouth with his, devouring it in a hungry kiss he'd been thinking about from the time he'd first looked into those incredible eyes of hers, and every time she had opened her mouth to sass him. Her mouth parted in a sigh of surrender as she closed her eyes and returned the kiss.

He felt the shudder that swept her beneath his fingertips and he slid his hand lower and cupped her rear, pressing her even tighter against him. Her rounded curves cushioned against him felt good. Warm. Soft. He burned to touch her breasts, to taste them.

Breathlessness forced them to break the kiss, and she leaned her cheek against his chest. He buried his head in her hair and thought of the next kiss.

"Let me go, Rico," she murmured when she had regained her breath.

He knew he should apologize, but he feared any words would only lead to an argument. He released her and she got to her feet. Her face was flushed as she looked down at him, but there was neither anger nor friendliness in her eyes.

He stood as well. "I thought you said you didn't know how to start a fire," he teased. "I guess I was wrong, and you're to be congratulated. Jenny, I didn't intend to embarrass you or prove anything. It was spontaneous and got out of hand. But I'm not sorry I did it."

"You shouldn't be. You build a good cot, Dan'l Boone."

Perplexed, he scratched his chin as she walked away. What in hell did she mean by that? He shrugged and returned to his labor.

Both Andrea and Don had dozed off. Jenny wished she could do the same and put the incident with Rico out of her mind, but that was impossible—her feelings were too turbulent.

She sat down and leaned back against the granite wall. What had just happened between them was nothing more than a physical attraction. But no soldier had ever caught her fancy, nor any rancher's son or town merchant. So why did she find Rico Fraser desirable?

She could tell herself that it was because he was heroic. That like the knights of old, he rode out to defend the helpless, to fight the dragons, to rescue fair maidens.

She snorted. When Rico Fraser rode out, it was to collect a reward. She recognized the need to uphold principles like duty, honor, and justice. But pursuing someone for money was reprehensible to her.

So why did his touch excite her to the point of surrender? Knowing he was near, she wanted to be even nearer, to feel the exciting energy he generated. And to her further distress, she wanted to experience the climax of that incredible sensation he had aroused within her. Now it was an unfulfilled desire until he did, and she would have to fight that temptation. The wisest way would be to avoid him whenever possible. Hopefully they could leave this place tomorrow, and once home, she would be rid of him once and for all.

With that firm resolve, Jenny stood up, brushed off her skirt, and walked over to see what he was doing.

Over the cot he had strung a rope around the trunks between four trees, making an approximately six-foot square.

"Don should have some food to help strengthen him, but you said to save the remaining jerky and nuts for the trip home," she said as an excuse for approaching him. She wanted to show it was back to business between them. "What do you think we should do?"

"Eat them. When I finish what I'm doing, I'll try to find some more." He grunted as he lifted a long, leafy tree limb.

"What *are* you doing?"

Once again he was shirtless as he lifted and arranged the heavy branches. He continued to lay the long limbs horizontally across the top of the strung rope until they formed a solid layer.

"I'm building us some cover before it starts to rain. Masters is too feverish to let him get wet." He laid another layer of branches crossways on top of the first one.

"As long as that rope holds we should have a roof over our heads, at least," he said. "I'm going to create the sides next. Meanwhile, could you gather up some smaller branches for a fire later?"

"Certainly."

By the time Jenny returned with her arms full of wood, Rico had propped enough leafy limbs against the roof to close up three sides of the square. Despite the shelter's crudeness, it would keep them dry.

"This is very clever of you, Rico," Jenny said.

"Let's just hope that a strong wind doesn't accompany the rain."

He strung another length of rope between the trees next to the shelter and roofed off a smaller area.

"Are you constructing private quarters for the women?" Jenny asked, very pleased at the idea.

Perspiration covered his brow and his muscular shoulders and chest. "No, your highness, this is for the horses," he replied gruffly. "I don't want to let them stand out in the rain all night. If they get sickly, we'll never get back to that damn fort."

"My, Dan'l, your consideration for everyone is truly commendable." She chanted,

"Of course, of course,
Protect the horse.
Nothing's worse, I'm told,
Than a horse with a cold."

The briefest of grins lit his expression, then he replied,

"Your attempt at rhyme,
Is a waste of time.
Let's get on with this cot,
For a poet you're not."

Her eyes rounded in amusement, and this time his grin was broader. "As soon as I move Masters into this shelter, I'll go hunting. Do you think you could manage to tote his saddle and saddlebags into the shelter while I'm gone?"

"I'll try," she said, returning his sarcasm.

He started to pull her against him with a grin, but she held him at arm's length. "I do not appreciate being mauled by someone dripping with perspiration."

"Princess, you've lived a sheltered life. You don't know what you're miss—"

"Spare me the details, sir."

Jenny left the shelter and Rico followed her over to

Don and Andrea. He lifted Don into his arms, carried him into the shelter, and laid him on the cot.

"This should be more comfortable, Masters."

"It is. I'm sorry to be such a problem. I can't believe what you did here."

"I agree, you're amazing, Rico," Andrea exclaimed. "I wasn't looking forward to getting soaking wet when the rain begins."

Rico wiped off the perspiration and pulled a shirt over his head. "I've got orders to find us something to eat," he said, and hooked the two canteens to the saddle. "Hopefully I'll be back before it starts to rain."

"And I bet I know who issued those orders. Why don't you go with him, Jenny?" Andrea said.

"Sure, come along," Rico said. "It will break up the boredom of your day."

"Or increase it," Jenny declared, unable to suppress her grin.

"Will you be okay until we get back, Andrea?" Rico asked.

"Of course. I have Don's pistol and rifle. If there's a problem, I'll fire the rifle twice."

"And I can sit up and fire a Colt if I have to," Don said.

Rico mounted Bucephalus, reached down a hand and pulled Jenny up in front of him.

"Don't think I'm not wise to what you have in mind, Rico Fraser. Keep your hands to yourself, and do not attempt to kiss me again."

"Miss Jenny, I have only your interests at heart. I could tell you needed something to keep you occupied. Idleness can be as dangerous as any disease or wound. So I want you to enjoy this outing, instead of hoping I'll kiss you."

"Hoping!" She laughed and said, "You do have an amusing imagination, Dan'l. I think I'll enjoy this little outing, after all," and leaned back against him.

9

Andrea gazed worriedly at Don. His eyes were closed and despite his brave front, she knew he was in pain every time he moved. Fear lurked in her heart that the wounds might become infected before they could get him proper medical care. She put a hand to his brow—he still felt feverish. If only they had something to fight it.

When she started to remove her hand, he suddenly reached up and grasped it. "Don't take it away. It feels good."

"I'm sorry I woke you," she said.

"It doesn't matter. I keep drifting in and out of sleep." Disgusted, he said, "This damn fever keeps me weak and useless."

"I was just wishing we had something to give you for it. Since you're awake right now, I'll change your bandages."

"Dare I ask where you got bandages?"

"I cut my petticoat into strips."

As Andrea removed the blood-soaked compresses that covered his wounds, she could feel his gaze. Drawn to it, she stopped what she was doing and looked deeply into his blue eyes. Then she blushed and returned her attention to his wounds.

"Are you aware that everything about you is beautiful, Andrea?" he murmured.

"I fear you're becoming more feverish, Captain Masters." Her light banter disguised the turmoil in her heart.

Andrea poured water onto some cloth and began to sponge his face and neck. His flesh felt hot beneath her fingertips. "Does this make you feel a little better?"

"Not as much as your touch does."

She met his gaze again, and once more her pulses pounded at the look in his eyes. Fearing he would read her thoughts, she turned her head.

"Please don't turn away, Andrea." He reached up and tipped her chin toward him, then he gently caressed her cheek. "Your face is the best medicine I could ever hope for."

Andrea returned breathlessly, " 'Tis said that a patient often falls in love with the woman who nurses him."

Don managed to chuckle. "I already *was* in love with the last woman who nursed me."

His words stabbed at her heart. "Were you wounded in the war?"

"No, I managed to get through that unscathed. It was my mother, my precious Andrea. She nursed me through measles and mumps; she set my broken arm when I fell out of a tree; massaged my aching body after the first time I rode a horse; and she stitched up my leg when I gashed it climbing a neighbor's fence after stealing apples from his tree."

Andrea couldn't believe her ears. Had he really called her "his precious Andrea"? "Is your mother still alive, Don?"

"No, she died shortly after the war ended. My father was a colonel in the army and was killed at Gettysburg. It broke my mother's heart, and she never got over his loss. She told me just before she died that she only stayed alive long enough to make sure I survived the war."

"Oh, Don, how sad. I'm so sorry. Did you choose a military career to please your father?"

"No. I joined because he was my hero. I loved and respected him. He told me a career was *my* choice to make, and said, 'All I ask is that you make sure you're good at it.' "

Don's expression shifted to regret. "He should see me now. Useless and flat on my back from a couple of simple wounds."

"Perhaps the leg wound, but the one to your shoulder is not a *simple* one. I know what damage a rifle blast can do to a body, and Rico said you were fortunate. A couple inches lower and the bullet could have torn your shoulder off. But there doesn't appear to be any internal damage; it was a clean wound. It's the fever and loss of blood that's keeping you flat on your back."

Drowsiness had returned to overtake him, for he closed his eyes as he clasped her hand. "But I have a good nurse to care for me," he murmured before he drifted back to sleep.

For a long time Andrea gazed lovingly at the sleeping man. Then she raised their clasped hands to her lips and pressed a kiss on his.

"I love you, Captain Donald Masters," she whispered tenderly. Dare she hope he felt the same about her, or were his words merely said in feverish gratitude? No matter, she would remember these moments for the rest of her life.

"Enjoying the outing, Princess?" Rico asked as they rode through a wooded area. He had tried a new direction and had come upon a lush, grassy tableland abounding with leafy oak, mountain laurel, and sweet-smelling pine trees. Patches of wildflowers and bushy shrubs convinced him there was a source of water nearby. If it was a stream, it might be a source of fish.

"It's so beautiful here," Jenny exclaimed. "And it's a pleasure to relax and not fear having to hide from pursuers. I hope you won't spoil it by making physical advances toward me."

"I said I wouldn't. But maybe you came because you hoped I *would.*"

"Don't be ridiculous. I came out of boredom," she scoffed.

He chuckled. "Whatever you say, Princess. But I'm

only here to find us some food and water." He reined up. "And I think I might have found what I'm looking for." Sliding off the back of the horse, he lifted her down and then walked over to two boulders set in a particularly green area. Water poured through a narrow gap between the rocks like a fountain and flowed into a stream. And silver streaks flashed back and forth in the water.

"Mountain trout," he told Jenny. "We're going to have fresh fish for dinner today, Princess. Could you gather up some of those chestnuts over there while I catch us some fish?"

"As you wish, Dan'l," she said lightly.

Within moments, Rico had carved a limb into a spear and waded into the stream. Jenny began gathering nuts. After stuffing several handfuls of them into his saddlebag, she decided it was enough—this opportunity was too good to waste. She ducked behind a bush, pulled off her gown and removed all her underclothes. Then she put her gown back on and gathered up the undergarments. So as not to disrupt Rico, who was standing ankle deep in the water spearing fish, she went a little farther downstream.

When she finished washing her underclothes, she spread them out on some bushes to dry.

"How are you doing?" she called to Rico.

"Good. A couple more and we'll have enough for a meal tonight."

Jenny began picking wildflowers, then sat down to make a bouquet. Rico soon joined her carrying six trout strung on a vine. He glanced at her clothing stretched out on the bushes.

"What happened? Did you fall in?"

"No, I washed my underclothes."

"*You* washed them! How did you manage to do that without Andrea?"

His remark irritated her, but she held back a retort. "Rico, will you cut off a piece of this vine so I can tie these flowers together?"

He did so and handed it to her. "What do you intend to do with those flowers?"

"I thought they might cheer up Captain Masters."

He snorted. "I think a dose of quinine would be a better cure."

Rico's mockery struck a nerve. "Must you spoil this day by making an issue about a few wildflowers? Is it truly that disturbing to you, or are you just trying to start an argument again?"

"What's disturbing me is knowing you have nothing on under your gown, Miss Jenny. It makes a man forget his good intentions."

His grin showed that his bad humor had passed, and she relaxed, and smiled back.

"Since you pride yourself on being a man of your word, I'm sure you have the willpower to suppress whatever thoughts may have entered your head."

"I'm trying, but you sure can jumble a man's brain, Jenny."

She raised the bouquet to her nose and drew in a deep breath of the sweet fragrance, unconscious of how the feminine gesture only added to his mounting desire for her.

"Don't you like the scent of flowers, Rico?"

"Sure."

"Then why are you frowning?"

"I believe flowers should remain where they grow. Once they're picked they wither, and their beauty and life is destroyed."

Jenny raised an eyebrow and glanced at the fish flopping on the ground beside him. "Just like those fish? Or the quail you shot yesterday? And the cattle my father raises to be driven to slaughterhouses? How does that differ from picking a flower?"

"Eating is necessary to our survival. Flowers are not."

"I disagree. I believe beauty in all its forms is necessary to life, as well. And new flowers will grow to replace those that are picked—just as new animals will replace those we eat."

She changed the subject. "Where did you grow up, Rico?"

"I was raised in a Catholic mission in California— *El Misión de La Dueña de Esperanza.*" The name rolled off his tongue melodically.

"What a lovely name. What does it mean?"

"The Mission of the Lady of Hope. Legend has it that a young Indian girl saved some missionary priests from being slaughtered by the Indians. In gratitude, the priests built the mission and named it in her honor."

"So you were raised in a mission. Were you orphaned at an early age?"

"No, my mother was the housekeeper there. My uncle, Father Chavez, was in charge of the mission."

Jenny marveled at the change in his expression. The tenderness in his eyes made him so handsome.

"And what about your father?"

"He died before I was born, so I never knew him."

"I never knew my mother, either. She died giving birth to me. Were you happy as a child, Rico?"

"I was. There were times I yearned for a father, but Father Chavez was a kind and loving man, and he tried to fill the gap."

Jenny nodded. "That's how I feel about Andrea. She's always been more than an aunt; she was the mother I turned to."

"I guess we were both lucky to have them in our lives."

A distant rumble of thunder reminded Rico of the approaching storm. "We'd better get back to camp before the rain starts."

Jenny lost her balance when she rose to her feet and fell against him, their mouths so close their breaths mingled. His gaze shifted from her parted lips to her eyes, and for a breathless moment he read the anticipation in their emerald depths.

"Like I said, Miss Jenny—you make it hard for a man to remember his good intentions." He released her and turned away.

Shaken, Jenny quickly gathered up her clothing. She had wanted him to kiss her, and was annoyed at herself. Fearing he had guessed her mounting attraction to him, she was too mortified to even look at him when she handed him the wet clothing.

He silently tied the string of fish to the saddle, then stuffed her clothes into one of the saddlebags. Grabbing the canteens, he hurried back to the stream to fill them.

"What the hell?" Rico murmured, as he stared at the ground. He squatted down for a closer look.

"What is it, Rico?" Jenny asked.

"These are horse tracks. Quite a number of them. And fairly recent."

"Maybe they're from wild horses?"

He shook his head. "No, the horses were shod." Standing, he grabbed his rifle from the sling. "Stay here."

He walked around until he found another sign to examine, and gazed thoughtfully in that direction for a moment before hurrying back to Jenny. "Let's get out of here."

They reached the campsite just as large raindrops began to fall. Rico made quick work of getting Bucephalus into the lean-to where Andrea had already staked Don's horse.

Then he entered their shelter and dumped his saddle and saddlebags in the corner and glanced at the pile of wood stacked neatly at the foot of the cot.

"It was wise to bring the wood in here to keep it dry, Andrea."

"I didn't build a fire because I wasn't certain where

you wanted it," she said. "You built a good house, Rico. It's not even leaking in here."

He laughed. "Let's hope it doesn't rain any harder, or it soon will be."

"All that wood certainly takes up a lot of space," Jenny complained. "There's no space to move. We'll have to crawl over each other to get in or out."

"That won't matter, because I'm building the fire at the entrance," Rico said. "At least we'll stay warm tonight."

"I had hopes of spreading out my clothes to dry." Jenny sighed. "After being stuffed into the saddlebag, they'll be totally wrinkled. I just didn't think about that rain."

"Just like those flowers you picked for Captain Masters?" Rico snorted.

"Oh, dear! That's right, I left them behind. But there's no need to be so nasty. You're the one who wanted to leave in such a hurry!"

With her usual efficiency, Andrea already had set about scaling and boning the fish. "If you want my opinion, what there definitely *isn't* room for in here is the two of you sniping at each other. Don't you agree, Don?"

Don tried to chuckle. "I figure all that hot air should help keep us dry until Rico gets a fire going, sweetheart."

The term of endearment caused Jenny and Rico to glance at him in surprise as Andrea calmly wrapped the pieces of fish in leaves Rico had brought back.

When he went out to feed the horses, Andrea

asked Jenny, "What happened between you two today?"

"Nothing. I think he's upset because he saw some horse tracks when we were leaving."

"I can understand that." Andrea looked serious. "I hope it's safe to have a fire tonight." Her worried gaze went to Don.

10

Rico returned a short time later carrying several more branches. He shook them out as best he could and brought them inside.

"We'll have a huge fire tonight!" Jenny exclaimed.

"These aren't for the fire."

Jenny exchanged a puzzled look with Andrea, but chose not to pursue it any further. She'd come to recognize when it was wiser not to intrude on Rico's thoughts.

"The fish is ready," Andrea said.

The meal of fish and roasted nuts was filling, and despite the dampness, the fire had heated the shelter to coziness. Jenny looked forward to a much warmer night's rest tonight.

When they had settled in for the night, Rico spread the fire across the whole entrance to thwart anything or anyone from entering. Then he sat down next to Don's cot.

"It's not safe to stay here any longer," he said softly so as not to alarm the women. "I saw some recent horse tracks at the stream today."

"You figure they're Slatter's?" Don asked.

"No. It looked like at least five or six shod horses, so I'm ruling out Indians, too."

"I doubt it's an army patrol," Don said. "If Colonel Hardy sent out a patrol to back us up against the Slatter gang, it would have been at least twelve men."

Rico nodded. "That's what I was thinking, too. So I figure it must be bandits."

"Dammit! We get rid of the Slatter gang and another one shows up."

"I can't hunt for food or water and leave you all unprotected, so we'll get out of here in the morning."

"You're right. If I can't get on a horse tomorrow, leave with the women and I'll stay hidden for a couple days. By then I should be able to make it out of here on my own."

Rico shook his head. "You need medical attention, food, and water. Without it, you'd be dead by the time I got back here. And if anyone spots this shelter, they're sure to check it out.

"I got those new branches for a travois. In the morning I'll break down this shelter to get the ropes, and tie a blanket to the poles. It'll be a little bumpy for you, but we can get you out that way."

"God, Rico, no wonder you wanted to come alone. You said if I was wounded or lost I'd be on my own, and I don't want to slow you up any more than I have already."

"My mind's made up, so save your breath, Masters."

"I know you want to go after Slatter. This will delay you more."

"I'll still find him. And if he's not dead, I'll kill that murdering bastard."

Rico was unaware he'd raised his voice at the end. Jenny glanced at Andrea and saw her aunt had overheard his last words, too.

The hatred and grim determination in his voice was a painful reminder of how much she abhorred what he did for a living, and her heart ached. No matter how much she quarreled with him, she couldn't deny this magnetism between them. It was a desire they had shared the first time they looked into each other's eyes.

But she couldn't let herself care for a man who didn't hesitate to kill for money, so she had to face reality. She could not give in to this temptation.

Jenny glanced at Andrea and saw the look of compassion in her eyes. Her aunt had finally come to realize it too.

With a muted sob Jenny whispered, "Do you believe me now, Aunt Andrea? Perhaps you'll get over those romantic notions you've been harboring. Rico Fraser's only interest in me is the reward on my head—the same as he is in Slatter's."

Andrea clasped her hand and squeezed it.

Rico returned to the fire and began to shave the

leaves off the poles and toss them into the fire. He said nothing to them about tomorrow's plans. Andrea shifted over to Don's bedside and Jenny curled up in the corner, listening to the rain and watching Rico until she fell asleep.

She awoke during the night and discovered the rain had stopped and the shelter had withstood the storm. Rico was still sitting up at the fire with rifle in hand, a silent sentinel on duty.

As if sensing her stare, he turned his head and looked at her. In the fire's flickering light his somber expression changed to one of wistfulness.

Or had she imagined it?

Jenny woke up to bright sunlight and the smell of brewing coffee to discover the shelter had been stripped down. Not only was she alone, even the cot was gone. She saw Andrea over near the rocks where a small campfire was burning. Jenny joined her and poured herself a cup of coffee from the pot set in the embers.

"Good morning. What's going on?"

"Good morning, honey. We're getting ready to leave. Here's the last of the jerky; you should eat it before we go. Then finish your coffee and give me the cup."

"You mean Don's well enough to ride?"

"Rico built him a travois."

As if on cue, Rico appeared leading Don's horse. Trailing behind it, Don lay on the simple conveyance. The two long poles that formed the shafts of the travois were tied to the saddle and elevated slightly to keep his upper torso from lying flat. Rico had tied shorter poles crosswise to the shafts to form a base to support Don's weight and padded it with a blanket to make it a little less uncomfortable.

"Daniel Boone, you have saved the day again," Jenny said.

"Or what's left of it, Princess. I thought you would never get up, and Andrea wouldn't let me wake you. Do you prefer to ride double with her or me?"

"That question is too silly to answer, Dan'l." She started to mount Don's horse.

"I'm flattered, Princess—I'm riding that horse, too."

"You aren't riding Bucephalus?" she said, lowering her foot to the ground.

"No, I need to control the horse pulling the travois. You and Andrea will ride Bucep."

"I'm surprised you let anyone else ride your horse."

"It's normally just the opposite: Bucep doesn't allow anyone else but me to ride him. But I had a long talk with him so it shouldn't be a problem. Bucep's very understanding."

Jenny smiled despite herself. Why did he have to be so darned amusing? "Does he ever talk back to you?"

"Not as much as you do," Rico replied, with a return grin.

Andrea mounted Bucephalus, and Rico lifted Jenny up behind her. "Your legs are much shorter than mine, Andrea; how do those stirrups feel?" he asked, tightening them.

"That feels fine now, Rico."

"Then let's get out of here." He swung up on the back of the other horse and started to ride on. Bucephalus didn't budge. Rico turned his head and whistled lightly, and the horse started to follow.

"I thought that you understood this arrangement, Bucephalus. It sure doesn't look like it to me," Jenny grumbled.

By noon, the heat bore down on them relentlessly as they slowly wound their way down the rugged terrain.

"I don't remember coming this way before," Jenny said to Andrea, looking around in confusion.

"We didn't. Remember, we just ran to get away from Slatter. I'm sure Rico knows how to get us back."

"Well, I'm uncomfortable from riding. I think I'll walk awhile."

"I will, too. It will give me a chance to see how Don is doing."

"You can see how he's doing; we're looking right at him," Jenny said. "You should stay off your ankle and let it heal."

"Maybe so, but I'm getting used to it. So there's no sense in having a sore rear end too," she said lightly.

Andrea reined up and they dismounted, then walked up to the travois. Don was awake.

"Are you feeling any better?" Andrea asked.

"Don't worry, I'm fine," he said. "How is your ankle?"

"Getting better." She put a hand on his brow.

"Don't lie to me, Captain Masters. You're still fever-ish. I wish we had a way of cooling you off." She put the canteen to his mouth. "Drink a little water. Maybe it will help."

"Thanks, sweetheart," he said when he finished. "How much farther to the fort?"

"Rico told me that if we get out of this rough ter-rain before sunset, we could push on and get to the fort around midnight. If not, we can get an early start at daybreak and make it there by noon tomorrow.

"You must be feeling every bump on this trail. I hope none of your wounds break open," she said wor-riedly.

"I'm fine, but what about you? You shouldn't be walking with a sore ankle."

"It feels a lot better than it did, so I wanted to stretch my legs."

He chuckled. "And start it hurting again."

They came to a tree line that offered some shade and Rico pulled into it. "Good place to rest the horses," he said.

"Are you familiar with this area, Rico?" Jenny asked.

"I tracked a man up this way last year. That's how I discovered Perdition." He handed her a canteen. "Sorry I can't offer you anything to eat."

"I'm not hungry. All I can think about is getting back to the fort."

"Tell you what. Tomorrow I'll buy you the biggest steak in town."

"With a fresh green salad and baked potato?"

"And a piece of apple pie to top it off." Laughter showed in his eyes. "What about it, Jenny? Is it a date?"

"The thought is tempting, Dan'l, but I have great expectations of being home by this time tomorrow. Not in town."

"I think you're in for a disappointment, unless you intend to leave Andrea behind." He nodded toward the travois, where the couple were holding hands. "She won't leave him until she knows for certain he'll pull through."

Grimacing, Jenny nodded. "You're right, I forgot about that. I'd like to know how two people can fall so madly in love in such a short time."

"Jenny, why do you think Masters volunteered for this job?"

"I hadn't really thought about it. I suppose because he's an officer and a gentleman."

"He's army, all right, so why wouldn't he have come with a patrol, in uniform? You're confident my motive was mercenary, but what was his?"

"What are you trying to say?"

"It should be pretty obvious that he had a deeper motive for volunteering for this mission." He got up and went over to water the horses.

Jenny sat for a moment, then glanced again at the couple deep in conversation. She jumped to her feet and rushed over to Rico.

"Did Don tell you he's in love with her? Is that it?"

"You'll have to ask him yourself."

"That's got to be it!" she exclaimed, and clutched his

arm in enthusiasm. "That's wonderful! Andrea thought he'd never be interested in a woman her age, and that his affection now was only due to gratitude."

"I'll never understand women. Why would one as lovely as Andrea think a man wouldn't desire her for a wife?"

Suddenly Rico's attention was distracted by Bucephalus, whose ears were pricked up alertly.

"What is it?" Jenny asked in a hushed voice.

"I don't know. Think I'll take a quick look around. Take Bucep with you and go join the others. Stay down and be quiet." He grabbed his rifle, and pulled Don's pistol out of the saddlebags. "Give this to Don just in case."

Jenny told them Rico's instructions and they quietly awaited his return.

In a short time, Rico came hurrying back. "Let's get out of here fast."

"What is it, Rico?" Don asked.

"There are six riders nearby. I remember seeing a couple of them in that barroom in Perdition. I don't know if they're following us, but we've got to get off this trail. There's a coach trail about a half mile from here, and once we reach it we can make better time. Trouble is, getting to it is going to be pretty rough on that travois, because the trail's practically straight downhill all the way. You'll be jostled around much worse than up to now, Don, and we'll be lucky if the damn travois holds together."

"We won't know until we try, so let's get going," Don said.

"It'll be wiser to lead the horses, rather than ride them."

"You won't get any argument from me on that," Jenny said.

Rico managed a wry smile. "It could be they aren't even after us, or probably they wouldn't have stopped. But we don't dare take any chances, so be as quiet as possible."

Rico hadn't exaggerated the difficulty. They struggled to keep their pace slow and the horses reined in. At times, the animals skidded and almost tumbled over. Fortunately, the damp ground helped to slow the descent. Still, Rico had all he could do to keep the army horse from losing its footing. Andrea and Jenny each held a rein on one side of Bucephalus and were straining to keep the animal's head up.

After about a quarter mile, Rico told them, "Let him go. He'll do better on his own."

The women released the horse's reins and Bucephalus continued down without their guidance. As they continued down, they tried to steady the travois to keep it from tipping over and dumping Don off.

By the time they reached the bottom, they were exhausted and splattered with mud, but the travois had held together and the horses had made it down without mishap.

Jenny slumped to the ground, and Andrea staggered over to make sure Don had made it without damage to his wounds. Rico took time to catch his breath, then began to check the legs and shoes of both horses.

Glancing down at her torn, mud-splattered gown, Jenny said, "It will give me great joy to burn this gown when we get home."

"I thought you might want to launder it and hang it up to show your grandchildren one day," Andrea teased.

"No, thank you. The sooner I put this all behind me, the happier I'll be."

"I never want to forget it," Don said weakly. He reached for Andrea's hand. "I can't wait for the day we can tell *our* grandchildren about it."

Andrea blushed and put a hand on his brow. "I'm afraid he's delirious."

"I know everyone is exhausted, but let's get moving," Rico said. "If that gang spots us, they're as capable of getting down that mountain as we were. Ladies, we have to pick up the pace, so get back on Bucep."

As Jenny climbed on behind Andrea, she grumbled, "Doesn't Dan'l Boone ever get tired?"

"Honey, I'm sure he's more tired than any of us. Every time I woke up last night, he was awake sitting at the entrance. I bet he didn't get a wink of sleep."

Jenny felt a stab of remorse, remembering the same thing. "You're right, Aunt Andrea. I'm being cranky and childish. I just wish he was more tactful and less bossy."

"He takes his responsibilities seriously, honey. I'm sure he wants to be rid of us as soon as possible."

"And collect his reward. I'm sure my father's will sweeten that pot, too," Jenny declared.

"And a well-earned reward, indeed. If I had any

money I'd throw it into the pot, too. Jenny, why do I have to keep reminding you that none of us would be alive right now were it not for Rico. I think you're trying too hard to convince yourself that you aren't attracted to him. I don't believe you're fooling him, either."

"I know I'm not." Jenny sighed deeply. "He laughs or shrugs off my insults, then orders me around as if I'm stupid and inept. But not knowing how to build a campfire, or preferring to sleep in a bed rather than on the hard, damp ground, are personal choices. They don't reflect a lack of intelligence. So why should I try to please Rico Fraser with capabilities I don't have, when he makes no effort to recognize the ones I *do* possess?"

She sighed again. "I tell myself not to be foolish enough to succumb to his occasional charm, but I *am* attracted to him. Yet I abhor what he does for a living."

"My poor darling, I understand what you're going through. Last night you told me you've only exchanged a kiss. I hope that's true, and that he and you haven't—"

"We've only kissed, Aunt Andrea."

"It was forward of me to ask, honey, but as you said, he has a persuasive charm when he chooses to use it. I was only thinking of the consequences if . . ."

"I understand, and I'm not offended." Jenny tightened her hold around Andrea's waist and leaned against her back in a hug. "I love you, dearly, Aunt Andrea."

*   *   *

They hadn't been riding for more than an hour when Rico reined up and motioned to them to get off the road.

"I thought we were going straight through to the fort," Jenny said.

"That's my intent, but there's a dust trail coming up from behind us. Andrea, do you think you can handle the travois? I'll catch up with you later."

"What do you plan on doing?" Jenny asked.

"If it's that gang, he intends to try and stop them. Don't you, Rico?" Andrea said.

"You said there were six of them, Rico. You wouldn't have a chance against six guns," Don protested.

"I see some good cover over there in those rocks. With two rifles and my Colt, I can hold them off for a few hours. By then it will be dark enough for me to slip away and catch up with you."

Troubled, Jenny's full lower lip curved down. "If you're still alive. Why don't we just try to outrun them?"

"They'd overtake us—and the travois isn't built for that kind of speed. It's a miracle it held together up to now. We've saved a lot of time and miles, getting down here the way we did. Andrea, stay on this road and don't stop. I figure you've got about a six-hour ride from here to the fort."

"Why don't I stay with you?" Jenny said. "I can keep loading the rifles for you."

"Not on your life, Princess. Get going—you're wasting precious time."

Jenny slipped her arms around his neck, tears misting her eyes. "You're not fooling me for a minute, Dan'l. You're just hoping to get out of that date we have for tomorrow night." She drew his head down and kissed him, then turned away quickly and climbed on the horse behind Andrea.

"God be with you, Rico," Andrea said, and goaded the horse forward.

11

"Let's find us some good cover, Bucep." Rico stationed himself behind a slightly projected boulder near a curve in the road. He figured he could pick off a couple of them right away as they came around the curve.

Within minutes, he heard the thundering pound of approaching horses. Hope leaped into his heart when it was followed by the sound of creaking wood and the crack of a whip. A coach came jostling around the curve.

Rico lowered his rifle and stepped out on the road and waved his hat. "Hey, Sam, pull up."

With grinding gears, the driver pulled it to a halt.

"Damn blast it, if it ain't Rico Fraser!" A shot of tobacco juice splattered the road. "You're lucky Tucson here didn't fill you full of lead with a trick like that. What in hell are ya doin' out here?"

"Looking for a ride to town. You got room for a few more passengers?"

Rico explained the situation, then galloped ahead and quickly caught up with the others.

The two coach passengers, a man and woman, moved together in one of the seats, making the other seat available for Jenny and Andrea. With the help of Sam and Tucson, Rico lifted Don off the travois and stretched him out on the top of the coach.

"No, Andrea, you are *not* riding up there with him," Rico declared, when she climbed up onto the box. He lifted her down, then plunked her firmly on the seat next to Jenny. With a wink at Jenny, he said, "Tie her down if you have to."

"Let's get movin', folks. I wanna get to town afore it shuts down for the night," Sam grumbled.

Rico tied the two horses to the rear of the carriage and climbed up on the box, then onto the roof. "What are you waiting for, Sam?"

"Yah-h-h!" the driver shouted, and whipped the reins. The coach bounced forward, jostling the passengers inside.

"How are you doing, Masters?" Rico asked after a short time.

"No offense, Rico, but it's more comfortable than that travois."

Rico chuckled. "This was the break we needed, Don. We should reach the fort in a few more hours, and you can finally get proper treatment."

"I don't believe it; you finally called me by my name," Don exclaimed.

"Like Andrea said, you're delirious. Go to sleep, Captain Masters, you've had a busy day," Rico grumbled.

"You can say that again—and the day's not over yet."

As the stagecoach raced down the road, Rico rested drowsily, his mind on Jenny and her kiss good-bye. Even though it had taken him by surprise, he had returned the kiss and it had felt good. Lord, how good it had felt!

The kiss was a reminder that they still had unfinished business between them. It had intensified their desire for each other, but as much as he desired her, he couldn't give in to the temptation of remaining at the fort. Until he knew Slatter was dead, he couldn't let anything or anyone deter him.

His head began to bob as his mind and body succumbed to exhaustion.

A gun blast startled him awake, and he turned his head to see six riders with blazing pistols pursuing the stagecoach. He handed his Colt to Don and grabbed his rifle, then faced the attackers. Tucson, kneeling on the seat of the box, was already returning their fire.

Dust swirled around them, pebbles bounced against the coach, and amid the sounds of thundering hooves, guns blasting, screaming from inside the wagon, and the crack of Sam's whip to prod the horses to a faster gallop, the noise was intense.

Two of the riders went down when Rico and Tucson's shots found their mark. Then Tucson dropped his rifle when a bullet shattered his arm. He slumped forward onto the top of the coach.

With only Rico returning their fire, the attackers gained ground on the coach when he had to reload. One of the outlaws succeeded in reaching the wagon and leaped onto it. Rallying his strength, Don raised himself on an elbow and fired the Colt Rico had given him. The blast caught the man in the chest and he fell to the ground.

Suddenly the front of the coach crashed to the ground when the right wheel rolled off. The women's screams filled the air as the stage rocked from side to side, threatening to topple over. Rico threw himself across Don to keep the helpless man from being thrown off, as Sam strained to rein up the galloping team.

When Sam finally brought the coach to a stop, Rico grabbed his rifle and jumped down. Able to take a steady aim for the first time in the attack, his shot found its mark and another of the gunmen perished. The two remaining attackers wheeled their horses and galloped away.

Rico opened the door of the coach and discovered the source of the screaming: the female passenger, who was crying hysterically.

"Anyone hurt in here?"

"Just our eardrums," Jenny said.

Andrea moved to the doorway. "How is Don?" she asked worriedly when Rico extended his hand to help her out.

"Last I knew, he was fine."

The man exited next. "My name's Walter Crane." Then he reached in and lifted the woman out of the coach. "This is my wife, Olivia. Can I be of any help?"

"We'll soon need help to get the coach rolling again, Mr. Crane. Until then, it would be a big help on all our nerves if you could quiet her down."

"I'll do my best."

"I think the worst of it is over now, Mrs. Crane," Rico said kindly, but the woman continued bawling. Crane put an arm around her shoulders and led her to the side of the road.

Jenny was the last one to exit. Their eyes locked in a deep gaze as she slipped her hand into his.

"You okay, Princess?" he asked tenderly.

"I am now," she said softly, as his hand closed tighter around hers.

"Rico, I need you," Sam yelled.

Rico released her hand and moved to the box. Tucson had regained consciousness, and Sam had folded his bandanna into a tourniquet.

"That shot busted a bone, Tucson. You won't be wieldin' that Winchester for a spell," Sam said. He followed it up with a splat of tobacco.

"It's worth a busted arm to get away from that durn tobacco spittin' of yours," Tucson grumbled despite his pain.

Andrea appeared with more strips from her petticoat. Between the three of them, they managed to tie a compress on Tucson's wound and help him off the stagecoach.

"Sorry about puttin' you folks out. As soon as we

mend that wheel, we should be on our way," Sam said, relieved to see that the passengers were unharmed. "What's that woman wailin' about?"

"Try to understand this has been a very harrowing experience for her," Crane said.

"Reckon it has for the other ladies, too, Mister Crane. Her wailin' ain't makin' it easier on none of us. Let's get that soldier boy off the top of that stage."

Under Andrea's watchful eye and orders to be careful, Rico, Sam, and Walt Crane lowered Don to the ground and carried him to the roadside.

Rico then went to check the horses that had been tied to the rear of the coach, and encountered bad news. A stray bullet had hit the army horse. The animal could no longer stand, and collapsed.

Rico patted the dying horse's head. "Sorry, old boy," he murmured sadly. He drew the Colt he had reclaimed from Don and put it to the horse's temple. Then he pulled the trigger.

There was little Jenny could do to be of help, except to try to calm Olivia Crane, who was still sobbing. Listening to the woman's continous litany that they might have been killed, Jenny realized the shallowness of the crying woman. Obsessed with self-pity, the woman was oblivious to all the pain and suffering going on around her, and Jenny had little sympathy for Mrs. Crane's anxiety. Not once had the woman even walked over to offer a sympathetic word to the two wounded men lying on the ground.

With startled awareness, Jenny realized that she was guilty of such an attitude herself. Her own welfare had always been foremost in her mind, whether dealing with her father or with Rico—and Andrea, too.

Was this how *she* was seen by others? Shallow? Self-absorbed? Dispassionate to others' suffering? Jenny lowered her head in shame and prayed to God to forgive her.

Then she glanced at Rico. Though she had been frightened during the attack, she also knew that Rico would bring them through it. She had developed the same trust in him that Andrea and Don had, a trust that had nothing to do with the physical attraction she felt for him.

Her heart ached for the grief he was suffering as she watched him attach the dead horse's reins to Bucephalus's saddle to pull it off the middle of the road.

She went over to him. "I'm so sorry, Rico. I know how much you love horses."

He looked up at her as he untied the reins. "Horses have great hearts. And army horses deserve medals when they're killed in action, the same as the troopers who rode them. But the horse losses are only measured as a head count."

Sam had backtracked and now appeared toting a couple rifles, with the wagon wheel tied to the rear of a horse.

"We're lucky, Rico. The wheel's bent a mite, but we should be able to get it back on the coach. It might not be the most comfortable ride, but Lord knows it's better than walkin' and totin' a couple wounded men."

"Where'd you get the horse?"

"It was standin' beside that last fella you shot.

Couldn't have been a day over eighteen. Asked me to take care of his horse. He also told me his name, and asked me to let his mom know he died. Said her address in Missouri was in his saddlebags."

"Did he say why they were after us?"

"They wuz plannin' to rob the stage. Sure picked a bad time to try."

Sam doffed his hat to scratch his head. "Funniest thing I ever did see, though. The kid had this little bunch of wildflowers tied to his saddle."

Jenny gasped when she saw it, and tears rose to her eyes. It was the nosegay she had dropped at the stream the previous day. Rico recognized it too, and they exchanged glances.

"May I have it?" she asked.

"Reckon so, ma'am," Sam said and handed it to her.

Although the night's rain had preserved it, the small bouquet was now wilted. Tears rolled down her face for the dead young man who had seen the beauty in it, too.

"Let's get that wheel back on and get out of here, Sam," Rico said quietly.

The sun had long set by the time the coach wobbled through the gates of Fort Redemption.

Within minutes, Don and Tucson were in the healing hands of the fort's doctor. A protesting Andrea departed with Jenny and the doctor's wife, who insisted Jenny and Andrea spend the night at their quarters, since her husband would be remaining with his patients at the dispensary for the rest of the night.

With a promise to Tucson to return in the morning, Sam departed the fort to deliver his passengers to the hotel.

Rico remained until the doctor assured him Don's condition was under control; he wouldn't be performing surgery on Tucson until morning. His patients were now sleeping peacefully.

Rico was too tired to report to Colonel Hardy, and returned to his quarters instead. Knowing Hardy, he figured the colonel would probably show up.

His hunch proved right. Rico had no sooner pulled off his boots when a knock sounded on the door, and Hardy entered without waiting to be invited.

Abandoning all military formality, Hardy rushed over, grabbed him in a handshake, and slapped him on the shoulder. "Dammit, Rico, if you were a woman I'd kiss you."

"A handshake's fine, sir."

"I knew you could do it, son," Hardy said, continuing to pump Rico's hand. "Doc said the Burke women are fine and are spending the night in his quarters. Tell me, Rico—were they abused?"

"If you mean raped, Colonel, the answer is no. Miss Andrea has a sprained ankle, and Miss Jennifer sustained some facial bruises and a cut knee, but other than that, after a hot bath, a good night's sleep, and a decent meal, both should be fine. They're two very remarkable women. And I wish to add that Captain Masters is an excellent officer."

"I knew he would be," Hardy said. "No one can say that Colonel Tom Hardy doesn't recognize an officer's capabilities in his command. And what about the Slatter gang?"

"All dead for sure except Slatter. I got a couple slugs into him but he got away, so I'm heading out tomorrow to find out if he's dead or alive. *If* I ever get some sleep tonight," he added.

"Doc said the shotgun rider's got a busted shoulder. How'd you hook up with the stagecoach?"

"It's a long story, sir, and I'm tired as hell and need some sleep. I'll make my report in the morning."

"You've earned it. Great job, son. Great job." Hardy paused in the doorway. "Don't suppose I could convince you to join the army? I could pull some strings and get you a commission."

Rico tried unsuccessfully to stifle a huge yawn. "Not interested, sir. Good night."

The colonel departed, and Rico turned off the oil lamp, fell onto the bed, and was asleep before his head hit the pillow.

Maude Evans glanced at the wall clock behind the bar of the Boots and Saddles. It was eleven o'clock, and she was looking forward to closing up the bar in an hour. It was Saturday night and Colonel Hardy didn't permit the sale of alcohol on the Sabbath.

She and Frank had barely slept in the four days since the girls had been abducted. She was too much of a realist to believe they were still alive, but she kept up a positive front for Frank's sake. Lord knows his grief would be tenfold when Rico Fraser returned with the bad news.

She loved Frank Burke. She understood the man better than most, and tolerated his gruffness and bombastic outbursts about his daughter. That's why she was content to let their relationship continue for fifteen years with no talk of marriage.

And she liked his daughter, too. As proper as the girl was, Jenny appeared to harbor no animosity toward her for her relationship with Frank. The same was true of his sister, Andrea. Neither woman was uppity like some of the women in town, who looked down on her because she ran a barroom.

It was an honest job. She didn't water down the liquor, didn't charge the soldiers as much for a drink as the fort tavern, and she didn't hire prostitutes—she left that to the ladies in the whorehouse down the street.

Frank and her husband, Cal, had been close friends in Missouri, and the two couples had come west together. Cal had opened a bar and Frank had gone into ranching. Then Ellie Burke had died twenty years ago giving birth to Jenny. Five years later, when Maude's husband had died from consumption, the twenty-five-year-old widow had decided to remain, rather than return to St. Louis.

Due to the long-existing friendship it was only natural that she and Frank gravitated toward each other, and somewhere along the way, the friends had become lovers.

Never in the past fifteen years had Frank asked her to marry him. She had come to enjoy her independence as the best of both worlds. Yet in her heart, she'd give it up tomorrow if Frank asked her to be his wife. For despite how much she liked her independence, she *loved* Frank Burke.

From habit, she poured a shot of whiskey when she saw Sam come through the door. "You're late getting in tonight, Sam. And where's Tucson?" she asked, shoving the drink at him.

Sam gulped it down, and motioned for a refill. "Had some trouble on the road. Half a dozen gunmen tried to rob us, and Tucson caught a bullet in his shoulder. He's at the doc's office in the fort."

"Is it serious?" she asked.

"Busted a bone. Long time before he'll be able to ride shotgun again."

"How come you're still in one piece, Sam?" one of the fellows at the bar asked. "You ain't gonna try to tell us you outgunned six men tryin' to hold up the stage?"

"Ain't said I did. We'd of been fish in a barrel if it weren't for Rico Fraser. He helped kill off four of 'em, and the other two turned tail and scrambled."

"Now we *know* you're blowin' hot air, Sam. Rico Fraser and an army captain named Masters are out trailin' the Slatter gang, who hit the Double B and took off with Burke's sister and daughter."

Sam was now the center of attention of all in the bar, and he made the most of it. "You got part of it right." He paused, downed his drink, then wiped his mouth on his sleeve. " 'Cept I jest left Rico at the doc's in the fort. Cap'n Masters got pretty shot up."

Maude slammed down the bottle. "For God's sake, Sam, what about the girls?"

"They looked to be in pretty good shape, Maude. Doc's wife took them home with her."

"Oh my God! *Frank. Frank!*" She raced up the stairs.

The patrons in the bar hurried out to spread the word.

Within moments Frank Burke came rushing down the stairway, pulling his suspenders over the unbuttoned shirt he'd donned. Maude followed as they left the bar.

Sam looked around at the suddenly deserted room. "Well I'll be durned!" he muttered, "They didn't even wait to hear about the wheel rollin' off." He reached for the bottle and poured himself another drink.

After delicious bowls of soup and chicken sandwiches, then hot baths and clean nightgowns and robes that the doctor's wife had dug out of a chest, Jenny and Andrea were relishing their second cups of tea for the evening when a pounding at the door interrupted their conversation.

"Evening, Mrs. Wallace," Frank Burke said. "I've been told my—"

The doctor's wife nodded and stepped aside, and Frank Burke rushed past her.

Jenny's eyes brimmed with surprised tears when her father's arms closed tightly around her. Her father never displayed any affection for her, and it felt good, feeling the strength of his hug.

As if embarrassed, Frank stepped back. "Are you all right?"

"I'm fine, Father."

Frank turned to his sister and gave her a hug and kiss on the cheek. "What about you, Andrea?"

"Nothing worse than a twisted ankle, Frank."

"That's good. How'd your face get so bruised?" he asked Jenny.

She shrugged off the question with her usual flippancy. "Compliments of Mr. Slatter."

Her father's jaw hardened in anger. "What *else* did he do to you?"

"Other than making a lot of threats, he just shoved us around a lot."

"That's not quite true, Frank," Andrea interrupted. "She came very close to Slatter killing her. Not only had he dragged her across the ground and ripped her knee open, but he was about to cut her throat when Rico and Don Masters arrived. She'd be dead today if not for Rico. We all would be, Don included. You owe that man a big debt, Frank."

"I always pay my debts, Andrea. You can be sure of that. I told him he could name his price."

Mrs. Wallace retired to the kitchen with Maude to give the reunited family some privacy. Shortly after, Frank and Maude departed and Jenny and Andrea went to bed.

As they lay side by side in the comfort of the bed,

Jenny said, "Do you believe, it's really over, Aunt Andrea? We're finally safe."

"Yes, we are. But I won't feel secure until I'm sure
Don made it safely, too."

Jenny reached for her hand. "He will, Aunt Andrea.
He's strong, and he has a great incentive to recover.
He has your love."

They slipped into slumber, still clasping hands.

12

Early the next morning, Jenny and Frank Burke rode back to the Double B. It was hard for her to believe she'd only been gone for four days—so much had happened that would live in her memory forever.

As they approached the house, she glanced at the small cemetery surrounded by a whitewashed fence. Her mother's grave was set apart from the crosses that marked the final resting place of crew members who had died while working at the ranch. She felt a lump in her throat at the sight of the two new additions.

"Maude came out and put the place in order," Frank said when they entered the house. "Those bastards tore it apart pretty badly."

"I heard they were looking for money."

"I'm going out to feed and water the stock. How soon before we head back to town?"

"I just have to change my clothes and pack up some clothing for Andrea."

"How long is she planning on staying in town?" he asked.

"You'll have to ask her, Father. Probably not until she's sure Captain Masters is out of danger."

"Just when did my sister and Masters get so friendly?" Frank asked gruffly.

"It could be when Captain Masters almost died trying to save her."

Her sarcasm was not wasted on him. "Well, just the same, she might be making too much of it. Some of these army boys—"

"Captain Masters is not a *boy*, Father."

He frowned. "Okay, some *men* wouldn't hesitate to take advantage of a softhearted woman like Andrea, no matter how old she is."

"That's right, Father. Just like you do."

His brow knit into a frown. "Blast it, girl, that's no way to talk to your father. You know what I meant! It's no wonder I get short with you." He thumped out, slamming the door behind him.

It never takes long for us to be at each other's throats, Jenny reflected as she climbed the stairway.

Opening the door to her bedroom, hot air swarmed to greet her. The sun always blazed in the western windows in the afternoon, and now, with the drapes left open and the room closed up for days, the heat was stifling. She opened the windows to let in the morning breeze.

For a long moment she gazed at the rainbow of

color below in the garden—her Garden of Eden. It was the only thing on the ranch that she devoted her heart and soul to maintaining.

Blooming cacti literally carpeted the white-picket-fenced area with the brilliant scarlet blossoms of Mojave cactus, stunning clumps of white from saguaro, the gold from fishtail, and the fragile strawberry blooms of hedgehog, set amid the shade of several palm and olive trees.

She breathed their sweet fragrance deeply and thought of the past few days. Soon Rico would be leaving. Her heart told her to try to convince him to remain; her common sense told her it would be wiser to let him leave, for once he found Ben Slatter, he'd simply move on to the next wanted man. That was the life he preferred; he'd never settle down to raising a family.

She moved away from the window. As she began to shed her clothing, she paused and studied her image in the mirror. Many had told her she was beautiful, but her looks were something she gave little attention to. She leaned closer and stared at her reflection. Did Rico think her body was beautiful? She certainly thought his was.

Jenny Burke, you're acting as lovesick as Andrea. Why? You aren't in love with Rico Fraser, any more than he is with you. The events of the last few days have created a feeling that normally wouldn't have developed between us, so what does it matter, whether he thinks I'm beautiful or not?

She turned away and dressed quickly, then sat down

on the bed to put on her shoes. The volume of Shakespeare she'd been reading before her abduction still lay open on the nightstand next to her bed, and as she picked it up, the words seemed to jump off the page.

"This above all: To thine own self be true."

I intend to do exactly that, Mr. Shakespeare. My eyes are wide open when it comes to Rico Fraser—and myself.

She closed the book and laid it back down on the table.

Rico decided to leave today rather than tomorrow, and he had a number of things to do before departing.

He had promised to take Jenny to dinner that evening, but decided he'd make it up to her when he returned. After a bath, a shave, and a hot meal, he packed up his saddlebags, replenished his ammunition, and checked on Bucephalus. Then he stopped at the dispensary before departing.

Doctor Wallace had completed the surgery on Tucson's shoulder and Don was sitting up in bed, on the road to recovery, his fever checked and new dressings on his wounds. Andrea sat at the bedside.

"Thought I'd stop and see how you're doing before I pull out," Rico said.

"So you're moving on?" Don asked.

"To find Slatter. Once I do, I figure on heading back to California."

"Did you say good-bye to Jenny?" Andrea asked.

"I will after I leave you folks," Rico said.

"I'm afraid you've missed her. She and Frank went

back to the ranch, early this morning but I expect them to be returning soon."

"I thought the two of you were staying at the doctor's quarters last night."

"We did. But Jenny needed a change of clothing, as do I. They should be back shortly, and she'd be upset if you rode off without saying good-bye."

"Tell her that as soon as I locate Slatter, I'll be back," Rico assured her. "I better get on my way."

Andrea hugged him and kissed him on the cheek. "Thank you. Those two words are so inadequate for the debt we owe you, Rico. Be careful, and come back safely."

"You better come back, Rico. We're hoping you'll stand up at our wedding," Don said as the two men shook hands.

"It would be an honor. When's the happy day?"

"I'd like it to be today, but my future bride says we wait until I'm back on my feet again."

"You need at least a week," Andrea replied. "You're still bedridden, you know."

"I was under the impression that's where most newlyweds spend most of their time," Don teased.

Andrea blushed. "Shame on you; you're embarrassing me."

"Well, I'm looking forward to the wedding, so get well, Don. I can't make any promises about getting back in a week. If I don't make it, I'll be thinking about the two of you."

"And you take care, Rico," Don warned. "I'm hoping Slatter has died from those gunshot wounds."

"If he did, I'll find out somehow."

Andrea sighed. "I still wish you would wait to say good-bye to Jenny."

"Tell her I didn't wait because it's not good-bye between us. She'll understand what I mean. And tell her that I haven't forgotten I owe her a steak dinner when I get back." He suddenly grinned. "Come to think of it, I'll tell her myself. How long does it take to ride out to your brother's ranch?"

"About forty-five minutes."

"Since I'm getting a late start already, another hour and a half won't make that much difference. Take care of Don, Andrea. He's a good man," Rico said.

She smiled at him. "I already figured that out. I wish you didn't have to go. Do you really need that reward money?"

"Don't you think it's time you let me tell her the truth about that, my friend?" Don asked.

"What truth?" Andrea asked.

Rico nodded. "I suppose you're right. But do me a favor and wait until I leave."

He left with Andrea looking at Don in wide-eyed curiosity.

In less than an hour, he reached the Burkes' house. It was much larger and more impressive than the sprawled ranch houses he was accustomed to. Clearly much had been done to improve the original structure. The lower walls were the original brick Frank Burke had used to build the house. Several rooms had been added to extend the first floor, but the biggest change was the addition of a second story clad in gray clapboard siding, with black shutters on the windows and a shingled roof.

Burke must have seen him coming, because he had walked up to the hitching post and was waiting to shake hands and thank him for rescuing his family.

"I figure you'd show up. Let's go inside and settle up," Frank said. "I said you could name your price, Fraser. How much do you want?"

"I don't want anything, sir. I never had any intention of being paid for trailing Slatter; you came to that conclusion on your own. Colonel Hardy will confirm that if you don't believe me."

"If that's the case, I owe you an even bigger debt than I figured. What brings you out here to the Double B?"

"I came to say good-bye to Miss Jennifer, sir. I'm moving on; I want to make sure Slatter is dead."

"I heard you put two slugs in him. You figure he could still be alive?"

"I just came from seeing Captain Masters. He took two slugs and he's very much alive. He and Miss Andrea are planning their wedding."

"*Wedding?*"

"Yes, sir. I'm sorry to surprise you. I assumed Andrea or Jenny had told you already."

"Those women don't tell me anything 'til they have to," he grumbled. "I keep a roof over their heads and food in their bellies, but I'm always the last to know what they're up to."

"I've got to get moving, sir," Rico repeated, "I'd appreciate it if you'd let Miss Jenny know I'm here."

"Sure you don't want to come in for a cool drink before heading out?"

"Thank you just the same, but I'm in a hurry, sir."

Burke shook his hand again. "Good luck, son. And be sure to keep your powder dry," he added in a lighter tone. "I'll call my daughter."

As he waited for Jenny, Rico looked around him. With the crew absent, the ranch was quiet.

When Jenny came out of the house, she had on the yellow gown she had worn the first time he saw her. Her auburn hair had been brushed to a satin sheen and was tied back with a yellow ribbon.

Her glance swung to his bulging saddlebags, then back to him. "So you're leaving."

"I told you I would be."

"I guess I didn't realize how soon that would be." She walked toward the garden, Rico following, opened a picket gate, and entered. She went over to one of the Mojave cactus and drew a deep breath of the scarlet blossom.

The gesture called up memories of the afternoon at the river, when she had picked wildflowers and made them into a nosegay.

"You're very fond of flowers, aren't you?"

Her smile was serene when she turned and faced him. "I planted all this myself, except for the olive and palm trees. I needed the help of a couple of the hands for that."

"Wherever did you get olive and palm trees in Arizona?"

"Father had them shipped here from California. He was excited when I asked for them, because he thought I was going to do something useful." She sat down on a bench. "He regrets it now."

"But why? This garden is a beautiful oasis in the midst of a desert."

"My father thinks it's a waste of time and money, and that I spend too much time here."

"I hadn't realized it was that difficult to maintain a cactus plant. After all, they grow wild in the desert."

"Maintenance isn't the issue. I spend most of my time here reading. That's what he considers a waste of time."

In a sudden change of topic, she dropped the idle talk and voiced what both of them had on their minds. "I'm not going to deny I hate to see you go, Rico."

"I'll be back, Jenny. As soon as I find Slatter."

"It seems you've made finding him a personal mission."

"It is. And has been for the past three years."

"You've been trailing Ben Slatter for three years and haven't caught him yet? What if it takes you another three years, or more? Because he's not going to sit and wait for you to catch up with him."

"Slatter's a desperate man right now. His gang is gone, and he has no one to back him up. This is the end for him. I can feel it. His luck has run out."

"But yours hasn't, has it? Not Rico Fraser's. It gives you the excuse you want to continue. You're content to tramp through the woods, living off what it offers. Wild game in the woods, fish in the stream, cold baths in mountain rivers. And a horse for companionship."

Her lower lip curved into a pout. "Damn you, Daniel Boone!" She turned away in frustration.

He put his hands on her shoulders and pulled her back against him. His arms felt so good, and added to her yearning for him.

The huskiness in his voice sent quivers of desire surging through her. "Don't damn me, Jenny. Leaving you now is damnation enough." He turned her to face him, the earnestness in his eyes a supplication for understanding. "There's nothing I'd rather do than remain here with you. But I have to finish something I've sworn to do. Then I'll be back; I promise you. We have had some unfinished business, and there's too much between us to let it go unanswered."

"Yes there is. But apparently your pursuit of Slatter is more important."

With incredible gentleness, he caressed her cheek. "Your bruises are beginning to fade, Princess."

Jenny raised a hand and covered his, sliding it to her lips. Then she pressed a kiss into his palm.

He took a step closer and drew her against him. Slipping her arms around his neck, she parted her lips as their mouths found a fit. The kiss was as hungry as it was persuasive. Intended to say good-bye, it deepened as their suppressed desire surged into an intoxicating passion. Her legs trembled and a shudder swept her spine when he slid his tongue into her mouth.

Breathlessness finally forced an end to the kiss,

and her startled stare met the astonishment in his. Her quivering breath met the rhythm of his, and their hearts beat as one.

Passion shimmered in his brown eyes as he studied her, as if seeking a matching response in her eyes.

Jenny blushed, thinking and feeling the same things.

"You aren't ready to let go any more than I am, Princess."

"Then why must we, Rico? Are you so driven in your pursuit of Slatter that you're willing to deny what we're feeling now? This is all new to me: I don't know if it's gratitude, or something deeper. But I do know that until this moment, I've never desired any man to make love to me."

"I'll be back, Jenny. What's between us is not going to end now," he said, reaching for her again.

She squared her shoulders and stepped back. "I've offered myself to you, Rico. And I'll never do it again." Tears misted her eyes. "I wish you luck wherever the trail leads you, Dan'l Boone. May God be with you."

She turned and hurried into the house before she burst into tears in front of him.

She raced up the stairway, ran into her room, and closed the door.

13

Rico was torn between leaving and going after Jenny. No matter how she felt about it, or his increasing affection for her, he couldn't abandon his search. He would never have peace of mind until he knew Slatter was dead. If luck was with him, he'd know the answer in a few days and then he would return.

What he had begun to feel for Jenny was deeper than a sexual attraction, but he suspected it probably wasn't so with her. She was used to getting her way, and that might be her motive whether she recognized it or not.

Regardless, the sooner he left, the sooner he could return.

Going to the hitching post, he mounted Bucephalus and was about to head out when Maude Evans galloped up. Frank Burke came outside to greet her as she slid off the horse.

"Rico, thank God I caught you before you left. I've got something important to tell the two of you."

"Come inside out of the sun," Frank said. "What's this important news?" he asked as they followed him into the house.

"Do you remember Ed Callahan, who used to ride for the Lazy R?"

"Yeah. He took to drinking heavily and Dave O'Malley had to let him go. What about him?"

"He came into my bar and told me he saw Ben Slatter."

Rico jerked up his head. "When? Where?"

"Early this morning, on the road leading into Redemption. Ed said he ducked behind a bush to take a leak and saw a man lying under a tree who looked to be dead. When Ed went over to check, he recognized Slatter."

"How could he be certain?" Rico questioned.

"I asked him the same thing," Maude replied. "He said he's seen Slatter a couple times before. And besides, the varmint's picture is plastered all over the county. Ed claims the whole county's been talking about Slatter ever since his gang hit the Double B and snatched the women."

"And this Callahan claims Slatter's dead?" Rico asked.

Maude shrugged. "He didn't say. As soon as he saw it was Slatter, he got out of there."

Frank snorted. "You can't believe a word that drunk says."

Rico shoved his hat to the top of his forehead. "Where exactly was this?"

"About ten miles south of town," Maude said.

"And Slatter was alone?"

"According to Ed. He didn't see anyone else with him."

Rico thought for a moment, then headed for the door.

"Where are you going?" Frank asked.

"Since your spread is north of the fort I figure you're safe for now, but there's two homesteads within ten miles south of Redemption. If that murdering bastard is around, those people should be warned.

"In the meantime, Mr. Burke, get Jenny back to the fort and keep her and Andrea there until I get back. Under the circumstances, I'm sure Colonel Hardy will offer your family sanctuary."

"I know Tom will," Frank said.

"Don't let either of those women step a foot out of that fort. And I advise you to do the same. Without any crew here you're not safe, either."

"Young man, I've fought Indians and outlaws from the time I came here," Frank said. "And anyone else who tried to drive me off my land."

"Then you have nothing to prove to anyone Mr. Burke. So do as I ask and stay at the fort with your daughter and sister, to make sure they don't try to leave."

"I'll see that he does," Maude said.

They followed him outside and Rico swung up on Bucephalus. "I'll be back as soon as I check out those homesteads."

"Slatter would be a damn fool if he tries to hit the Browning house," Frank said. "Jake Browning has three grown sons and they're all deadly with a rifle. I'm more worried about the Coles. Pete and Maggie are up in years, and they've been alone since their son got killed in the war."

"Thanks. I'll check them out first." Rico took off at a gallop.

Jenny came out of the house carrying a carpetbag just as Rico rode away. "All right, Father, I'm ready to leave." She set the bag down when she saw Maude.

"Hello, I didn't know you were here. Was that Rico riding off? I thought he had left already." When she saw her father and Maude exchange a worried look, a shiver of apprehension spiraled down her spine. "What's going on? Is it Don? Has his condition worsened?"

"Jenny, Maude brought word that Slatter might be back in the area," Frank said. "Rico wants us to go to the fort and stay there."

At the thought of the crazed madman, her heart began thudding in her breast.

"He went to check out the Cole place since Slatter was sighted near there," her father continued. "You best hurry up and throw some clothes in that carpet-bag for yourself, too, no telling how long we'll have to remain in town."

"Should I pack some for you, Father?"

Frank blushed and cleared his throat. "Uh . . . I figure I can always . . . ah . . . buy some at the general store."

"Good Lord, Frank, who are you trying to fool?" Maude declared. "He's got a change of clothing at my place, Jenny. So quit your hemming and hawing, Frank Burke, and go hitch up the carriage." She slipped her arm through Jenny's. "Come on, honey, I'll give you a hand."

Rico pulled the pair of binoculars his cousins had given him for Christmas out of his saddlebags. Although his eyesight was excellent, the spy glasses proved helpful at times.

He focused the glasses on the distant house and surveyed the countryside surrounding it. Nothing appeared to be out of the ordinary. The Coles' dog was stretched out asleep on the porch, and smoke was coming out of the chimney.

"Looks peaceful enough, Bucep." He started to return the binoculars to the saddlebag, then stopped, struck by an afterthought. He lifted them back to his eyes.

"Why are the shutters closed, Bucep? Doesn't make sense that the Coles would shut out the breeze on such a hot day unless . . ." He quickly put the glasses away and pulled his rifle out of the sling.

Rico approached the house slowly and cautiously. Near the clearing he dismounted, tethered Bucephalus, and proceeded on foot. He crossed the clearing unchallenged. Even the sleeping dog didn't stir, and he soon discovered why. The dog wasn't sleeping; its throat had been cut.

Rico cocked his rifle and then kicked the door open.

The body of Pete Cole was lying near the window, shot through the head. The old man had attempted to fight off the attacker; a rifle was lying nearby. Rico picked it up and checked the chamber. The gun had been fired recently. Maggie Cole was lying on the floor, also dead.

Broken pieces of china and dresser drawers dumped on the floor reflected a hurried search. A bloody bandanna and torn strips of a plaid shirt lay on the table next to a crock of bloody water, indicating the culprit had cleansed and bandaged his wounds. The plaid strips were similar to the shirt he'd glimpsed on Slatter when the wounded man had escaped from him.

There was no doubt in Rico's mind who had murdered this couple.

He grabbed two blankets from the bedroom, then went back into the kitchen and looked down at the bodies of the aged couple. His hands curled into fists.

This could so easily have been Jenny's body. Well, Slatter would have to come through *him* to get to Jenny.

After wrapping the bodies in the blankets, Rico hitched up a wagon and laid the bodies in its bed. As a final respect to the dead couple, Rico hurriedly dug a shallow grave and buried their dog. Then he drove the wagon to the Brownings' ranch.

As Frank had thought, their home had not been

molested. Rico told them of the murders of their neighbors and advised them to stay alert.

The trip back to the fort gave Rico plenty of time to think. There could only be one reason why Slatter had come back to this area: revenge. And he wouldn't leave until he got it.

But this time the murderer would be up against him, and not defenseless women. Although, no doubt, the madman would try to include them in his scheme, Rico told himself. *What that bastard doesn't recognize is that his madness has driven him to make the biggest mistake of his life—he narrowed the battlefield to this one area.*

So I don't have to go looking for him; he's come here to find me, too. All I have to do is to be sure the women are safe and make myself visible enough to draw him out into the open. And then I'll have him where I want him.

Rico flicked the reins to goad the horse to a faster gait.

A crowd gathered around the wagon when Rico stopped in front of the undertaker's office. One of the men stepped up and gave him a hand to carry a body inside. "Is it Slatter, Rico?" he asked hopefully.

"No, it's Pete and Maggie Cole."

"What happened to them?" a woman asked when Rico came back for the other body.

"Shot," he replied succinctly.

The crowd, buzzing among themselves, asked him a dozen questions when he returned from inside again. Rico climbed back on the wagon and drove away without answering. He left the Coles' wagon and horse at the town livery, then watered Bucephalus.

The fort's gate had been closed by order of Colonel Hardy, and only authorized people were permitted to enter. The sentry recognized Rico at once and passed him through.

"Colonel Hardy has instructed me to tell you to report to his office as soon as you arrive, Rico."

"Did Frank Burke and his daughter arrive?"

"Yes, earlier this morning."

Rico nodded. "Thanks."

The usual cigar was protruding from Hardy's mouth when Rico entered the colonel's office.

"Sit down, Rico, and report what you've found."

"I'm no longer employed by the army, Colonel Hardy so stop addressing me as if I were one of your privates."

Hardy chuckled. "You underestimate your worth—I think of you as at least a lieutenant. And if you're no longer employed by the army, I'd have to kick you out of those quarters you're occupying. They're government property." He shifted the cigar to the side of his mouth and shoved the box at him. "Help yourself and let's hear your report. Any truth to this Slatter rumor?"

"Sure is. I just brought in Pete and Maggie Cole."

"Cole? Is that the old couple who live about five or six miles from here?"

"*Did* live five or six miles from here," Rico corrected. "They're dead. Shot." Rico told him the condition of the house when he found the bodies.

"Do you have any proof it was Slatter?"

"I've got a plaid strip from the shirt Slatter was wearing the day I wounded him." Rico pulled the cloth out of his pants pocket and tossed it on the desk.

Hardy picked up the strip and examined it. "Shirts like this can be bought at any general store or trading post between here and St. Louis, Rico.

"With all the talk and those wanted posters, every one's on edge. Two of my troopers were shot at by some crazy woman because she claimed one of them looked like Slatter.

"I don't believe the man would ever come back to this county, much less this close to the fort. Sounds more to me like some drunken Indians."

Rico snorted. "Right—drunken Indians wearing plaid shirts. Why didn't I think of that?"

"Cool down, Rico. You said that all the shutters were closed. That's a sign the old man might have been fighting off an Indian attack."

"Or a sign to make anyone riding past think that the Coles had gone away. If it had been an Indian raid, they would have scalped the couple, taken the horse with them, and killed the rest of the stock."

"Not if they were drunk, rather than on the war-path," Hardy said.

"I know Indian sign, sir, and I know Slatter sign when I see it."

Tom Hardy slumped back in his seat. "Well, I respect your judgment, Rico, so I'll send out a couple of patrols to search for him. And while I don't blame

Frank for wanting his family at the ranch, army regulations prohibit non-army personnel being quartered on the post for longer than a week unless they're visiting a family member. They'll have to go or bunk at the hotel after that."

Rico stood up to depart. "I've got my own plan how to locate Mr. Slatter, Colonel."

"And I don't suppose you intend to share it."

"The less you know, sir, the better."

14

Rico had just put Bucephalus into a stall when Frank Burke entered the horse barn.

"Rico, I heard you were back. I've been looking for you."

"Then you know I brought back the bodies of Pete and Maggie Cole."

"Yeah." Burke shook his head. "They were fine folks. Salt of the earth. Pete and Maggie were the closest neighbors we had when Ellie and I first came out here. Helped get us through our first winter. Did the same for Cal and Maude Evans." His gaze turned to steel. "Figure it was Slatter who killed them?"

"No question in my mind."

"See any sign of their dog Ginger? That dog was damn protective of them."

"Probably the first to go. Its throat was cut. That

might explain why the shutters were closed. The dog could have tried to fight off Slatter while the couple closed up the shutters. I'm going back in the morning to try to pick up any trail."

"This world sure would be a better place without him," Frank said. "That's what I want to talk to you about. If Slatter's in this area, why leave it? Tom Hardy told me that we could only stay a week here at the fort. With my crew not due back for at least a month, I'm hoping you'd be willing to stay at the ranch with us. We could use your protection until they get back."

"Can't you just hire a couple hands?" Rico asked.

"I tried. There's no one to hire on such short notice."

"Have you considered sending the women away? Maybe to some relatives they could stay with until this is over?"

"There aren't any. Why do you think my sister lives with me? She ain't got nowhere else to go."

Rico admired and respected Andrea, and Burke's words rubbed him the wrong way. "I thought it had something to do with loving her," he said sarcastically.

"That ain't what I meant," Frank said in an angry huff. "Sure I love her, and I don't want to see anything happen to her or my daughter."

"Did you mention this idea to either of them? Jenny's pretty angry with me right now."

"Don't pay her no mind. She's always in a snit about something."

Rico shoved his hat up on his forehead. "Well, if that bastard doesn't turn up in the next week, I guess I could hang around for a while. If Don has his way Andrea will be getting married soon, and then she'll be safe here at the fort. But it's been my experience that Jenny doesn't take well to obeying orders."

"Humph! You think I don't know that? Then it's a deal."

"Only if you're willing to take my orders, too, Mr. Burke. I can't protect three people if they're going off in different directions."

Frank offered his hand. "My handshake's my word, Rico."

Rico returned to Colonel Hardy's office and informed him of his change of plans, then headed to the dispensary to see how Masters was doing. For a change, Andrea wasn't sitting at his bedside.

"Where's your nursemaid?" Rico asked.

"In town buying material for a wedding gown."

"In town! My orders were that neither of those women were to leave the fort. I suppose Jenny went with her?"

"Yes, *and* a military escort. Relax, Rico, they're in good hands."

"So you're getting married right away."

"Yep. Dr. Wallace said I should be up and around by tomorrow, so we're getting married at the end of the week so Andrea doesn't have to leave the fort. I don't intend to let her out of my sight. By then, hopefully someone will have tracked the murdering bastard down."

"Don, are you sure you aren't rushing into this wedding?"

"Good Lord, Rico, I told you I was in love with her before we even went on that mission."

Rico grinned. "I'm not referring to that. I've heard honeymoons can be very . . . ah, tiring for a man."

"I'm sure I'm up to the challenge." Don grinned back. "My wounds were in my shoulder and leg, old man."

Rico chuckled. "Sounds like you've got a little bit of each of my cousins in you."

"What do you mean?" Don asked.

"You've got the imaginative vision of Clay, and my cousin Colt's tendency to follow the letter of the law. I recognize some of Jed's tacit reserve in you, and now, most assuredly, Garth's cocksure presumption of his ability to . . . perform."

"And do you see these traits as strengths or weaknesses, my friend?" Don asked.

"You could never hope to assemble a finer group of men," Rico replied. "They're Virginians. With the exception of Colt, who's a lawman in New Mexico, the others—and their continually increasing families—live on a compound in California. Clay became a vintner and one by one the others have joined him; and now they've built one of the most successful vineyards in California. I hope to join them when I finish up with Ben Slatter."

Rico told Don his plans for remaining, and the agreement with Frank Burke. Don's relief was evident, and when Rico returned to his quarters, it was with thoughts of Jenny.

He'd had his share of beautiful women in the past, but none had the effect on him that she did. She constantly challenged him, which kept him guessing about how he really stood with her.

In truth, all women were beautiful to him. The women his cousins married were all outstanding beauties, and in his heart, no woman could ever compare to his mother. A woman's beauty came from within, and all the women of his family possessed it.

From the beginning there had been a powerful physical attraction to Jenny, and at first he had let his body do his thinking for him. Her physical beauty and his desire for her had initially blinded him to the courage and sensitivity she concealed under a flippant façade, and as a result he had unjustly accused her of being lazy and self-absorbed.

Lord knew she'd been as scared as Andrea when they were Slatter's prisoners, but from what Andrea had told him, Jenny had the spunk to not give in to that fear—and she still bore the injuries that Slatter had meted out in punishment.

And what he had once looked upon as her taking advantage of Andrea was in truth just the opposite. Andrea thrived on nurturing people. It was her purpose in life, and Jenny had the sensitivity to recognize how important this was to her aunt. Instead of teaching the young girl the hows and whys of life, Andrea had done everything she could to make her niece's life easier. Just as she had taken on the responsibility of becoming her brother's housekeeper and cook when his wife had died, and had remained at Don's side from the time he was wounded.

As loving and caring as Andrea was, *she* was the one who had coddled and spoiled Jenny.

He needed to make peace with her, and based on the way they parted that morning, it wasn't going to be easy. He tossed his shirt aside, then sat down on the edge of his bed and took off his boots. Stretching out, he tucked his hands under his head, and lay there trying to figure out how he was going to handle Jenny. As he closed his eyes, the thought of her stirred his blood, and he wondered how long he could have stayed away from her if he had ridden away.

As if he had conjured up a vision of her, she suddenly knocked and slipped through his doorway.

"Father told me about the Coles. How can that man continue murdering innocent people? That couple didn't have an enemy. Even the Apaches left them alone!"

Her expression and rising voice reflected the panic building in her. Rico reached for her and held her in his arms.

"You'll be safe here, Jenny. I won't let anything happen to you."

"I'm not worrying about just myself, Rico."

"I meant you and your family," he said.

"And I meant *you.*"

"Princess, you don't have to worry about me. For the past three years I've shadowed every move that man has made, and I know what to expect from him."

"Explain that to Pete and Maggie Cole, because frankly, I'm confused. If you've been trailing him for three years and know how he thinks, why is that murderous fiend still on the loose? How many people has he killed this week alone? Stumpy, Charlie, Pete and Maggie Cole—and those are just the ones we know about. There could be more victims out there not discovered yet."

"What do you expect me to do, Jenny?"

"Get over the idea that you're smarter than he is, because his insanity gives him a cunning greater than your logic. You can't do it alone, Rico. Colonel Hardy has offered you the help of a patrol, but you've turned him down. Why? Is the reward money that important to you that you would let this man continue his carnage until you finally outsmart him—or he succeeds in making you another one of his victims? Frankly, I think you already *are.* You're so obsessed that you've already wasted three years of your life. How many more do you plan on wasting?"

"You condemn my leaving for the reward on Slatter's head, then in the next breath offer me yourself as a reward if I remain. I'm damned if I do and damned if I don't. Either choice makes me nothing better than a mercenary—as you so often remind me."

"If that's what you believe, so be it." She lifted her

chin in defiance. "I guess it's another example of your tendency to underestimate people?"

She spun on her heel to depart, but he caught her shoulder. "Dammit, Jenny, why are we arguing? Have you forgotten we have a date tonight?"

"That date was off when you rode away this morning."

He pulled her into his arms. "Are you going to waste the evening pouting, when we could be enjoying each other's company?"

Her sense of humor prevailed. "You mean like we are now?"

He grinned. "Princess, do you really want us to be at odds?"

"Of course not. But sometimes you make me so angry, I could scream." She nestled against his chest, and glanced up at him with a shy smile. "What time are we going out to dinner?"

"I figured at seven. But it really would be better if you remained inside the fort."

"Surely Slatter wouldn't attempt to harm us in the restaurant. It's only a block away from the gate."

"I guess it's safe enough—but I don't want you to leave my side. Why don't we go to Maude's? Her cook makes a pretty good steak."

"Whatever you want. I feel safer with you than I do with this fort full of soldiers. I know you aren't going to let anything happen to me."

He cupped her cheeks between his hands. "I wish I could be certain of that. You're taking the danger too lightly. You were right when you said Slatter's madness makes him more cunning than I am. I figure the only way I can win is to draw him out in the open."

"And risk your life doing it."

"The risk and danger already exists. He wants revenge because I killed his gang. That's why I should avoid your company. I'm his main target, but he won't hesitate to kill you too, Jenny. You've got to take the threat seriously."

"Of course I'm taking it seriously. I can still see the madness in his eyes, hear his maniacal laughter. My skin crawls just recalling his touch. Until that man is dead, I'll live in fear of him, Rico. But my belief in you is stronger than my fear of Slatter."

"Then promise me you'll do whatever I tell you to."

"I promise," she whispered, right before his mouth covered hers.

The gentleness of the kiss quickly spiraled into the arousing heat of passion, and only the awareness of where they were prevented Rico from pursuing it further.

"Where are you quartered?" he whispered when he broke the kiss.

"Colonel Hardy put us in the quarters of an officer who was transferred."

"And your father is staying there with you and Andrea?"

"Of course," she said, amused.

"I figured he would be, but hoped I was wrong."

She arched a brow, and said teasingly, "Why, sir, what could you possibly have in mind?"

"You for dessert, after dinner."

His hunger matched the one he read in her eyes as she slipped her arms around his waist and hugged him closer. "You're pretty confident, Dan'l."

His tongue circled the outline of her lips. "You taste mighty fine, Princess. I could devour you right now."

Sighing, she parted her lips and he slipped his tongue past them, and began to brush the roof of her mouth with an erotic touch that made her legs tremble and reduced her breath to gasps.

Her core tingled with every exquisite stroke as he continued the teasing assault on her eyes and the curve of her jaw before he reclaimed her lips.

When he lifted his head, Jenny rested her head on the brawn of his chest until her trembling ceased. Her desire for him had passed a point of no return. Drawing a deep breath, she murmured, "Maybe we should have dessert before the steak."

"Honey, anyone could walk in on us here."

"Isn't there a bolt on that door?"

"Yes, but if anyone saw you enter, your reputation could be destroyed. The wisest thing you can do is get out now while it's just a rumor."

Her eyes lit with devilment. "Why try to put out *that* fire, when the one within me is much greater?"

"Because regardless of how much I want you right now, you have to live among these people." He took her by the hand and walked over to the door.

"I can't believe you! You're turning me down *again*? Twice in the same day!"

"I'm only warning you of the risks." Then he

slipped the bolt on the door. Grinning, he turned and lifted her into his arms. "And having done so, what are we waiting for?"

He lowered her to the bed. She offered no resistance when he stripped her of her clothing, then stood up and shed his own.

She had seen him bare-chested before, but nothing had prepared her for the long muscular length of him. Fascinated, she swept her gaze from his face to his long, muscular legs, then returned to the extended organ at the junction of them. She swallowed hard.

The burning desire she saw in his eyes incinerated any reservations, and stoked the flame of her own need for him. She opened her arms and lifted them to him. He raised them above her head as he lowered himself and covered her with his body. His flesh was warm against her own, and the feel of it incited her passion even higher.

He slid his palms up her stretched arms and laced his fingers through hers, then trailed a string of kisses up one arm and down the other. She arched against him, but his weight kept her captive beneath him.

Closing her eyes, she gave herself up to the sensuous kisses he began to rain on her face and eyes, then covered her mouth and let his tongue weave its magic.

Needing to embrace him, to feel him in her arms, she struggled to free her arms, but he held her firmly as he dipped his head and trailed quick kisses along her neck to her breasts. She writhed in rapturous torture when he laved the sensitive tips of her nipples, then took one into his mouth in an erotic suckling that caused her to cry out under wave upon wave of imploding carnal tremors.

His kiss smothered her outcry and he released her arms. She clutched his shoulders, pulling him closer, tighter, molding herself even more against the muscular length of him.

"Dear God, Rico, I can't stand much more of this."

"The best is yet to come, Princess," he murmured. She parted her lips for the kiss that followed.

A loud knocking on the door caused him to break the kiss. "Mr. Fraser," a voice called out.

"Who is it?" he barked.

"Private Scott, sir. Colonel Hardy has summoned you to his office."

"Tell him I'm indisposed, and unless the fort is on fire, I don't wish to be disturbed. You can also tell him I'm no longer under his command and don't have to obey any summons."

"Come on, Rico," the soldier whined. "You know he always kills the messenger. I'll end up mucking out horse stalls for a month."

Rico sighed. "All right, Scotty. Tell him I'll be there as soon as I get dressed."

"Thanks, Rico." The private left to deliver the message.

"I can't wait until I ride out of this fort for the last time," Rico grumbled as he got to his feet and pulled on his clothing.

He leaned down and gave Jenny a drugging kiss, then moved to the door.

Jenny propped up an elbow and cradled her head in her hand. "Well, like they say, Dan'l, you can't have your cake and eat it, too. Or is it you can't eat your cake and have it, too?"

He turned his head for a final glance. "Dinner's at seven o'clock, Princess. You can stay where you are, or we can go to Maude's."

15

Rico stormed through the colonel's office door. "What?" he snapped. "It better be important enough to get me out of bed."

He nodded to the buckskin-clad figure who'd been staring out the window. Jake Bedford grinned, and leaned back against the wall.

"I'd appreciate your showing some respect for my rank," Hardy retorted. "It's hard enough keeping up the men's morale, much less their respect in this god-forsaken fort. And what in hell were you doing in bed at this hour of the day?"

Rico had no intention of replying, any more than Hardy expected him to. It was just the colonel's way of having the last word.

As he waited impatiently for Hardy to continue, he wondered if Jenny would wait for him to get back.

The sight of her stretched out naked in his bed was hard to forget.

"Jake here said he sighted some Indian sign southwest of here."

"And were they wearing plaid shirts?" Rico asked dryly. "You know as well as I that there's been no serious trouble with the Apaches since Cochise surrendered to General Crook."

"What do you call what they did to Private Hanson?"

"Hanson knew better than to cross the river. Naturally some of them remained behind when the tribe was moved to a reservation. After seeing what that San Carlos reservation looked like, you can't blame them for breaking away. It's a sun-baked hell hole, unfit to even grow crops. They're starving to death. It's no wonder the Indians don't trust the government."

"Cochise and his Chiricahuas were put on the reservation at Warm Springs. There's no comparison," Hardy declared.

Jake Bedford spoke up. "They put them there because the Chiricahua Apaches refused to go to the San Carlos reservation. They don't get along with the Mescolaro Apaches already there."

"Well, now with Cochise's death, there's probably a lot of younger bucks who can't wait to break out of the reservation."

"It's not the government's fault these Indian tribes can't get along," Hardy said. "These settlers come out here from all parts of the country and get along. Maybe the Indians should try doing the same."

Rico winked at Jake. "Heard tell there was a war between the North and South. Seems there was a big difference among the white folks there, and thousands of them died over that disagreement."

"You don't have to remind me about the War Between the States, sonny. I was there," Hardy said impatiently. Gray cigar smoke was beginning to circle his head like Indian smoke signals.

Rico saw Hardy's growing irritation and was in no mood for a face-off with the colonel.

"I'd say the Apache have honored the terms of the agreement and not crossed the river, sir." But unable to resist the temptation, he glanced at the colonel. "Even drunken ones."

"Jake, tell him what you told me," Hardy said, and took another fuming puff on his cigar.

"We were about twenty-five miles southwest of here, between the fort and the river. I was scouting along the bank when I come upon their trail. I figured it was Indians because the horses weren't shod, so I followed it for a distance."

"How big was the party, Jake?" Rico asked.

"I made it out to be about dozen or so," the scout said. "When I came upon them, they had stopped and set up camp. So I skedaddled back to the patrol to keep it from crossin' their path."

"Were they wearing paint?" Rico asked.

"Not that I could see from a distance."

"Were there any women and children with them?"

"Didn't see any."

"What do you make of it?" Rico asked.

Bedford shrugged. "Best guess, just a hunting party looking for game. Worst guess, a hunting party looking for trouble."

"Want it or not, my guess is that they found it at the Cole cabin," Hardy declared.

"If it was a raiding party, we'd have heard more word about it by now," Rico said. "I know Slatter killed that couple, and since I planned on riding out tomorrow to look for him, I'll keep my eyes open for any further Indian sign."

"You'd better, if you want to return with your scalp intact," Hardy called after him as Rico headed for the door.

His room was empty when he got back to his quarters. "Dammit!" He slammed the door and plopped down on the bed.

He trusted Jake Bedford's opinions, and he respected Colonel Hardy's instincts. Both men were seasoned veterans of Indian wars.

So on top of having Jenny on his mind, he now had to consider not only Slatter lurking in the shadows, but the possibility of raiding Indians.

As soon as Rico left, Jenny got up and slipped the bolt in place. The last thing she wanted was for someone to walk in and find her naked in Rico's bed. If her father didn't shoot him, "Uncle" Tom would probably put him in front of a firing squad.

She dressed slowly, her body still tingling from his touch. Nothing she had ever read had prepared her for it—a rapturous feeling building and building within her until she thought she would explode from the pure ecstasy of it. And Rico said the best was yet to come.

Was it possible?

If only the knock on the door had come later. Then she would have known the fulfillment of that moment. But tonight she would be in his arms again. Tonight she would find out. And tonight couldn't come fast enough for her.

She glanced at her reflection in the cracked mirror hanging above a chest of drawers. Her hair was disheveled, and she searched for a comb or brush. Finding none on top of the chest, she opened the top drawer and found it was empty. A check of the others met with the same results.

That caused her to pause and look around the room again. There was nothing personal of Rico's in the room at all. Not a garment on the row of hooks on the wall, in the drawers, or on top of the chest.

Other than his saddle on the floor in the corner, and his saddlebags flung over the back of the chair, there wasn't another article to reflect that Rico Fraser occupied the room.

Her gaze swung back to the saddlebags and she sat down to open them. A rain poncho was shoved in on top of one of them holding most of the articles she had seen before. Ammunition, utensils, a flint, a bag of oats, and the usual hygiene items. There she found a hairbrush, and as she ran it through her hair she continued the search and discovered a rosary, a Bible, and a small bound copy of *Alexander the Great*. She flipped through the pages, many battered and dog-eared.

He was such a man of mystery. Her curiosity led her to open the other saddlebag. There were several changes of underclothes, stockings, several shirts, a couple pair of jeans, a neatly folded pair of black trousers and short suit jacket, a white shirt, and a black string necktie, the ends tipped with silver studs. For formal affairs, no doubt, wondering what type of formal affair he would attend, considering his wandering ways.

As she replaced them, a package fell to the floor. It contained a narrow gold chain with a tiny cross attached, and a small, silver-framed photograph of a woman. She picked them up and studied the picture. The woman had high cheekbones, a rounded chin, and dark eyes and hair that reflected her Hispanic ancestry.

She was quite lovely, and for an instant Jenny felt a pang of jealousy. Then a closer look at the picture caused her to reconsider. The eyes of the woman in the photograph were identical to Rico's.

The woman was his mother.

She swallowed the lump that had suddenly formed in her throat. His life seemed so pitifully sad. All his possessions contained in worn saddlebags; his home a stark room in an army barracks; moving from place to place with only a horse as a companion. The loneliness seemed devastating.

Her heart bled for him, and she replaced the items in the package, retied the strings on the bags, then left the room.

Andrea was all smiles when Jenny arrived at their quarters. "Look, dear, Cynthia Hardy loaned me her sewing machine. I'll have my wedding gown finished much sooner than I expected!"

"That's good," Jenny replied.

"I thought the pattern was too severe for a wedding gown, so I changed the cut of the neckline and sleeves a bit."

"I'm sure that will look lovely, Aunt Andrea." Jenny walked over and gazed out the window.

Andrea stood up and moved to her side. "What is it, dear? Has something more happened? Did they discover more deaths?"

"No, nothing that tragic, Aunt Andrea," Jenny quickly replied.

She was too confused to discuss her mixed emotions about Rico. Besides, this was Andrea's shining hour, the selfless woman's moment in the sun. Jenny resolved she would not do or say anything that would detract from that glow.

Then her spirit lifted as she recalled those rapturous moments in his arms. Yes indeed. Rico Fraser was definitely *her* problem. One she welcomed with open arms. She grinned. *And I mean that literally,* she told herself, amused. *Talk about wanting your cake and eating it too, Jenny!*

She turned with a wide smile. "I wish I had some of your energy, Aunt Andrea. I guess the events of the past few days have finally caught up with me. I think I'll try to take a nap." She hugged and kissed Andrea on the cheek, then sped from the room before her aunt could question her more.

*   *   *

Frank Burke opened the door when Rico knocked promptly at seven o'clock.

"Come in, Rico. What can I do for you?"

"I'm here to pick up Jenny. I promised her a steak dinner when we got back to the fort."

"And I'm hungry enough to eat a whole steer," Jenny said lightheartedly, entering the room.

She looked lovely in a light green gown that matched her eyes. Her hair was tied back with a green ribbon, and hung past her shoulders like a young schoolgirl's.

He had expected she might act more reserved since their earlier encounter, but as usual he underestimated her. She greeted him warmly but politely. And anyone observing her would never have suspected that only a few hours before, she had lain naked in his bed.

Get that out of your mind, Rico. She's not the first girl you've kissed, so stop thinking like a raw schoolboy.

But he sure as hell felt like one, as if he expected Frank to point a shotgun at him for molesting his daughter.

"Maude's steaks are better than the restaurant's," Frank advised.

Rico nodded. "I think so too. I thought that's where we'd go, if Jenny has no objections."

"I'll do whatever pleases you, Dan'l." The devilment in her eyes indicated she wasn't referring to steak. "I just hope the dessert will be as good as the steak."

"I didn't think you were that fond of desserts,

Jenny," Frank said. "You barely touch them at home."

"Since the abduction, I've developed a hunger for them. I never realized what I'd been missing."

Frank frowned in thought, then shook his head. "The abduction and a dessert? I don't get the connection."

"Connection—the perfect word to describe it! I must say, neither do I."

The woman is going to get me shot for certain, Rico thought. "Are you ready to leave, Jenny?"

Again, the message in her eyes could have set the room ablaze. "I've been thinking about it for hours, Rico."

Two could play at that game. "Gotta admit it's crossed my mind as well. A man doesn't have an opportunity too often in these parts to be able to sample a really good dessert."

"Then you're in for a treat, Rico. Maude's good at cooking up a dessert," Frank said. "She often makes a delicious pastry with chocolate frosting that she calls an éclair. My mouth waters thinking about it. I have half a mind to join you."

Rico could tell by Jenny's expression she was as appalled at the idea as he was.

Then Andrea entered the room. "Good evening, Rico."

Rico nodded. "Evening, Miss Andrea. "

"We're going out to dinner," Frank said. "Would you care to join us?"

"No, thank you. I'm working on my wedding gown. Saturday will be here before we know it."

"It can't come soon enough for Captain Masters," Rico said. "He sure was excited about it when I spoke to him earlier."

"Remember, Rico, you promised to be here. Don will be so disappointed if you aren't his best man."

"Wouldn't miss it," he said, shifting nervously. His mind was still on the plans that were now jeopardized by Frank inviting himself to join them.

"I'm so happy to hear that. You and Jenny will make such a handsome couple."

Jenny hugged her. "Not so, Aunt Andrea. We'll pale compared to the bride and groom."

Andrea's enthusiasm was so contagious, Rico couldn't help smiling. He had never seen her looking lovelier; she glowed with excitement.

"Well, there's much to do and a short time to do it in, so I'm getting back to my sewing. You all enjoy your dinner."

From habit, Rico surveyed the occupants of the Boots and Saddles when they entered. As close as Maude's was to the fort's gate, he didn't doubt that Slatter's madness could make him attempt anything.

As his gaze swept the room Colonel Hardy stood up and waved them over to his table.

Frank hurried over to them. "You're the last two people I expected to see here," Frank said. "I'm glad I decided to come. Evening, Cynthia." He bent down and kissed the colonel's wife on the cheek.

"You can thank Cynthia. Instead of staying home and preparing a meal, she pulled rank and had half the troop sawing limbs off the pine trees that I had previously ordered were not to be touched."

"Oh, fiddle-faddle, Tom Hardy. It was a single patrol and we only cut a few limbs off your precious trees." She raised her head to accept Jenny's kiss on the cheek. "Do sit down and join us, darling. And where's our blushing bride?"

"She's sewing her wedding gown. What do you need pine boughs for, Aunt Cynthia?" Jenny asked her godmother.

"To decorate the room for the wedding. And you're the very person I wanted to talk to. I'm planning a luncheon on Friday, and you mustn't breathe a word of it to Andrea. I want it to be a surprise. Setting up housekeeping at the fort, she'll need just about everything, I imagine." She laid a hand on her husband's. "I'm giving her that set of china my mother shipped us years ago that you dislike so much, Tom."

"I know she has some favorite utensils and pans," Jenny said. "I'm sure she'll bring them with her when she leaves the ranch."

"Hold on there, daughter. Everything in that house belongs to me," Frank said.

Jenny looked at him in shock. "Consider them a wedding gift, Father," she said in a disgusted tone. "In my opinion, you should give her at least a third of the Double B. She's worked as hard as you have to run it."

Colonel Hardy chuckled. "Makes sense to me. What do you say to that, Frank?"

"Just like I said: *everything* on that ranch belongs

to me." He directed the reply to Jenny, and they exchanged a hostile glare.

"Does that include me, Father?"

"You bet it does, if you've got any smart ideas about running off and getting married, too."

Cynthia Hardy looked aghast. "There's such a thing as a dowry, Frank. Surely you don't expect your daughter to remain on the Double B the rest of her life. She would naturally go wherever her husband chooses."

"Then she better marry a local rancher who can run the Double B."

"You're mistaken about two things, Father," Jenny said. "Number one, I would never marry a rancher. Number two, even if I were ever desperate enough to marry one, he'd be running his *own* ranch, not yours."

Good for you, Princess, Rico thought.

Some of Jenny's attitude was beginning to make sense to him now. Hardy appeared to thrive on issuing orders; Jenny disliked being told what to do. From the beginning Rico had figured her father had spoiled her, but it was the very opposite. He had tried to break her spirit with ridicule—even now, in the presence of company. But that incredible spirit of hers had enabled her to stand against even a man as ruthless as Ben Slatter.

When they left Maude's, Rico accompanied the Burkes to their quarters.

"Come along, Jenny, it's late," Frank ordered, and went inside.

She looked at Rico and hesitated. "Good night."

Her disappointment to the night's ending was as obvious as his. "Good night, Jenny. I'm leaving first thing in the morning to search for Slatter. I'll be back no later than Saturday morning."

Jenny nodded. "I know. Be careful."

"I will. Promise me you'll stay inside the fort while I'm gone."

The door opened suddenly. "Jenny, come inside," Frank ordered. "Good night, Rico." This time he remained in the open doorway.

"Promise me, Jenny," Rico repeated.

"I promise." Ignoring her father's presence, Jenny pulled Rico's head down to hers for a passionate kiss. Then she turned, brushed past her father in the doorway, and went inside. Frank closed the door and Rico heard the slide of the bolt.

For a long moment he stared at the closed door, then he slowly returned to his quarters.

16

In the days that followed, Rico checked every gorge, canyon, cave, and abandoned mine. There was no sign of Slatter, much less any Apaches.

All that remained to check out was the section along the river that Jake Bedford had described.

"Of course, Bucep, the old-timers say that you don't see an Apache unless he wants to be seen," he said, patting the horse's flank as it drank from the river.

He continued to follow the river and came upon the tracks Bedford had mentioned. About a mile beyond there, he discovered tracks indicating where the Indians had crossed back to the other side. He followed and saw where they came out and continued on their way.

The tracks appeared to be as old as the original

ones Jake Bedford had found. Even an occasional spoor dropping had been baked dry, but he continued to follow them until they swung away from the river and into the mountains.

"Looks like the fort can stop worrying about an Indian attack, Bucep." But what had caused the Apaches to even cross and risk the chance of being shot or captured? It didn't make sense.

Returning to the proper side of the river, Rico scaled a nearby bluff and gazed at the frothy water that snaked between the granite walls of the canyon.

What if Slatter had tried to cross the river but the rapid current had swallowed him up and carried him downstream?

"Reckon that sonofabitch's body could be feeding the fish in the Pacific Ocean right now, Bucep. But why those Indians crossed this river is still bothering me. I think we'll take another look at that Cole cabin."

The area around the house had been trampled by army patrols and neighbors rounding up the Cole stock. Any hope to distinguish an unshod horse among the wagon tracks and trampled footprints was futile. He was confident that had there been, he would have noticed them the day he discovered the bodies.

The inside of the house had been thoroughly cleaned by well-meaning ladies. It was unlikely any possible clue would have been salvaged in the cleanup, but he still looked for some sign that might offer a clue. He had no doubt the culprit was Slatter, but the possibility of hostile Indians in the vicinity might dictate otherwise. Especially in the mind of the fort's commander.

"For damn sure, Bucep, that old couple didn't kill each other," Rico murmured as he rode away.

It was after midnight when he arrived back at the fort, so he went directly to his quarters and went to bed.

As he lay in the dark, his thoughts returned to Jenny. During these past five days he had purposely forced thoughts of her out of his mind to keep from being distracted. But when he had bedded down at night, thoughts of her had filled his head as he drifted into sleep.

Even now, he could see that devilish sparkle in her eyes and hear the warmth of her laughter when she teased him, or her unconscious gesture of brushing the hair off her cheek. He buried his face in the pillow and breathed in the faint scent of jasmine, as intrinsic to her as her incredible green eyes and auburn hair.

But most of all he relived the heat of her flesh against his own, the sweetness of her lips, and her tremors of arousal when he caressed her.

If this Slatter situation wasn't resolved, how in hell would he ever be able to ride away from her?

He'd sworn he'd never permit himself to fall into this kind of predicament, and until now, it hadn't been a problem.

The ludicrous part of it all was that he couldn't figure out how she really felt about him. One moment she would welcome his kiss, and then he'd feel the sting of her scorn for being a "bounty hunter."

Right now it was better that Jenny didn't know his real motivation for pursuing Slatter. He hadn't found any sign that Slatter was nearby, which meant he would have to leave her again.

"I wonder if you spend as much time thinking about me as I do about you, Miss Jennifer?" he murmured as he drifted off to sleep.

Jenny tossed restlessly. She hadn't had a decent night's sleep since Rico rode away. Despite the preparations and excitement of the wedding, the past five days had passed like months to her. At least she knew nothing bad had happened to him. She'd heard Colonel Hardy tell her father today that a patrol had met up with Rico and he'd told them he would be back by morning.

It was hard to believe that in such a short span of time he had come to mean so much to her. Every feature, everything he did, was etched on her mind: his smooth glide of a walk, his effortless grace mounting a horse, the sensual-edged huskiness of his voice, his warm chuckle when he was amused, the way his beautiful dark eyes would brim with laughter or smolder with passion.

And Lord, how she missed his touch. The gentle brush of his fingers on her cheek, the warmth of his palm when he caressed her.

She closed her eyes, reliving the way his kiss could set her blood burning through her body.

No other man had ever had this effect on her. She couldn't wait for his return, and wondered if he even gave a thought to her when he was away.

Jenny sighed and tucked her hand under her cheek.

Would morning ever come?

The following morning Andrea was perfectly calm, but pandemonium reigned around her in the form of Cynthia Hardy.

The colonel's wife had already organized the lunch the previous day, and the women of the fort had generously opened up their hearts as well as their china cabinets and cedar chests, resulting in such gifts as a rocking chair once occupied by General Ulysses S. Grant, a pair of candlesticks cast by the famous silversmith Paul Revere, embroidered napkins and tablecloths, and a patchwork quilt.

Now, on this morning of the wedding, Cynthia's voice, pointing fingers, and flying arms could be heard or seen nonstop as she issued one order after another to the minions under her command.

She had assigned the task of preparing specific foods and desserts including a three-tiered wedding cake, to a dozen officers' wives.

She had seen to the collection of white tablecloths, punch bowls, glasses, plates, and utensils for the food.

She had discussed with Sergeant Dugan, the leader of Fort Redemption's band, the selections of music she wanted and the time each song should be played.

She had sent out patrols to gather flowers off the blooming cacti for the bridal bouquet and centerpieces.

She had formed a decorating committee to make bows and ribbons to decorate the pine boughs that now filled the room with their aromatic scent.

She had even assigned the task of pressing Captain Masters's uniform and Rico Fraser's suit and shirt to the wife of one of the noncommissioned officers.

But her greatest accomplishment had been convincing Maude Evans to donate kegs of beer for the dancing that would follow dinner.

"With our door open, I can hear Aunt Cynthia giving orders all the way over here," Jenny said.

"I can't imagine how I'd have done it without her help," Andrea replied.

"I know, she's incredible. I wish I could have been more help to you, but she made it my responsibility to get you dressed and ready on time," Jenny said, as she added the final pin to Andrea's hair.

She stepped back and looked at her aunt's smiling face in the mirror. "I've never seen you look so lovely, Aunt Andrea."

"I feel lovely. Don makes me feel that way when he looks at me."

Jenny carefully picked up the tiara of woven white blossoms and satin ribbon and placed it on Andrea's head; then she pinned it firmly to her aunt's upswept blond hair.

"The crowning touch. You look like a queen, Aunt Andrea. A beautiful queen."

"If so, then you're a princess, honey. The golden blossoms against your auburn hair are lovely."

Jenny felt the rise of tears and turned away, but An-

drea had already caught her reflection in the mirror.
"Jenny, dear, what's wrong?"

Andrea's remark had been a poignant reminder
of how Rico often called her Princess. Her father
had told them earlier that Rico had returned late last
night, and the wedding was less than an hour away,
yet he hadn't made any attempt to come see her, to let
her know he was back. Was that too much to expect?

Perhaps she had foolishly read too much into his
previous attention to her. After all, he had been ready
to ride away until the Coles were killed. He had even
said good-bye. So maybe she really meant nothing to
him. He had merely been satisfying a man's needs, as
they said.

Well, she had discovered a woman has needs, too.
She'd been such a fool, fretting over her true feelings
for him while he had made his intentions clear.

*What a stupid, naïve fool you've been! Well, not
anymore.*

She wiped her eyes and turned around with a
smile. "Nothing's wrong, Aunt Andrea. I was just
thinking of how much I'll miss you, now that you'll be
living at the fort."

Andrea hugged her. "We'll only be a few miles
apart, honey. I'll always be here for you." Tears glistened in Andrea's eyes, too.

"Hey, what are we crying about?" Jenny declared.
"This is a glorious day—the happiest day of your
life!"

Then they both broke into tears and hugged each
other tightly.

*   *   *

A knock on the door awoke Rico. He had ignored the last two times someone had knocked, but from the steady rapping on the door, it appeared whoever it was had no intention of leaving this time.

A woman's voice called loudly, "I know yer in there, Mr. Fraser, so haul yer skinny ass out of bed and be openin' this door."

There was no mistaking the voice of Molly Shannon, the sergeant major's wife.

Yawning, Rico asked, "What do you want, Mrs. Shannon?"

"I'd be thankin' ya to be takin' yer clothes off me hands. I've been totin' them back and forth so often today, they'll soon be worn thin."

Rico got out of bed and pulled on his pants, then he padded across the floor and opened the door.

"Good morning, Mrs. Shannon," he said to the woman who was almost as tall as he, with shoulders to match. "What are you doing with my clothes?"

She shoved them into his hands. "I've been ironin' them."

"They looked perfectly fine to me when I hung them up before I left."

"Well, maybe ya should be tellin' that to the colonel's wife, 'cause she's the one who told me to do it. Faith and begorra, we'll not have ya shamin' the regiment at Captain Masters's weddin' by lookin' like a scraggly mutt. So get yerself to a barber while there's still time."

"My very intention, Mrs. Shannon. Be sure and save me a dance at the wedding."

A grin softened her face. "Oh, be off with ya, ya handsome dev'l. Bye, Rico."

"Bye, Molly. And thanks for pressing my clothes."

Rico hung the clothes on the wall pegs, then sat on the edge of the bed. Thoughts of Jenny had resulted in a restless night, and it had been almost dawn when he finally slept. Good thing Molly showed up when she did.

He had anticipated stopping in to say hello to Jenny, but now he was pressed for time. Besides, she probably had her hands full with last-minute wedding preparations. After he stopped at Hardy's office, he'd go into town, get a haircut, shave, and a hot bath, then return to the fort to change for the wedding.

Colonel Hardy was rooting through his desk drawers when Rico entered his office. "Dammit, what did I do with it?"

"With what, sir?" Rico asked politely.

"With the letter I'm writing to Washington."

Rico reached down and picked up a sheet of paper lying on the floor. "Is this it, sir?"

Hardy perused it quickly, then settled back in his chair. "Thanks. I don't know what in hell I'm running here. Half my men are out searching for Slatter's ghost, and my wife has the other half picking posies."

"Maybe they'll find Slatter hiding behind one of them."

"Did you find any sign of him?"

"No."

"But you still think Slatter's around here."

"Could be I'm wrong," Rico said.

"Damn right you're wrong. Between your search and the patrols I've sent out, every foot of this area's been scoured. There's not a sign or sighting of him by anyone except Callahan."

"The bodies of Pete and Maggie Cole weren't any figment of the imagination."

"What about those Indians Jake saw?"

"Looked like they remained close to the spot where he saw them. Their tracks led back across the river and into the mountains."

"Well, in this report to Washington, I'm blaming the incident on the Apaches."

"It's no skin off my ass, Colonel. By tomorrow at this time, I'll be working for Frank Burke," Rico said. "That's all I have to report, and since I need to prepare for the wedding, I'll be leaving."

"I hope that includes a shave and a haircut," Hardy called after him.

The wedding was open to any army personnel who weren't on duty. Coupled with the civilians who were friends of the Burkes, Jenny figured there had to be at least three hundred people in attendance.

Due to the size of the crowd and the glorious sunshine, Cynthia Hardy had instructed that the flower-adorned bower, under which the couple would exchange their vows, be moved outside in front of the small chapel.

Jenny took a deep breath at the sight of Rico as he approached her shortly before the ceremony. Clean-shaven, his dark hair trimmed short, he looked like a refined young Spanish nobleman instead of the rugged frontier scout she had grown accustomed to. His black suit fit his tall, muscular body flawlessly, and his white shirt was a striking contrast against his olive skin.

"You look beautiful, Princess," he whispered.

"I could say the same about you," she said, her heart in her throat.

He took her hand and led her up to the bower where Andrea and Don awaited them.

Andrea was a vision of loveliness in her white satin gown. Her hands were shaking when Jenny handed her the bridal bouquet and kissed her on the cheek.

Don was handsome in his dress uniform, his sword on his hip.

Jenny stole a glance at Rico, and discovered his eyes were on her. His gaze was inscrutable before he shifted it away again.

When the ceremony ended, Don kissed his bride and the attendees hooted and applauded.

Throughout the reception that followed, Jenny had little opportunity to speak to Rico. When she sat down at the table next to Andrea, her father and Maude sat down beside her, and Rico sat on the other side of Don.

Although the food was delicious, Jenny was restless through dinner and the many toasts that followed. Though she smiled and nodded on cue, her mind was on Rico's true feelings for her—and her heart yearned for what she would never have.

17

Day had faded into twilight by the time most of the tables were cleared away. Kegs of beer were rolled out for the men's refreshment, punch bowls for the women, and the band struck up the music for the dancing to begin.

The single officers made a rush to claim Jenny as a partner, and by evening she had been passed from one pair of arms to another. Rico had not made any attempt to ask her to dance.

She was at a loss what to think. He had greeted her warmly at the wedding ceremony. Granted, he was besieged with questions about Ben Slatter and the death of the Coles, but surely he could have slipped away for one dance?

For the sake of her pride, she had to convince him it didn't matter if that was how he wanted their relationship to end. Resigned to her fate, she continued to dance with one officer after another.

When Rico finally stepped in, she said, "Why, Mr. Fraser, I thought you had left. Where have you been hiding?"

Having been detained with endless questions all night, he had only been able to catch glimpses of Jenny flitting from one partner to another. Finally able to dance with her, he was in no mood for small talk and smoothly waltzed her across the floor and out the door.

Small groups of guests stood outside talking among themselves, so he led her behind the chapel to a small garden for privacy.

"Finally! It's been killing me to watch all those other men with you all night. I can't blame them, you're the most beautiful woman here. But they don't know you've also the bravest, and the feistiest."

His warm chuckle curled around her heart, a reminder that the attraction between them was far deeper than just the sexual one.

"I owe you an apology, Rico. I thought you intended to ride away once you had your way with me."

"Once I had my *what* with you?" he asked.

"You know . . . become intimate."

"Lady, I'm no miracle maker. I've discovered it's impossible around this army post for even two dogs to become *intimate* with each other."

A burst of laughter carried back to them from afar. "See what I mean? We can't even have a quiet talk or a dinner for two without interruption. And while I'm on that subject, need I remind you, Miss Jennifer, *you* came to *my* quarters . . . which, I have to say, I don't consider intimate."

"Really! Well then, what *do* you consider it?"

"Spooning. Maybe heavy petting."

"Spooning! You call being in bed with a naked woman heavy petting?"

"That's as far as it went."

"Because someone knocked on the door, Rico Fraser."

"And unless my memory has failed me, you also chose to kiss me in front of anyone who might have been looking at the time—your father among them!"

A grin curled at her lips. "Well, that was supposed to be dessert."

Any argument, sadness, regrets, apologies, or the foolishness of wasting a day trying to ignore one another became dissipated by the friendly reminder to both of them of how much they enjoyed being together.

Rico's grin matched hers. "That sure as hell wasn't the dessert *I* had in mind for the evening. I'd like to see you brave enough to try that kiss now when we're alone."

Slipping her arms around his neck, she raised her head until their lips were barely touching. "I never thought you'd ask, Dan'l."

She kissed him with reckless abandon, savoring each moment. Her need for him intensified as shivers of desire raced through her.

"That's not how I remember it, Princess," he murmured huskily when she broke the kiss. "Seems it was more like this."

He crushed her in an embrace, and his mouth covered hers with a devastating hunger and need. She returned it with all the fervor of her own craving.

"Do you think we'd be missed if we don't go back inside?" she murmured when breathlessness forced them apart.

"We'll never know if we don't try," he whispered.

They hurried to his quarters hand in hand, unaware of the figure nearby in the shadows whose steady gaze followed them.

Rico closed and bolted his door.

"Don't light the lamp," he cautioned. "And if anyone knocks on this door, I'm not answering it."

With only silver moonlight to illuminate the darkened room, Rico drew her into his arms. Their lips met hungrily in a kiss that left her trembling.

"Are you certain this is what you want, Princess?" he murmured. "Once we begin, there'll be no turning back."

"I've wanted this from the moment we met," she whispered. She took his hand and placed it on her breast. "My heart's pounding so hard, I fear it'll burst."

He kissed her again, and her head seemed to whirl.

"Let's get rid of this." Hairpins and the flowered tiara fell to the floor, then he removed the remaining pins until her hair cascaded down her back. Burying his nose in its tumbled mass, he breathed in the scent of jasmine.

He laced his fingers through the auburn thickness as he reclaimed her lips, sweeping the heated chamber of her mouth with darting forays of his tongue.

The rest became an endless flow of ecstasy: his removal of her clothes, the discarding of his own. When he picked her up, when he laid her on the bed. His mouth, his tongue, his hands seeking, tantalizing, finding her lips, her breasts, her stomach, the core of her womanhood.

His whispered words of endearment and encouragement. His groans when her hand or kisses found the sensitive parts of him. His scent, his heat, the weight of his strong body on hers—it all merged into the shared rapture as her body climbed toward fulfillment.

And when that moment came—that blinding release—she cried out his name in ecstasy.

As they lay entwined, Rico asked, "Are you sure you have no regrets, Princess?"

"I only regret I didn't do this sooner. It was incredible, Rico."

"I was only fifteen when I had my first offer of marriage. He was a rancher thirty years older than I was, and when my father refused, the man made the same offer to Andrea.

"Also, being raised near an army post, there's been an endless number of eager suitors since then. Many of them were handsome young officers with great futures in the army. And then there were lonely widowers looking for a wife to replace the woman they loved and lost.

"All with different ages, different backgrounds—yet none of them held my interest or appealed to me."

"After a while, I began to doubt myself for refusing all the offers. But then one day, I decided to stop worrying about the dictates of society, to live my life to please myself rather than other people."

"So why me, Jenny?"

"I've asked myself that same question a dozen times. And I think I finally know why. Fate, Rico. At the most perilous time in my life, you rode in like a young Lochinvar and swooped me up into your arms.

"Rico, to me you are that dauntless young knight. You're King Arthur at his Round Table, Leonidas at Thermopylae. You're Washington crossing the Delaware or a fervent Patrick Henry crying, 'Give me liberty, or give me death.' "

She raised her hand to his cheek in a tender caress. "You're my hero, my Daniel Boone, Rico," she murmured softly. "Haven't you realized that?"

"Princess, there's nothing unique about me. You're looking at heroes every time the cavalry puts on their uniforms and ride out in pursuit of marauding Indians. Whenever a lawman faces down a gunman. Or a settler and his wife raise a barn in the wilderness.

"No one is born heroic. The decisions we make and how we handle the circumstances we encounter in life are what make people heroes. And whatever the cause, the danger, or the choice we have to make, we need the courage to see it through, because we're all throwing the same ante in the pot—our lives."

"That brings to mind something I once read," Jenny said.

> *Cowards die many times before
> their death:*
> *The valiant never taste of death
> but once.*
> *Of all the wonders that I yet have
> heard,*
> *It seems most strange that man
> should fear;*
> *Seeing that death, a necessary end,*

Rico finished the quote for her.

> *Will come, when it will come.*

Jenny looked at him with surprise. "You really do know Shakespeare."

"His *Julius Caesar,* for sure," he said. "The wisdom of some words you read, you can never forget."

She sighed and leaned her head on his chest. They lay in silence for a long moment, his arm holding her close. This was the feeling of contentment she had been yearning for since his return.

"It's one thing to say differently, but when you, or one of these heroes you pointed out to me, is actually in a life-or-death situation, don't you fear death then?"

"I can't speak for everyone, Jenny, but I imagine if I had a wife and child I'd fear dying. I'm a God-loving man, but how does one welcome eternal life without fearing what will become of family he left behind?"

"But does one really think of eternal life when facing death?"

"Did you, when you were at the mercy of Slatter?"

"I knew he intended to kill me, but I guess I was more revolted by that horrible man himself to think about eternity."

"So you defied him, rather than cower. That's courage, Princess."

"I think it was just downright anger."

"But there are happier things to think about on a wedding day," Rico said.

Jenny raised her head again and stared down into his incredible dark eyes as his warm palm slid to her breast.

"Oh? And what is the best man thinking about?" she murmured.

Rico rolled over on her, pressing her to the bed. "The same thing that he's been thinking ever since he laid eyes on the maid of honor," he whispered.

Frank Burke had stepped outside to smoke a cigar when he saw Jenny and Rico cross the clearing and disappear into the darkness near the bachelor quarters. He remained in the shadows for a long time, staring thoughtfully at the darkened area. Then he crushed out the cigar with his boot and went back inside.

18

The following morning, Jenny and Andrea said a tearful good-bye as the newlyweds prepared to leave for a honeymoon in St. Louis.

"I wish you would reconsider and come with us, dear," Andrea said as she prepared to board the coach.

"Aunt Andrea, we've been through this before. I have no intention of being the third person on your honeymoon. This is the time for you to be alone enjoying each other."

Andrea hugged her. "Just promise me you'll be careful with this Slatter scare. Do whatever Rico tells you to do."

"I promise. And you have a wonderful time! I'll be thinking about you."

"Sweetheart, they're waiting to pull out," Don interrupted. "We have to get on board."

Jenny and Andrea exchanged another hug and kiss. "We'll be back in a month, dear," Andrea called out as Don practically lifted her into the coach.

As the carriage began to roll forward, Jenny waved and called out, "I love you."

She sighed and turned to Rico and her father, who had stepped back after saying their good-byes.

"I've seen enough of this fort to last me for a month of Sundays," Frank Burke said. "Let's get back to the ranch."

It felt good to be back in familiar surroundings. Before doing anything else she hurried to check her garden, Rico following closely behind. To her relief, it was undisturbed.

Rico made a check of the barn, and then joined Frank and Jenny at the corral, where Frank was filling the horse trough.

"Looks like nothing's been disturbed here," Rico said as he glanced around. "That same horse was in the corral a week ago."

"I've been coming out here every couple days," Frank said.

"I told you to stay close to the fort for your own safety," Rico said.

"Slatter or Indians, I still have a ranch to run— stock to feed, a cow to milk. And Andrea needed to pack up her belongings before she left. But I'm no fool, boy. Hardy sent a patrol with us."

Nevertheless, when they went inside the house,

Rico checked all the rooms to make sure there was no hidden intruder.

"You best take the room at the end of the hallway," Frank said. "It gets a good cross breeze at night."

Jenny spun around in surprise. "But Father, that's Andrea's room. Some of her things are still in there."

"Then move them into the guest room. Makes no sense to tie up a good bedroom," Frank grumbled, and thumped back downstairs.

Rico went over to her and took her in his arms. "If you prefer, Princess, I can take the other room."

She cuddled against him. Just being in his arms soothed her. "No, Father's right. It's just hard to imagine anyone other than Andrea there. It's always been my sanctuary to run to, and be welcomed with open arms. I feel like I've lost a mother and best friend."

"I understand, Princess." He pressed a kiss to her forehead. "And there's no need to move anything."

Jenny raised her head and smiled at him. "Well, I hope you're planning on staying long enough to unpack your saddlebags. Now you'll excuse me, I intend to take a bath."

Rico opened the windows to get the promised circulation through the room, then took a good look around. It was clearly intended for a woman. His attention was drawn to a large armoire and he went over and opened the doors, carved with trailing roses running the lengths of them.

He couldn't help thinking what charm the armoire would add to the barren quarters at the fort Andrea would now occupy. The night they'd joined Colonel Hardy for dinner, he had been as surprised as Cynthia Hardy at Frank Burke's adamant refusal to let his sister take any household items with her when she left. Rico shook his head in bewilderment. Andrea must have cherished this piece of furniture. What loss could it be to Burke to part with it?

He was beginning to understand more about the conflict between Jenny and her father. Though there were always two sides to every story, why did so many people find it difficult to play the hand dealt to them?

Rico hung up his clothing, put the rest of his items in one of the empty drawers, then closed the doors of the armoire.

After he'd familiarized himself with the layout of the ranch yard, the intense heat drove Rico back inside.

He stole a glance inside Jenny's room and saw that she had fallen asleep. Frank's bedroom door was closed, so he was probably napping too. Returning to his room, Rico removed his gun belt, boots, and shirt, then lay down and stretched out.

The bed was considerably more comfortable than the one at the fort, which had been only a thin straw mattress on a wooden frame. This bed actually had springs, a luxury he hadn't enjoyed since he'd left the mission. Within minutes, he drifted into sleep.

*   *   *

When he awoke, the light had shifted away from the windows of his room, and he realized he had been sleeping for a couple hours. He lay there for a few moments, thinking about Jenny and how his life had changed in these past few days.

He walked down the hallway to her room and discovered she was no longer in bed. The door to Frank's room was still closed.

Rico pulled on his boots and went downstairs. Jenny wasn't in the kitchen or parlor, and he began to feel uneasy. A search of the rest of the rooms met with the same result.

Fully alarmed, he went outside. There was no sign of her in the barn, either, and he cursed himself for falling asleep. She was his responsibility and he had let her wander off unprotected.

Then he realized where he would most likely find her, and hurried to her garden. She was sitting there reading.

"I've been looking everywhere for you, Jenny. I wish you wouldn't do this."

"Good heavens! You sound like my father. This is my favorite spot."

"I know, but until things settle down, I'd like you to stay close to me."

She laughed lightly. "And I'd like to stay close to you, but since you were sleeping, I doubt my father would have appreciated that. Besides, I don't think Slatter will venture this near to the house, knowing you're here."

Rico put his arms around her and drew her to him.

"It's still best to use caution, Princess. Since you were once his prisoner, I didn't think I'd have to remind you of that."

He kissed her and they remained in an embrace as he slid kisses down the column of her neck, then opened the buttons of her blouse and slid his hand inside. She drew a shuddering breath as his warm palm cupped her breast and his thumb toyed the nipple into a hardened peak. Then he lifted her chemise and dipped his head to close his mouth around her.

The erotic suckling sent ripples down her spine, and she slipped her arms around his neck. Groping for her skirt, he drew it up to her waist, then slid his hand into her pantalets.

The divine sensation drove her to boldness, and she fumbled at the buttons on the fly of his pants and opened them. He shifted her up and she looped her legs around his hips.

Her groans became constant as he continued to suckle the turgid peaks of her breasts when he entered her, and for endless seconds moved in and out of her. Their passion soared, their breaths quickened, their hearts pounded, blind to everything except sensation as the rhythm of his thrusts increased, building to the explosive climax.

For a long moment she remained limp in his arms as they both struggled for breath, then he pulled out of her. Her legs felt too weak to support her when she lowered them and she clung to him.

The kiss that followed robbed her of breath, and

she buried her head against his chest until she was able to speak.

"Did that really happen, or am I dreaming?"

"It happened, Princess, and I'm counting my blessings." He gave her another quick kiss, then released her and buttoned his fly. "Let's get you restored properly."

Jenny quickly buttoned her blouse and adjusted her skirt. "How do I look?"

He smoothed down her mussed hair. "Good enough to eat." Then he grinned. "But we'll have to cover that lesson at a later time."

She looked up at him perplexed. "What do you mean?"

"Dessert." He handed her the book she'd discarded.

Frank met them at the door when they reached the house and glanced at the bound book in her hand. "I might have guessed you'd be loafing in that garden, as usual," Frank declared. "You planning on putting some food on the table soon?"

"No."

"Well, it's time you do. I haven't eaten since early morning, and I'm hungry as hell. Do you know how to make the potato and dumpling dish Andrea always made that I like so much?"

"I haven't the vaguest idea." She stepped past him into the house. "So perhaps I suggest you'd better make it yourself."

*　　　*　　　*

To ward off any further argument between Jenny and her father, Rico made them cheese sandwiches and fried potatoes for supper. But the tension between the two was so thick he could have cut through it with a knife. Neither of them spoke a word to the other throughout the meal. And as soon as she finished, Jenny retired to her room, and Frank to the library.

Rico stabled the horses, then fed and watered them for the night.

"I sure as hell can't figure out what we're doing here, Bucep," he said as he curried the stallion. "I don't like being in the middle between them. They're both two very stubborn people."

He couldn't help but compare their relationship to that of his cousins: Garth's wife, Rory, and her lovable father, Pop O'Grady; or Jed's wife, Caroline; or Colt's wife, Cassie. The three women were all close to their fathers, and their love and friendship for them was obvious. That sure wasn't true between Jenny and her father.

"Looks like we've found ourselves smack in the middle of a hornet's nest, Bucep, and there's no getting out of it without being stung."

Returning to the house, Rico decided to go to his room to read Cooper's novel *The Last of the Mohicans,* which he had found on the library shelves earlier. But first he checked to make certain the doors and shutters were closed and locked.

Frank Burke was still in his library, and Rico stuck his head in the doorway.

"Good night, sir. Will you be sure to close and lock the windows and shutters in here?"

"Come in and sit down, Rico," Frank said cordially. "I'm just enjoying a smoke before retiring."

Rico began to feel a trifle uneasy when Frank handed him a glass of whiskey. "Cigar?" Frank asked.

The rancher's extreme mood change made Rico leery. "No thank you, sir."

After several puffs on his cigar, Frank said, "Rico, as we both know, you declined my reward for rescuing my daughter and sister. I appreciate that, son, because I worked hard to get what I have today. It's one of the biggest spreads in Arizona, as a result."

"No doubt, sir."

"No need for formality here; just call me Frank." A pause followed again and a smoke ring drifted past. Then Frank leaned forward. "How would you like half of it?"

"Half of what, sir? Ah, Frank?"

"The Double B."

"Why would you give me half of your ranch?"

"As a wedding gift."

The words hit Rico like a slug in his gut. The old man was putting his daughter up on the trading block.

He put aside his glass and stood up to leave. "The answer is no. Thank you for the drink."

Frank's laugh sounded more like a snort. "That's what I like about you, Rico: you shoot straight from the hip. But don't be so hasty, son. Just think about what a rich man you'd be."

"I have no inclination to be married. Have you mentioned this to Jenny?"

"No call to. She's my daughter; she'll do as I say."

It was Rico's turn to snort. "Really? I haven't seen any evidence of that."

"Don't think I don't know what's going on between the two of you. Your actions speak louder than words, Rico."

"My actions are not subject for your approval, Frank."

"They are when my own daughter is involved. I saw you sneaking off together last night. That's what gave me this idea."

"Is this when you pull out a shotgun and march us to the preacher, Frank?"

"Hell, no." Frank leaned back in his chair. "I like you. I'd be proud to have you as a son-in-law."

"And is this plan to get Jenny married for her benefit, or yours?"

Frank laughed. "Like I said, Rico, you shoot from the hip, so I'll lay it out in the open. With Andrea gone, I'm gonna be needing Jenny here to run the house. If she gets married, she's most likely to leave me, too."

"So you're willing to buy your daughter a husband who is willing to remain here, just to keep your own life from changing? You don't care whether the man she marries loves her, just as long as it doesn't disturb your routine?"

"Sure, I care. I told you that I like you—that's important to me. And I figure Jenny wouldn't be averse to marrying you since she's sleeping with you. You're the only man she's paid any attention to in her twenty years. And let's face it, Rico: she's not much good for anything except sitting in that garden and reading her damn books. How could she ever go off and set up housekeeping for any man?"

"I don't see her that way at all, sir. I find Jenny to be as intelligent and witty as she is beautiful. Sure, she's independent and has an inquisitive mind that often gets her into trouble. But that only adds to her appeal. She deserves far better than to be put on the trading block like one of your prize steers."

"Then you ought to be more than willing to marry her."

"I won't deny it's crossed my mind that when this Slatter situation is over, I might consider settling down with Jenny if she's willing to marry. But if that time comes, you can be damn sure we wouldn't remain here on the Double B. We'd be moving to California."

"What's in California that you can't find here?" Frank asked.

"A bit of paradise called Fraser's Keep. My family lives there, and I know Jenny would be happy there."

"Thought you didn't have any kinfolk?"

"Only my parents are dead, Frank. Not my family. And I'm looking forward to when I can get back."

"Then why did you become a bounty hunter? Just for the money?"

"That's another misconception you have, Frank. I'm not a bounty hunter; my motive has never been money. When I finished my education, I earned my living as a scout on a cattle drive, the railroad, and finally for the army."

"Then why were you so fired up to catch Ben Slatter if not for the price on his head?" He snorted. "Don't try to tell me it was for the good of mankind."

"The Slatter gang raped and murdered my mother three years ago."

Frank's expression shifted to shock. He got to his feet and walked over and stared out the window for a long moment, then poured himself another drink.

"You sure bushwhacked me, Rico. Does Jenny know this?"

"No. I thought if she didn't know my motives, then when the time came to leave her, it would be easier on her if she resented me for leaving."

"What about Tom Hardy? Does he know the truth about you?"

"Colonel Hardy only knows that I've been trailing Slatter for three years."

"So you only remained here because you think Slatter's around these parts, and you'll take off again if he's not. That don't bode well for Jenny, if she's smitten with you."

"Your concern for her is coming a bit late, isn't it? Only a few minutes ago, you were willing to sell her to suit your purposes."

"You trying to say your motives are any better? You're getting what you want out of her, too, know-

ing all the time you intend to ride away," Frank accused.

"That's right, and she knows that," Rico said. "Both
you and I are guilty of serving our own purpose where
Jenny's concerned. And out of consideration for her
feelings, let's forget we ever had this conversation.
Good night."

19

Another sleepless night, Jenny got out of bed and walked to the open window. The night breeze that ruffled her hair was a soothing contrast to the smothering heat of the day.

The latest disagreement with her father had disturbed her more than prior ones had. Though she acted as if she shrugged off his attitude, she now had to deal with it without Andrea as a buffer.

She had considered the solution many times: just give in to his demands. But doing so would make her life even more miserable. The more Andrea gave in to please him, the more he expected of her. There could never be a compromise with him. He was an insensitive, selfish man who always considered his own needs above anyone else's. He'd proven that in the way he treated her, Andrea, and Maude. He regarded women as if they were chattel.

A tender smile softened her face. Rico was just the opposite. He might issue commands when it was necessary, but he was protective of women and respected them. When he spoke of his deceased mother, or his cousins's wives, it was always with love and admiration. It made her wish she could meet those women.

She bet Rico would make a wonderful father if he had a daughter. She sighed deeply. He would make a wonderful husband, too.

He was intelligent, understanding, tolerant, and had a sense of humor. Lord knows he was handsome, and he made her heart skip a beat every time she looked at him, and her toes curl when he touched her.

Rico was a decent man, there was no denying that. So what had led him to become a hired mercenary?

She started to return to bed, but drew up sharply when she detected a movement in the nearby trees. Recalling Rico's warning, she stepped back quickly. Could it be Slatter?

Staying concealed, she peeked out for another look just as a man stepped out from the shadows. She smiled and relaxed. The man's walk was engraved on her heart.

She stepped up boldly to the window, placed a hand to her breast, and called out theatrically, " 'O Romeo, Romeo! Wherefore art thou, Romeo?' "

Rico walked over and stood beneath her window. Grinning, he said, "You're mistaken, Juliet, if you think you're going to get another line of Shakespeare out of me. Once is enough."

"You're a spoilsport, Rico Fraser. Couldn't you have played out the scene with me?"

"Come down here and I'll be glad to play *with* you."

"I can't. I'm in my nightgown."

"More's the reason."

"Shame on you. Why are you roaming around in the dark?"

"Couldn't sleep. I've been having that problem since I met you, Princess."

"Why don't you come upstairs, and we can spend our sleepless nights together?"

"What do you have in mind?"

"Oh, I'll think of something by the time you get up here."

When he slipped into her room she was stretched out in bed, her discarded nightgown on the floor.

The next morning, in an effort to impress Rico— certainly not her father—Jenny attempted to prepare a breakfast of French toast, bacon, and fried potatoes. Cooking had always been Andrea's forte, so years ago they had agreed that Jenny would stay out of the way and leave it to her.

Frank came into the kitchen when she was peeling the potatoes, and started a harangue that she was cutting away too much of the vegetable.

Agitated, Jenny chopped haphazardly at the potatoes and cut her finger.

Frank thumped out of the kitchen shaking his head.

After wrapping a bandage around her finger, Jenny returned to her preparation of the meal.

A search of the cupboards revealed the heavy cast-iron skillet that Andrea used to fry the bacon. Jenny laid the strips in it, then got out a fork to turn them over.

Unfortunately, the stove was too hot and the bacon began to sputter. Several drops of the hot grease splattered her hand, and she dropped the fork into the skillet.

She quickly tried to lift the heavy skillet off the stove, but the bulging bandage on her finger interfered with her grasp. The skillet slipped out of her hands, and the pan, bacon, and hot grease ended up on the floor.

Jenny couldn't decide whether to scream or cry. Her cut finger was throbbing, her grease-splattered hand was stinging, and now the floor was a mess.

Tempted to walk away from it all, she told herself, *You may not be a cook, but you're not a quitter, either.*

She got down on her knees and picked up the bacon and threw it back into the skillet; then she wiped the grease up with a towel. She was cutting slices of bread for the French toast when Rico came in carrying a bucket of milk.

"Okay, the cow's milked. What do you need now?" he asked.

She read the recipe Andrea had written in her tidy script. "Two eggs from the chicken coop," she said.

"What happened to your finger?"

"I cut it."

"Well then, can I help you make breakfast?"

"Yes, get me two eggs from the chicken coop," she

repeated tersely. Then she softened her tone. "I'm doing just fine. Breakfast will be ready as soon as I make the French toast, but I need the eggs, Dan'l."

"I had the impression you didn't know how to cook, Jenny."

"Whatever gave you that idea? Doesn't every woman? The eggs, Rico," she repeated, smiling though her teeth were clenched.

He hurried out the door.

Abandoning making the toast until his return, Jenny began to put plates and mugs on the table, but he was back before she could finish. "Are you sure I can't be of help?" he asked.

"Positive, so please get out of here," she said, shoving him out the door. "I don't like anybody watching me cook." Not that anyone ever did, since Andrea had barred her from the kitchen years ago. But he didn't know that.

The short delay was enough to cause another mishap. The coffeepot began to sputter, and before she could remove it from the stove, the coffee boiled over and ran across the hot surface, leaving a dark stain that began to smoke and emit an unpleasant odor. Jenny rushed to open the window to get out the smoke, then hurried back to the stove where the unattended bacon had begun burning. The acrid smell of the burning meat set her to coughing.

Waving aside the steam and smoke, she shifted the heavy skillet to the center of the table and reached for the coffeepot. The handle was hot, and she pulled her hand back and stuck it under cold water in the sink to soothe it. The towel was too greasy to use, so grabbing the hem of her skirt, Jenny picked up the hot coffee-pot and set it beside the skillet on the table.

Now ready to prepare the toast, she beat the milk and eggs together, then dipped the slices of bread into the mixture as directed. Transferring the dripping bread to the skillet, she had to immediately wash up the spill so that it wouldn't burn on the stove's surface.

As she sautéed the bread, she realized she had forgotten to put the potatoes on to fry, and quickly tossed them into the remaining skillet.

The kitchen was in shambles when they finally sat down to eat. Messy dishes were piled high in the sink, the kitchen floor needed scrubbing, the surface of the stove needed a thorough scouring, and the odor of burned food still hung in the air.

"This food is cold," Frank complained, shoving his plate away in disgust.

"It was hot when I put it on the table," she said.

"You must be the worst cook in creation, girl. The toast is soggy, the bacon is burned, the potatoes are half raw, and the coffee's so weak it tastes like piss."

"I don't like the taste of strong coffee," Rico said. "This suits me perfectly." He winked at Jenny and poured himself another cup.

"The only good thing about it is that it's hot," Frank grumbled.

"I think it's a very courageous first attempt," Rico said.

"It's a pity you're not the cook your mother was," Frank continued.

"Nor do I strive to be, Father. So I suggest you either learn how to cook yourself, or hire one."

She shoved back her chair and left.

When Jenny came down later, the kitchen had been cleaned and restored to order. It had to have been Rico, since her father never offered a helping hand in the house.

Deciding to make another attempt at being domestic, she sliced some bread and made a cheese sandwich. That was so successful, she decided to make one for Rico.

She wrapped it in a napkin, tied a red ribbon around it, and grabbed an apple from the pantry. Then, pouring some milk into a glass, she carefully carried them out to the barn.

Her father looked up when she entered.

"Where's Rico?" she asked.

"Callie strayed off this morning and he rode out to find her."

"Oh, I see." Unable to hide her disappointment, she handed him the sandwich and glass of milk. "Would you like some lunch?"

Frank took the glass and plate from her. "I figure this sandwich wasn't meant for me."

"If you don't want it, throw it away." She walked away.

"Food's hard to come by, girl," he called to her. "Time you took note of that." He took a big bite of the sandwich and washed it down with the milk.

Jenny grabbed her book from her bedstand and

went down to the garden to read. She hadn't realized before how long it took for minutes to pass into an hour, and how long it took for daylight to pass into evening. And still Rico hadn't returned.

It was dark when he rode in. He put Callie in her stall and was about to unsaddle Bucephalus when he heard Jenny cry for help. Colt in hand, he dashed out of the barn and saw her kneeling over her father, who was lying on the ground.

"What happened?" Rico asked.

Frank sat up, holding a hand to his head. "I can't rightly say. I guess someone conked me on the head. I heard you ride up so I came outside, and as I was walking over to the barn I heard a sound behind me. Before I could turn my head to see what caused it, I was knocked out."

"Did you get a look at who did it?"

"No. It happened too fast."

"What kind of sound did you hear?"

"Dammit, Rico, it was just a sound. A shuffle or something like that."

"How long do you figure you were unconscious?"

"My guess is just a couple minutes, Rico," Jenny said. "I heard you ride in, too, and I came downstairs when I heard the door slam as Father went outside. When I came out to follow, he was lying here. And I saw a man running into the pine trees over there."

"Do you think it was Slatter?"

"I don't know. It was dark, and I barely caught a glimpse of him."

At the sudden sound of hoofbeats, Rico said, "Whoever it was is getting away! Get inside, lock the doors, and don't go near a window." He gave two sharp whistles, and Bucephalus came thundering out of the barn.

Rico grabbed the saddle horn with both hands and swung himself up before the horse even came to a halt. Snatching up the reins, he galloped away.

Frank was sitting in the library holding a bag of ice against his head when Rico returned a short time later.

"It's too dark to follow a trail. I'll try to pick it up in the morning."

"Do you figure it was Slatter?" Jenny asked, joining them.

"At this point I'm blaming anything that happens on Slatter. I can't get over my gut feeling about the man."

"But it's been two weeks since Ed Callahan claimed he saw him," Jenny said.

Frank nodded. "And if it was Slatter coming here for vengeance as you believe, why didn't he kill me? He was close enough to do it."

"Because you're not his target. I am. My hunch is that he figured he had the opportunity when I was alone in the barn. Your sudden appearance spoiled his plans."

"Or maybe it wasn't him. There's been drifters and thieves passing through these parts for as long as I can remember," Frank said. "And a damn lot's at stake for you to be playing a hunch."

"You'd be surprised how many times I've shoved all my chips into the pot on a hunch, and managed to stay in the game."

Frank gave him a crooked smile. "If that's so, then why jeopardize our lives? Can't say I want me and my daughter to be the ante in your game."

"You're the one who asked me to remain, Frank. I intended to move on. I'm not using you people as decoys; I'm using myself."

"My life was in your hands before, Rico, and I trust your judgment now," Jenny said. "Father, you have no right to make an accusation like that. Rico *saved* Andrea's and my life, and risked his own doing it."

"Don't talk to me about gratitude, girl. Who's responsible for the roof over your head and the food in your belly? Who pays for all them damn books you're always ordering, or those clothes you have on your back right now?"

Undaunted, Jenny said, "Maybe I don't have a right to complain, but let's take Andrea as an example. She gave twenty years of love and devotion to you, cleaning your house, cooking your food, doing your laundry, mending your clothes, even keeping the ranch's books for you. Yet rather than being happy for her because she found love and happiness with a man who loves her dearly, all you can think of is that she ran out on you."

"I never did no such thing." Frank turned with an accusing glare to Rico. "Did you tell her I said that?"

Frank had definitely referred to Andrea running out on him when he'd tried to bribe Rico into marrying his daughter, but Rico wasn't about to bring that up. She would only be hurt by it.

"Keep me out of this, Frank, because you know where my loyalties lie. And the trouble between you and Jenny is too deep for an outsider to get in the middle."

"You mean too much to me to ever think of you as an outsider, Rico," Jenny said.

"Yeah—my own daughter thinks of *me* as the outsider here, even though it was my sweat that built the Double B. All these years keeping the Double B—"

"The Double B! The Double B! Is that your only concern in life, Father?" she lashed out. "You look upon this place as paradise, but I see it as Hades. There's no love here, no happiness. Thank God Andrea was lucky enough to escape from it. I have to wonder if my mother was ever happy here."

Frank's face reddened in anger; his hand clenched into a fist. Fearing the man intended to strike her, Rico moved to Jenny's side.

"Don't even mention her blessed name, daughter. If it weren't for you, she'd still—"

"That's enough, Frank," Rico warned. "I'm not going to stand by and let you do any more damage to Jenny than you've done already. Let's go, honey."

"No, I want to hear it all. She'd still be alive—is that what you were going to say, Father? I always suspected you resented me because she died giving me life."

"No, that ain't so," Frank said. "I didn't . . . I meant—"

Rico interrupted. "You're both beginning to say

things to each other that apologies won't cover later. There's no taking them back and they wouldn't be forgotten, so it's best to stop now."

"There ain't gonna be no more," Frank declared. "I've got a headache, I'm going to bed."

There was a long silence after he left the room. Finally Jenny lifted her head. Tears glistened in her eyes, but she forced a game smile. "I guess you can tell I'm not exactly Daddy's little princess."

Rico put his arm around her shoulders. "You're still mine, Princess." He led her to the foot of the stairway. "Go on to bed. I'll lock up down here and then stop to say good night. I think we all can use some sleep."

Rico watched her climb the stairs. The scene between Jenny and Frank disturbed him more than he wanted to admit. It wasn't just another quarrel between them. It was the revelation of *why* these quarrels existed between them. And Jenny could only be hurt more if they didn't settle it.

She turned at the top of the stairway and gave him a brave smile that made him want to kiss her.

"Good night, Dan'l."

"Good night, Princess."

20

Frank's outburst had shocked Rico. The poor girl had clearly grown up without experiencing any affection from her only parent.

In his own youth, he had often watched wistfully as his friends' fathers taught their sons how to ride a horse, shoot a rifle, and catch a fish. He had watched longingly as a father held his son's hand when they went to Mass, bounced a son on his shoulders, or carried him in his arms if the boy tired.

But when he grew into manhood, he had realized that despite the absence of his father, he had had a mother's love and devotion, as well as the love of his uncle, Father Chavez. Though his kindly uncle couldn't offer all the attention a real father would, by setting an example, he had taught his nephew the meaning of love, compassion, and honor. And foremost, his uncle had taught him an everlasting love and gratefulness for the Divine Father of all of us.

After witnessing the scene between Jenny and her father, he knew she was hurting, and his heart ached for her.

He tapped lightly on her door, then opened it. Jenny was crying, her cheeks wet with tears.

Rico sat down beside her and gathered her in his arms. "Cry it out, Princess."

She clutched a handkerchief in her hand. "I can't cry away twenty years. When I was very young, I never understood why I couldn't please him. As I grew older I began to suspect that he didn't love me, and that no matter how I tried, I would never be able to please him. So I finally stopped trying."

"Jenny, I can't believe that deep in his heart, your father doesn't love you. He's a proud man who, driven to building a successful ranch, expects those around him to have that same dedication."

"If that weren't reason enough for me to hate it, the heat is unbearable in summer, and so much of the ranch is barren and rocky. Though the dramatic beauty is startling in some places, I prefer green grass and trees, and the scent of flowers to that of horse manure. I want the evening breeze to soothe me, not blow sand in my face. This land is as uncompromising as my father."

"Have you thought of moving to a city?" he asked.

She sighed. "I tried once—but Father hired a Pinkerton agent to bring me back. I thought that next year when I'm twenty-one, I'd leave and he couldn't stop me. But now it's too late. How can I leave with Andrea gone? At least it's worked out for her. Don is a wonderful man."

"You are entitled to do what you want, with no guilt. Tell me, Jenny, would you consider marrying a man you didn't love just to get away from here?"

"Is that a proposal, Dan'l?"

He chuckled. "I'm only playing devil's advocate. No doubt there are many men who would happily marry you and remain on the Double B. But what if the proposal meant leaving the ranch? Would that be an incentive to marry?"

"Why would I marry a man I didn't love? That would just be jumping from the frying pan into the fire. If you were that man, I might consider it if you agreed to give up being a bounty hunter. I enjoy your company and . . ." The words suddenly seemed to lodge in her throat.

"And what, Jenny?"

". . . and your making love to me. Is that what's meant by being in love? To like being together and making love?"

"I don't know, Jenny. I have nothing to compare it to."

"Would the woman you marry one day have to be a good cook?"

"I wouldn't make it a prerequisite, but I'd hope she'd have some skill at it."

"Then I guess that would eliminate me as a possibility."

"What about your choice for a husband?" he asked.

"He wouldn't be a bounty hunter, that's for certain. And since I've bared my soul to you, Rico, will you tell me why you chose such a profession? Any woman would want to marry you, if not for that."

"A man elects to do what he thinks he does best."

"I think you'd be good at anything you tried doing. But I've thought about your pursuit of Ben Slatter. You said you've been trailing him for three years. Other than his face on a wanted poster, would you even recognize the man if he was standing next to you in a bar?"

"I met him on a previous occasion in California," Rico said.

Jenny settled back in his arms. "When was that?"

"Shortly after my mother's death," he said, determined not to reveal the whole truth to her. "I stopped in a bar and Slatter, Kansas, and the Carson brothers were there. They weren't wanted by the law then.

"Slatter started complaining to the bartender about serving *breeds* drinks, meaning me. One word led to another, and we started exchanging blows. Trouble was, it was four against one. After they finished beating me until I was almost dead, Slatter decided to hang me. Only the local sheriff's intervention saved my life. Later, the gang shot him in the back while escaping from jail."

Jenny's surprise was evident. "So your pursuit of Slatter is more for personal reasons."

"Yes. For very personal reasons."

Since her sobbing had ceased and she had composed herself, he thought he'd get back to her relationship with her father.

"Jenny, when you and your father were arguing earlier, you said you knew he never loved you. What gave you that impression?"

She didn't reply immediately.

"I couldn't have been more than five or six when Father took me for my first ride on a horse. He held me in front of him on the saddle, but I was petrified and started crying."

Rico could feel her trembling and cursed himself for being foolish to have encouraged her to dredge up her past. He tightened his arms around her protectively when she drew a shuddering breath and continued.

"Disgusted with me, he deliberately prodded the horse to a faster gait and began jumping the animal over obstacles. The more I screamed and cried, the more reckless he became to force me to stop crying."

She looked up at him, her eyes pleading for understanding. "But I couldn't stop, Rico. I tried, but I couldn't stop. Father was furious with me, and shouted that no child of his would grow up to be a crybaby. Every day for a week, he took me riding until I was able not to cry when he did. I suppose that's why I'm not comfortable on a horse to this day. And no matter what he's said to me in the years that followed, I've never shed a tear in front of him again."

Jenny half-laughed. "But he never hugged me, or held me on his lap."

Rico hugged her close. "I'm sorry, Princess. I'll bet that's why you were able to stand up to Slatter, though. Go to sleep now. Things will look better in the morning."

She grasped his hand. "Stay with me until I do?"

"I will."

"Rico, do you think the man who attacked Father tonight was Slatter?" Her voice trailed off as she began to drift into sleep.

"I'll know more in the morning," he said softly.

Rico held her hand until he was certain she was sleeping. Then he brought it to his lips and pressed a kiss on it. He knew at that moment that whatever lay ahead for her, he would be a part of it.

"Sleep peacefully, Princess," he murmured softly. "I won't let the Ben Slatters or Frank Burkes of the world ever hurt you again."

A rising sun had already brightened the sky when Rico awoke the following day. In his concern for Jenny last night, he had shoved the attack to the back of his mind. By oversleeping, he had lost several hours that would give Slatter a chance to slip through his fingers again. He shouldn't have let it happen.

Rico just finished pulling on his boots when he heard the hoofbeats of multiple horses. He grabbed his gun belt and moved to the window just as an army patrol rode up to the house. Strapping on his gun belt, he hurried down the stairs.

Frank Burke had already stepped outside to greet them. "Morning, Lieutenant. What can I do for the army today? If you need to water your horses, there's a trough over at the barn or the corral."

"Good morning, sir," the young officer replied.

Rico moved over to Jake Bedford, who was the

scout with the patrol, and they shook hands. "What's this all about, Jake?"

"We're trailing a prisoner named John Cramer who escaped from the army stockade at Fort Apache a month or so ago. The army figured the Apaches had gotten him, but he's been sighted in this area," Jake said.

"And since the trail led us nearby, we rode over here to make sure you folks are all okay," the lieutenant added.

"Matter of fact, we had an incident last night," Frank said. "Someone snuck up behind me and conked me on the head, but he rode off before we could catch him."

"If it was Cramer, sir, you were lucky. The man is quite dangerous. He was scheduled to hang for shooting an officer in the back. Then he stabbed the guard to death, and shot two of the post sentries while escaping."

"You figure he's the one who killed Pete and Maggie Cole?" Frank asked.

"I have no idea, sir," Lieutenant Brothers replied. "If he did, we can only hang him once. We'll be moving on now, Mr. Burke. I'm relieved to see none of you have been harmed, and I advise you to keep an eye open."

The door slammed behind them and Jenny came out of the house in time to hear the officer's last words. "What happened?"

"A killer escaped from an army prison, Miss Jennifer. I'm relieved you're . . . I mean all of you . . . are unharmed, Miss Jennifer."

The young officer was practically tripping over his own tongue at Jenny's appearance.

"May I offer you and your men a cup of coffee or something to eat, Lieutenant?" Jenny asked graciously.

"That's very kind of you, but we must be moving on. It's a pleasure to see you again, Miss Jennifer." He turned to Rico. "If you see any sign of Cramer, will you let us know?"

Jake Bedford added, "Don't kill him if you see him, Rico. There's a couple more deaths to clear up that Cramer might be guilty of." Then he slapped Rico on the back. "But don't take any chances, friend."

"Mount up," Lieutenant Brothers shouted, and the patrol moved on.

"Could be all this time we've been blaming Slatter when it was this Cramer," Frank said as they turned toward the house.

"I wouldn't be too sure of that," Rico said.

Frank snorted. "Wouldn't expect you to, since it would show you up to be wrong."

When they all stepped inside, they were met by a burning odor and a stream of black smoke emanating from the kitchen.

"The toast!" Jenny cried. "I forgot about it when I went outside."

"More waste," Frank grumbled.

Within minutes they had aired out the kitchen and disposed of the blackened bread. Rico then chopped up some smoked bacon and fried it with a half dozen eggs while Jenny made more toast.

Breakfast was a quiet affair. Rico couldn't figure out which was worse: having the Burkes bickering with each other, or the silence between the two.

He tried to get a neutral conversation started, but his efforts were met with only one- or two-word responses, nods, or shrugs. He finally finished his meal in silence.

A smirk crossed his face as he watched the cavalry ride along the riverbank on the other side of the river. Then he crawled back into the cave where he'd been hiding. Even the Apaches hadn't discovered him on their side of the river. They were all so stupid: the cavalry, the Indians, and those scouts that kept riding up and down over there, looking for him. He'd outsmarted all of them.

In the days that followed, Jenny's cooking skills improved. She still had much to learn, but had mastered cooking oatmeal for breakfast and frying bacon and making toast without burning it.

However, she and Frank avoided each other and continued their silence throughout the meals. Evenings, he would retire behind the closed door of the library, and Rico and Jenny would entertain each other with a card game or some such diversion. By the time another week passed, the strain was beginning to show on all three.

Then they heard the good news that the army had finally caught John Cramer. Although it did nothing to ease the antagonism between Jenny and Frank, the convict's capture was a relief to all, and the fact that there had been no sign of Slatter for weeks led Rico to believe that perhaps he had been wrong, and his nemesis was either dead or had fled. If so, he was not needed here, and should be seeking some confirmation of Slatter's whereabouts, dead or alive.

After an evening of losing three straight games of backgammon, Rico shoved back his chair in defeat. "You may have some shortcomings in the kitchen, Jenny, but you're lethal at a backgammon board."

"You crying uncle, Fraser?"

"He who fights and runs away, lives to fight another day," Rico recited. Then he sobered. "Why not do the same, Jenny?"

"I'm not the one losing, sir," she teased.

"I'm referring to this situation between you and your father."

The laughter left her eyes. "What do you expect me to do? Beg his forgiveness for being born?"

"How long can you go on living together like this? You said yourself you suspected since you were young that he didn't love you. So it couldn't have come as a big shock to you."

"The 'shock,' Rico, was his *reason* for not loving me. How can I be blamed for my own birth? Isn't that all in God's hands?"

"Perhaps that's the real problem your father's unable to accept. Is he very religious?"

"If you're talking about the Commandments, I'd have to say he lives pretty much by them. But if you're talking faith, my father's faith lies in himself. And as for morality, he's been carrying on a relationship with Maude Evans for the past fifteen years, and condemning us for ours. That's an example of his moral hypocrisy."

"Then why remain here? As long as you do, you have to expect to make some compromise."

She shoved away from the table and stood up. "For a while, you had me believing you understood. But I see the message is the same—you're just delivering it more kindly."

She left and went upstairs.

21

As Rico locked up the house for the night, he cursed himself. Why hadn't he kept his thoughts to himself? He hadn't meant to suggest she was the only one who needed to compromise. Nor had he made it clear that he felt Frank was wholly responsible for the bad feeling between them.

If grief had driven Frank to attach blame to his wife's death, why hadn't he blamed himself for getting her pregnant? But to heap that blame on the infant! He shook his head in disbelief.

Rico knew unless he made peace with Jenny it would prey on his conscience all night, so he tapped on her bedroom door. When there was no reply, he turned the knob.

The sight of her caused his heartbeat to quicken. She was asleep, the book she'd been reading still lying open on her lap. She'd brushed out her hair before retiring, and it now lay on her shoulders like a mantle.

He felt the draw at his loins when his gaze shifted to her bare shoulders and the swell of her breasts beneath her nightgown.

He sat on the edge of the bed, closed the book and put it on the nightstand, then leaned down and pressed a light kiss on her lips.

Startled, she opened her eyes. Her expression softened to a smile.

"I'm sorry for what I said, Jenny. I didn't mean to hurt you."

She caressed his cheek. "I know. This situation has put us all on edge. We mustn't let it affect our feelings for each other."

Rico kissed her, and the tantalizing heat of arousal began to wash through her body. He pulled her nightgown over her head, quickly divested himself of his clothing, and then stood above her, his worshipful gaze sweeping her nakedness in the lamplight. A shiver swept her spine and her nipples hardened as she returned his scrutiny with her own inspection of the muscular brawn of his chest, the mat of dark hair tapering down to his flat stomach, and the erection that already swelled between his legs. Her heartbeat quickened and she shifted restlessly, moistening her lips in anticipation.

"I knew I'd never be able to sleep if you went to bed angry with me," he said, sitting on the bed.

"I'm glad you didn't."

Rico slowly trailed his finger down the column of her neck to the cleavage of her breasts. He circled each peak until her breath became gasps.

"And now that all is forgiven, I'd hate to leave without a proper good night."

"Of course," she agreed throatily.

The muscles of her stomach leapt beneath his finger as it slowly continued its descent. She parted her legs as it drew nearer and nearer to its destination, which was now throbbing in expectation.

He had her fully aroused already and he'd barely touched her. That was the power he had over her; the power she couldn't resist—and didn't want to.

Her restless movements turned to writhing as his finger began an erotic massage of her heated chamber, building her passion higher. She gasped under the siege of ecstatic whorls that spiraled through her.

Rico dipped his head and pressed a light kiss on the tip of each nipple, then on her navel. Then his hands closed firmly on her parted thighs and he lowered his head between them. As his tongue teased her, the erotic sensation kept building until she was mindless. She grasped the metal frame of the headboard as if it were a lifeline to keep her from drowning in the rapture flooding her senses.

As her body imploded with wave upon wave of climatic tremors, she cried out his name again and again.

The crush of his lips silenced her cries and he rained kisses on her mouth, her eyes, on her neck, her throat. Then she felt the incredible warmth of his body on hers, pressing her deeper into the bed.

He rolled on his back when she clung to him, pulling her on top of him, and she smothered him with kisses, her seeking tongue finding his, her roaming hands caressing, possessing.

Driven by a passion out of control, she trailed quick kisses to his chest and stomach as she slithered down the length of him until she found his erection, then paused. It felt hot and throbbing in her hand. This was all so new and wondrous to her, but knowing the feel of it inside her spurred her to a greater boldness, and she put her lips on it.

His muffled groan was music to her ears, and she gloried to the sound of it, her excitement escalating with satisfaction at seeing how she could reduce him to the same mindless rapture he always aroused in her.

Driven now by her newly discovered sense of power, her exploration grew bolder and increased in intensity.

With a sound that was more a growl than a groan, he flipped her onto her back and entered her. And locked together, they soared to rapturous fulfillment.

Exhausted, Jenny lay curled against Rico's side as he slept, her head nestled on his chest and the comfort of his arm holding her close.

This is the most contented moment I have ever known.

Even if they were never intimate again, these glorious moments in his arms would remain in her heart forever.

"Trust me." That simple phrase he had uttered

during their lovemaking—when she tottered between sanity and madness—now danced melodiously in her head.

In the past she had trusted this man with her life, and tonight she had trusted him with her entire being, surrendering more than just her body. She had bound her soul to him forever.

When the day came that he rode away, her heart would ride with him. But until then, she would cherish every moment they had together.

Soothed by the rhythm of his breathing and his steady heartbeat, she pressed a kiss to his chest, then closed her eyes.

"I love you, Rico Fraser," she murmured as she drifted into sleep.

Rico was digging a ditch a few days later when Frank strode up to him.

"What in hell are you doing?" he barked.

"I found this piping in the barn—"

"Yeah, it was left over when we installed the inside plumbing."

"So I thought I'd put it to good use and run it between the barn pump and Jenny's garden. That way she won't have to haul heavy buckets of water when she waters her flowers."

"I don't give a damn if those posies get watered; water's scarce enough around here. You never know when a well's gonna go dry," Frank declared. "Besides, hauling those buckets is the only exercise she gets."

"I disagree, sir."

"Like I give a damn! I'm running this ranch, Rico, and I give the orders. If you don't like it, then haul your ass out of here."

"Have you forgotten why you hired me? If I thought Jenny would be safe, I wouldn't hesitate."

"I ain't forgotten, but there's no need for it now. It's plain to everyone that if Slatter's not dead, he sure ain't around these parts."

"Before they hung him, John Cramer admitted to knocking you out, but claimed he didn't kill the Coles."

"And you believe the word of a back-shooting murderer?"

"Can't say I normally would, except he had nothing to gain by lying. It wouldn't save him from hanging."

Frank was silent for a moment, then eyed him with a cautious glance. "If you figure on riding on, you plan on taking Jenny with you?"

"You know why I can't, Frank."

"You tell her that yet?"

"No. And I asked you not to, either, when you tried to bribe me into marrying her."

"Where is Jenny?"

"In the garden."

"If she'd pay as much attention to the vegetable garden as she does to that damn cactus, we'd have vegetables to sell," Frank grumbled, then strode away.

"What about running this pipe?" Rico called out.

Frank looked back. "Ah, what the hell. Go ahead, if you're crazy enough to be digging ditches in this heat."

*   *   *

Jenny glanced up from her book when her father entered the garden. He walked over and picked up the glass of lemonade she'd been drinking, and gulped it down. Disgusted, she got up and started to leave.

"Sit down, girl," Frank ordered. "We have to talk."

"I suggest you save your words for one who wants to hear them," she said, and tried to move past him.

"I said to sit down, daughter."

There'd been enough confrontations between them for her not to recognize when it was wiser to tolerate his anger.

Jenny sat down and folded her arms across her chest. "Very well, Father, if it makes you feel any better, then go ahead and say what you came to say. But I have no intention of arguing with you."

"When do you intend to do some laundering?"

"I just laundered my clothing. They're drying on the line."

"I'm talking about *my* clothes."

"Why, Father, are you implying that you expect my duties around here to go beyond cooking and cleaning?" she asked with mock innocence. "I had no idea."

"Don't you dare try mocking me, girl. I'll not tolerate it."

"Father, are you ill? You look quite flushed. I suggest you calm down—I'd hate to think that you would add nursemaid to the list of your intended duties for me."

Frank broke into laughter. "You've got a good wit, daughter, I'll give you that. And if I'm to believe Rico

Fraser, a lot more grit than I gave you credit for. But just because you read all those fancy books, don't think the day's ever dawned when you can outsmart your father."

"Do I detect a bit of innuendo in that statement, Father? It appears you still have some canary feathers on your mouth you haven't swallowed. What are you hinting at?"

Frank chuckled. "Got your attention now, don't I?"

"Then get on with it, please. What do you want to say?"

"No sense in pretending that I don't know you and that drifter's been playing hanky-panky at night, girl."

"What drifter?"

"You know damn well who. Rico spends more time in your bed than he does his own. For a scout who's supposed to be such a good tracker, he sure has trouble finding his own room at night."

"As usual, Father, you're jumping to the wrong conclusions."

"No point in denying it, girl. He doesn't."

"Nor do I. What I meant is Rico and I don't limit our . . . affection . . . for each other to only evenings."

The cat-and-mouse game he was trying to play with her was so blatant she had to conceal her amusement behind an impassive expression as she watched him choke back his mounting irritation.

"Like I said, girl, you have a sharp wit so I'll cut right to the chase."

"Please do, Father."

"Now that this Slatter scare's over, there's no call for Fraser to remain."

"Go on," she managed to murmur calmly, even though her heart had leapt to her throat.

"I just talked to him and told him I'd kick his ass out of here if he didn't start showing me some respect."

"And what did he say?" She dreaded to hear the answer.

"He said he could care less. And he's clearly anxious to get on with his pursuit of Slatter." Frank smirked. "Apparently you're not enough of a diversion to hold his interest."

Jenny held onto her temper "I'm aware of Rico's intention to leave when he feels it's safe to do so."

"And what if he thinks Slatter *is* around?"

"He's never been fully convinced that Slatter isn't."

"So, what if he finds some evidence that his suspicions are right?"

"His concern for our safety would prevent him from leaving."

"My thought exactly."

Suddenly, his intent was clear to her. Appalled, she asked, "Are you suggesting planting false evidence to keep him here?"

"Why not?"

Jenny stood to leave. "No matter how much I want him to stay, I care too much for him to deceive him."

"Sit down, girl. I'm not asking *you* to. I'm sure I can make it worth it to him to remain."

"Bribery won't work, Father. Rico's too obsessed with catching Slatter."

"I know—I already tried that and it didn't work. But I'll think of something."

"Why?"

"Because you don't want him to leave."

"Suddenly you're concerned about *my* welfare?" She shook her head. "I'm not that naïve. What do you expect to get out of it?"

"A compromise from you. I'll convince your lover to remain if you take over running the whole household. I know you can't do it as well as Andrea, but it's better than nothing. I'll even make it easier for you and do the bookkeeping myself."

"Good heavens, why don't you just hire a housekeeper? I intend to leave next year anyway."

"Housekeepers cost money. As long as you're here, why should I pay someone else to do it?"

"And you won't lie or deceive Rico about anything?"

"No. As poor as you are at it, he seems pleased that at least you're attempting to cook. And you'll have your lover right where you want him—in your bed."

As blunt as that was, he was right. Rico would be pleased to see her trying to compromise with her father. He had even suggested as much. She'd be doing it for him, not her father.

"All right, Father, I like that offer. If you convince Rico to stay, you've got yourself a housekeeper. I wish you the best of luck."

22

Jenny opened the library window and gazed at Rico, hard at work digging the pipeline to her garden. She never tired of looking at him.

His bare back and chest glistened with perspiration. Fascinated, she watched the bulge of his biceps and the ripple of muscles across his back as he tossed aside shovels of dirt. He paused to wipe his brow with the back of his forearm, then walked over to the pump, tossed aside his hat, and stuck his head under the spigot.

Dressed up, her father walked over to him. "Rico, I'm going into town. I have some important business to attend to."

"Why don't you wait until I clean up and Jenny and I will go with you?" Rico said.

"Naw, no call for you to do that, son."

"I can't keep an eye on both of you when one is here and one is in town."

Frank put a hand on Rico's shoulder. "I appreciate your concern, but you know I'm convinced the danger's past. But I respect your opinion, so I'll keep my eyes open, and *you* see to Jenny's safety. Why don't you get out of this hot sun and go inside and have a glass of lemonade?"

You're overdoing it, Father. Rico's no fool.

"Thank you, sir, but I'm fine. I want to get this digging over with."

Frank mounted his horse. "As you wish. By the way, I won't be home until tomorrow since Andrea and her husband are due back on the stage then. Thought I'd stay in town and greet them." He winked at Rico and then galloped away.

Rico stood leaning on his shovel, watching him ride off.

Jenny smiled. *I know just what you're thinking, sweetheart.*

She turned away and returned to aligning the books and dusting the shelves, but her thoughts remained on Rico.

From the time the Slatter emergency had died down, she had dealt with the heartache of when he would ride away. Right now Rico felt the danger still existed. That was why her father's proposition had intrigued her, even though it felt like shaking hands with the Devil. Whatever had happened lately between Rico and him, it had been evident Frank Burke would prefer to see the last of Mr. Rico Fraser. Rico was too strong an individual, with unrelenting principles and integrity, for her father to deal with.

And what her father didn't realize was that she would never align with him to deceive Rico for *any* reason. In truth, he was the one she would be deceiving. She knew Rico would never leave as long as he thought she was in danger, so let her father think Rico was willing to leave if ordered to do so.

So she had agreed to the compromise to keep him from harassing Rico. No one knew better than she how exasperating her father's constant nagging could be, and if she could prevent Rico from having to bear it, so be it.

But she'd never give her father the satisfaction of telling him her real motive. Let him think he won the personal victory between the two of them; that submissiveness that he had always tried to demand from her. Let him believe he had convinced her that they each would profit by exchanging one favor for another.

Actually, she didn't find housecleaning that difficult physically. The issue with her had never been the work involved but from her father's demands that she do it rather than read a book or work in her garden, because to him those things were wasted time.

She went upstairs to clean her father's bedroom, while the opportunity presented itself.

Actually, she didn't find housecleaning that difficult physically. The issue with her had never been the work involved but from her father's demands that she do it rather than read a book or work in her garden, because to him those things were wasted time.

There was no place in Frank Burke's world for
fiction or make-believe. He measured people by their
labor, and in his thinking there was no need for a
young woman to be educated, so he condemned her
continually with accusations of laziness and stupid-
ity. He just would not accept that learning about the
past was just as productive as developing the skill to
ride a horse or prepare a new recipe in the kitchen.
His judgment lay in what you produced—and the
acquisition of knowledge did not fall under that consideration.

She in turn found the acquisition of knowledge
fascinating and stimulating. Andrea, who thrived on
nurturing and embraced the household responsibilities with enthusiasm, always placated her brother's
demands and had prevented any need for Jenny to
even consider the need for compromise with him.

Andrea would be back tomorrow. It was hard to
believe the month had passed so swiftly.

When she entered her father's room, she sat on the
bed and picked up the framed picture of the smiling,
dark-haired woman, and smiled back at it.

"You were so lovely, Mother. It's no wonder Father's so bitter over losing you."

She set to work cleaning the room, and after finish-
ing she undressed to take a bath. She was just about to
step into the tub when Rico came inside.

"Anybody home?" he called.

Jenny slipped into her robe and went to the top
of the stairway. "My *unregrets*, sire, the master of the
house is not here."

"And the mistress?"

"Alas, sire, there is none in this household."

He leaned his arms on the newel post and grinned up at her. "And what is your name, fair maiden?"

"I am called Jennifer of the Garden, sire. I am but a humble servant who is more than happy to service you. What is your wont, sire?"

"My *wont* is the humble servant."

"Well, you can keep on *wonting*. This humble servant is about to bathe forthwith. And you, my lord, are all sweaty and dirty." She raised an eyebrow invitingly.

"The maiden is not only fair, but incredibly prophetic."

"She is, indeed."

Jenny returned to the bathroom and had just settled into the water when the bathroom door opened and Rico walked in buck naked.

"I'll wash your back if you wash mine, Princess. Just slide your pert little derriere forward." Then he sat down behind her, stretched out a leg on each side of her, and slid her back between his legs. "Just like riding double in the saddle."

Jenny snuggled back against him. "Oh, I do like this." She sighed when he massaged her neck and back with his soapy hands. He kissed her shoulder, then cupped her breasts in his hands. "Mmm, I like that, too."

She closed her eyes and lay encircled in his arms until he finished the erotic bath, then she turned and bathed him in like fashion, exchanging kisses as she did.

When restraint was no longer an option, he lifted her out of the tub and they dried each other off, then he swept her up in his arms and carried her to his bed.

Night had descended when Jenny awoke. Rico was asleep beside her. For a brief moment she stared yearningly at him, wishing it were possible to always awaken and find him beside her. But she had him for now, and she wasn't going to waste a moment of it.

She slipped out of bed and went to her room to dress; then went downstairs to prepare something to eat.

Jenny had set an intimate table in the kitchen with candles and a lace tablecloth by the time Rico joined her. She had even put a small bouquet from her garden on the table, and gone down into the root cellar for a bottle of wine.

"I hope you're not too hungry," she said, when they sat down to a simple meal of cheese, bread, baked potatoes, and a fresh garden salad. "I didn't want to spoil this perfect day by burning the food."

He reached over and squeezed her hand. "Princess, you're doing great. None of us are born knowing how to do anything. Do you have any idea how long I had to practice to learn how to fire a rifle and hit what I was aiming at? And I fell off a horse many times while learning to ride?"

"You're so kind Rico—and so generous. Guess what I did today?" she asked with an impish smile. "When I dusted the shelves in the library, I rearranged the books alphabetically."

"By title or author?" he asked.

"By title. Father would never find a book by author. He should be very pleased."

"Speaking of your father, Jenny, I had two short discussions with Frank today. In the first one he threatened to kick my butt off the Double B, and in the second discussion he stopped just short of kissing it. What's that all about?"

Jenny giggled. "He thinks being nice to you will convince you to remain."

"But I thought he wanted me to leave."

"He does, but he approached me with a proposition to compromise. He knows I don't want you to leave, so he said if I agreed to take over all of the household duties, he'll persuade you to remain. So I agreed."

"Why in hell did you do that, Jenny?" Rico declared. "You're giving in to him."

"But not for the reason *he* thinks, Rico. My motive is not to please him, but to make things more pleasant around here for *you.*"

"But he's getting what he wants. You know I wouldn't leave here as long as I thought there's a possibility you can be harmed."

"I know that, but he doesn't. Surely he didn't think I would let Andrea do them alone? I only complained because he *demanded* I do them. As I told you previously, I reached a time when I made up my mind I would stop trying to please him. As childish as it was, at least I made a stand against it. So now, I'm only doing what he wants for my own selfish reason—as unfair as it is to you, I'm ashamed to admit. Do you really think polishing a room or scrubbing a floor is that difficult? Of course not."

She grinned. "Now cooking to me is much harder, and I'm only doing that so you won't have to do it."

"Jenny, I don't want you to do anything for my sake."

"And why shouldn't I? Aren't you remaining on the Double B for my sake, when you want to be elsewhere? Why is that so different from what I'm trying to do?

"You had a good chance to catch up with Slatter, but for the sake of Andrea, Don, and me, you remained with us. And even now, you still are, despite my father's nagging at you."

"Don't make me sound so noble. I've been well rewarded beyond any expectations," he said.

"Then count your blessings, Dan'l, because my father isn't known for his generosity."

"I'm not referring to *his* generosity. I'm referring to yours."

"Mine?" she asked, surprised. "I don't understand."

"We spend a lot of our time making love. Is that your way of thanking me?"

Jenny choked on her wine, and she looked at him in disbelief. "Are you serious?"

Rico chuckled. "I love to rile you. You know, Princess, for the very proper young virgin you were when I met you, you sure learned quickly how to make a man *rise* to the occasion. It's so refreshing to meet a woman as completely uninhibited during intimacy as you are. It's another reflection of your honesty."

"I can't be any other way about you, Rico. I'm in love with you."

Rico knew he would only be fooling himself to deny he didn't feel the same about her. But he couldn't say it, or let that change why he had to leave.

Perhaps the sooner he left the wiser it *would* be. He had allowed his feeling for Jenny to distract him from his mission. Had convinced himself that Slatter was nearby as an excuse to remain.

Everyone else believed the murderer was either dead or elsewhere. So maybe he *was* fooling himself. Had held on to the false belief as an excuse to remain because he didn't want to say good-bye to her.

Rico looked at Jenny and realized how much she had come to mean to him. He was so proud of her. Every day, he'd witnessed her growing maturity. Or was he the one who lacked wisdom? Maybe he *should* have abandoned this search for the men who had murdered his mother a couple of years ago, and left it in the hands of the law.

But it was too late to turn back now. He had made a vow over her grave.

So now he was in love with Jenny and every minute he continued to remain made it ten times harder to try and leave. But the time had come to do so.

All he could hope was that Jenny would wait for him to finish this mission. He would tell her tomorrow, when they went to town to welcome back Andrea and Don.

Not tonight. He wouldn't be the one to spoil her perfect day.

*   *   *

Knowing he would leave her the following day, he made love to her tenderly that night with gentle caresses and confessions of love, rather than the breathless, fiery passion their lovemaking usually became.

And long after she fell asleep, Rico lay awake, feeling the warmth of her in his arms, the sweet fragrance that was Jenny teasing his nostrils.

23

*H*is eyes gleamed with malevolence as he peered through the brush at the man on the opposite riverbank rounding up a couple of stray cattle.

Rico Fraser! He remembered the bastard all right! Too bad he hadn't succeeded in hanging the damn breed back in California.

If it weren't for Fraser, he'd be in Mexico now instead of hiding out here, crippled.

Fraser and his rotten cousins! He'd have liked to have killed them all. It was them Frasers's fault him and his gang had been arrested and locked up in jail. Their fault he had to kill that stupid sheriff in Napa when they escaped. And it was Rico Fraser who shot and crippled him.

Well, this time he'd make sure he finished him off. He had his strength back and could probably pick him *off with a rifle right now. But there was no pleasure in killing him from a distance. He wanted Fraser to suffer before he died. Tonight he'd catch the bastard when he least expected it. He'd cut him up enough to hurt him, then make the breed watch while he raped and cut up that wise-mouth gal he was so fond of.*

Anticipation gleamed in Ben Slatter's eyes as he lowered his rifle and watched Rico ride away.

He drew back quickly at the sound of an approaching horse, and saw a young Indian girl dismount. She was alone and Slatter watched her as she let the pony drink. It had been a long time since he'd had a woman.

Hot anger surged through him and his mouth curled in hatred. Thanks to that half-breed Fraser.

Rico had that itch on the back of his neck that said he was being watched the whole time he rounded up the strays. Probably an Indian on the other side of the river, seeing if he intended to cross.

When he returned to the house, Jenny was ready to leave. He harnessed Callie to the carriage and they headed for Redemption.

Jenny was on pins and needles until the coach arrived. Her heart leapt with joy when Don stepped out and then assisted Andrea out of the stagecoach. Her beloved aunt glowed with happiness.

"Doesn't she look beautiful," she told Rico.

"She certainly does."

Jenny rushed into Andrea's open arms, and the

women hugged and kissed as the two men shook hands.

"Welcome back," Rico said.

"I can't say I was looking forward to it," Don replied good-naturedly.

"Where's Frank?" Andrea asked, after giving Rico a kiss on the cheek.

"At Maude's. They want us to join them once you get settled in."

Jenny linked her arm through Andrea's as they followed the men carrying the luggage.

"You must tell me all about St. Louis, and what the latest fashions are."

"Honey, everything was so fascinating! And wait until you see the new gown Don bought me."

As soon as they reached their quarters, the men dumped the luggage and boxes on the bed and left. Jenny and Andrea remained in the bedroom to talk.

"What's happened with Slatter?" Don asked when they stepped outside to smoke a cigar.

"There's been no further sign of him. I've searched every nook and cranny on the Double B and didn't find a sign."

"So he's still on the loose."

Rico nodded and told him of the John Cramer incident. "Folks around here appear to think that it was Cramer and not Ben Slatter who killed the old couple."

"And what do you think?" Don asked, as if sensing what the answer would be.

Rico snorted. "Seems I'm not thinking right these days. Jenny is a major distraction."

Don broke into a wide grin. "I don't believe it! You're in love!" He broke into laughter. "The way the two of you were at each other's throats when you met, I figured that you'd end up in bed. So what are your plans?"

"I'm riding out tomorrow. I guess I should accept the popular opinion that Slatter's not around here, and search farther out."

"I'm sorry to hear that, Rico. I can tell by looking at Jenny that she's in love with you. And you mean a lot to Andrea and me, too. It's going to be hard to see you go. You sure this is what you want to do?"

"It's what I *have* to do, pal."

"Have you told Jenny and Frank you're leaving?"

"Frank will be glad to see the last of me, but I haven't told Jenny yet. She knows I intend to leave; she just doesn't know it's tomorrow. Keep an eye on her for me, will you? She and Frank don't get along. And without Andrea right there to give her moral support, her life will be misery."

"She has a lot of inner strength, Rico."

"More than you can imagine," Rico said. "I just hate the thought of her being so unhappy."

"We'll do our best, but try and hurry back. I regret the precious time I wasted by not telling Andrea sooner how I felt about her. Ah . . . does Jenny still think you're a bounty hunter?"

"I believe so."

"So I imagine you've never told her you turned down Frank's reward for rescuing them, either."

"That would only make her feel she owes him a favor, and he'd take advantage of it immediately. I did tell Frank my personal reason for pursuing Slatter, but I don't think he'd tell Jenny. It's to his advantage not to. He wants to keep her close by to pick up where Andrea left off."

"That's what Andrea was afraid of."

"Have you told her any of the truth?"

"Yes. She said she sensed from the bottom of her heart that you aren't the coldhearted mercenary you pretend to be. Why in hell don't you tell Jenny the truth, too, Rico? She deserves to know. I think you're wrong in believing it will be easier to see you go if she resents why you're leaving. Nothing you do or say is going to make it easier for her to say good-bye to you."

"Don't think it will be easy for me, either. If I knew how long this would take, it would be easier to make plans. I'd like to take Jenny to my cousins in California until I get back. I know they would welcome her, and she'd be happier there."

"Where are you going to begin to start looking for Slatter?"

"I thought I'd head back to Perdition in case anyone has seen him. It's a lot to hope for, but I have to start somewhere."

"I still feel that bastard's out for revenge, and that I'd be his target since I wounded him and destroyed his gang. With Frank's crew due back soon, Jenny will be safe on the ranch."

"Rico, have you asked yourself if avenging the death of your mother is worth the price of losing

Jenny? I'm going to be frank with you. Your mother is dead, so there isn't one damn thing you can do to change that. If you have faith that she's gone to a better life, and you love Jenny, this is the time you must make a choice between them."

"Dammit, Don, it's not a question of choosing between them."

"No?"

"I made a vow over my mother's grave. You made one to protect this country. If Andrea asked you to, would you desert the army and that pledge you made to your country?"

"Rico, you made that vow at the height of your grief. You've devoted three years of your life already to honor that pledge. Is it worth the possibility of another three years and the cost of losing the woman who loves you? It's your life, and your decision to make. And if you insist upon leaving, all I can say is that Andrea and I will do our best to make Jenny's life as pleasant as possible while you're gone." He tossed down his cigar and ground it out with the heel of his boot. "What in hell is keeping those women?"

"Oh, it's so lovely," Jenny exclaimed when Andrea showed her the gown Don had bought her in St. Louis.

Andrea sighed. "I can't remember the last time I had a gown I didn't make myself."

She pulled a flat package wrapped in tissue paper out of one of the bags. "And this is for you."

"For me!" Jenny exclaimed, and opened the package to discover a fringed white shawl embroidered with roses and trailing green stems.

"Oh, it's lovely!" Jenny draped the shawl around her shoulders.

"I thought it would look nice with any of your gowns, dear."

"Thank you so much. I can hardly wait to find a time to wear it." Jenny took it off, folded it neatly, and wrapped it back up.

"There's so many stores and merchandise, it's hard to make a selection. We bought Frank and Rico new plaid shirts, and Maude a clip for her hair. Speaking of Frank, how did you and your father get along this past month?"

Jenny arched an eyebrow. "How do you think? Now he's resorted to bribery. Yesterday he concocted this scheme that if I took over the household responsibilities, he would convince Rico to remain on the Double B."

Andrea sat down on the bed next to Jenny. "I don't understand. I thought that was Rico's intention, in order to protect you."

Jenny told her about the events that transpired in her absence. When she finished, she said woefully, "So it looks like Rico will be leaving soon. He's still obsessed with finding Slatter."

"Honey, did Rico ever tell you why he is so insistent on bringing the man to justice?"

"Only that he's not pursuing Slatter for the reward. It's something to do with Slatter and his gang trying to hang him. And if he finds him alive, Rico intends to kill him. His mind is made up and there's no changing it."

Andrea appeared as if she intended to say more, then clasped Jenny's hand instead. "I'm so sorry, dear."

"What aren't you telling me, Aunt Andrea?"

"I think it would be better if you hear it from Rico himself. It's something the two of you have to resolve without any interference from the rest of us. Are you prepared to wait for him, no matter how long it might take?"

"I could never love anyone else, Aunt Andrea. I'm sure of that."

"Have you told him how you feel about him?"

"Yes, and he's promised to return as soon as he's certain Slatter is dead."

"Does he love you?"

"I believe he does."

"Honey, have the two of you become intimate?"

Jenny blushed. "Of course. I love him very much."

"Since you knew he intended to leave, wouldn't it have been wiser not to?"

"I don't regret that we did; I love Rico too much. Even if he doesn't love me, it doesn't change how I feel about him. So whatever happens, I'll at least have the memory of those moments in his arms."

Andrea reached out and gently stroked her cheek. "Oh, my dear, I wish I could be happy for you. But I know how it will break your heart when he leaves."

"Would you have done anything differently if our roles were reversed and it was Don?"

Tears glistened in Andrea's eyes. "No, you're right. I just can't bear the thought of you being hurt any more than you have been all through your life. But you're no longer a child. You've made that decision as a woman. So how can I censure you for it?"

"And believe me, Rico didn't take advantage of me. I went to him. So be happy, knowing that I've had that love for however little time it may be."

Andrea cupped Jenny's cheeks between her hands. "I do adore Rico. It's understandable why you would fall in love with him." She smiled tenderly. "My little girl has become a woman right under my eyes, and I've ignored that. I wanted you to stay a girl forever."

Jenny forced a mock frown. "Aunt Andrea, aren't you the one who tried to point out Rico's virtues to me?"

Andrea kissed Jenny on the cheek and stood up. "And here we sit chatting away, keeping those two handsome men we love waiting."

Jenny stood and put her arms around her aunt's shoulders. "Welcome home, darling. I'm glad you're back."

Later that evening, Rico told Jenny of his intention to leave in the morning. Without any attempt at subterfuge, they spent the night together in a room at Boots and Saddles. Their lovemaking was tender and emotional.

As Jenny lay in his arms, perhaps for their last time, she forced herself not to reveal her heartache to him. Whatever Fate had designed for her, there was no changing it.

"I wonder why?"

"About what?" he asked.

She hadn't realized she had voiced the question. "I was just wondering why certain things happen in a person's life. Take us, for instance. Obviously, it was intended for us to meet. Which we did, under the worst circumstances, and thus now are intending to part. So why even have us meet to begin with? What purpose was served by it?"

"Princess, if you're expecting an answer to life and fate, you've overestimated my intelligence. I take things as they happen without trying to delve into the reason behind them."

"But don't you think it's ironic that Ben Slatter brought you into my life, and now is the one who is taking you out of it."

"Slatter was in my life before I even knew you existed, Jenny."

"That's my very point."

"There's nothing provident about that. I followed him here from California."

"But why raid the Double B? There are other ranches in this area?"

"Nothing prophetic about that, either. Your father's the wealthiest rancher around here, and Slatter probably heard his crew was on a cattle drive. Easy pickings."

"And, of course, with an army post right here, and a whole regiment of United States Cavalry, it was a lone scout who saved our lives."

He chuckled. "I told you I'm good at what I do." Then he rolled over on her, and gazed down at her somberly. "Is that why you think you love me? Because I saved your life?"

"Because you *are* my life," she said.

The pain in his dark eyes wrenched at her very soul as he battled to restrain his emotions. She felt the rise of tears but fought them back.

"Rico, my life has been haunted by *if onlys*. But they all seem trivial compared to *if only* you love me as I do you."

He hugged her tighter. "I *do* love you, Princess. Lord, I don't want to leave you. I don't have the words to tell you how hard it is to do so."

It was a bittersweet moment. How long had she waited to hear that confession? "Then why *are* you leaving me?"

"Jenny, I've told you that there's a personal issue between Slatter and me. But I didn't tell you all of it. I'm pursuing him until I kill him or know for certain that he is dead."

"And finding him—killing him—is more important to you than I am?"

"Dammit, Jenny, it's not that simple. It's a question of honor. Remember when we spoke of the choices we have to make in life and the courage we need to see them through? There comes a time, no matter how much it hurts, we have to be true to ourselves. Because honor, duty, and self-respect are all part of that message."

"What's honorable about spending years of your life tracking down a man to kill him? Do you actually believe I can accept that as justification for leaving me? I'm not implying Slatter shouldn't pay for his past crimes. The man intended to rape and kill me, as he had done to others, but thanks to you I survived. And if I can put that grievance aside so we can go on with our lives, why can't you do the same? Let the law or the army bring him to justice."

"If loving you was the only issue, it would be so easy to do that. Three years of my life was enough. Then like your young Lochinvar I *could* ride into your life, sweep you off your feet, and we'd ride off into the sunset and live happily ever after."

"So why can't we, Rico? Why make his death a burden of guilt on the living?"

"Because I made a vow over my mother's grave."

"What kind of vow?"

"To find and kill the men who raped and murdered her."

For a long moment she was too stunned to speak. "You mean . . . Are you saying—"

"Ben Slatter and his gang raped and murdered my mother."

"Oh, dear God! Why didn't you tell me this sooner? All this time I thought . . . I believed you to be a mercenary and—"

"I wanted you to think the worst of me. I didn't want us to fall in love, because I knew this moment would come. I thought it would be easier for us to say good-bye if you resented my reason for leaving. But I was totally mistaken, because neither of us could have avoided falling in love."

Jenny drew a deep breath. "If I begged you not to

leave me, would you abandon your search for Slatter? If I told you you're breaking my heart, would you forsake your vow and remain?"

"I guess I'd have to, Jenny, because I'd have no other choice. I love you too much."

"And I know it would destroy you if you did, Dan'l," she said tenderly. "So I won't ask you to make that choice. Because if you did, you would no longer be the man I fell in love with."

"Then this I swear to you, beloved: if I find him, I'll turn him over to the army. And if there's been no sign or knowledge of Slatter in Perdition, I'll accept that he's dead, abandon the search, and come back. We'll marry and go to California."

"But what if he is alive and finds you first? He's smart and treacherous."

"Have faith that's not going to happen. My mother taught me a lesson I've carried all through my life: When you're on the side of righteousness, always put your faith in the Almighty. So whenever things look the darkest, Princess, look up for His help."

She slipped her arms around his neck. "Things look pretty dark right now, so hold me, my love. Let's not waste another moment of this night, for dawn will come too swiftly."

Early the next morning, after kissing Rico good-bye, uncertain whether she'd ever see him again, Jenny's vision became a tearful blur as she stood at the window and watched the morning mist swallow him up until she no longer could hear the sound of hoofbeats.

24

Jenny had no desire to talk to anyone, to see the sympathy in their eyes, to listen to their words of support, and receive their hugs of comfort.

The fear that he might not return was the battle she must wage alone, one minute at a time, one day, one month, one year. One eternity!

As soon as the sun cut through the mist, she left the Boots and Saddles, climbed into the carriage, and drove back to the Double B.

The early morning breeze was refreshing as Jenny sat deep in thought in her garden.

How would she go on without Rico? She no longer could visualize the rest of her life without him, any more than she could conceive remaining with her father the rest of her life.

Sighing desolately, Jenny got up to greet Andrea when she drove up in a carriage. "Good morning. What brought you out here at this hour?"

"Is Rico gone?" Andrea asked.

"Did you know yesterday that he intended to leave this morning?"

"He told Don. Oh, honey, I'm sorry. I know how you must be feeling."

"Why didn't you tell me? It wouldn't have been such a shock when he told me last night."

"I almost did, but it was Rico's to tell. I hoped in my heart that he wouldn't go."

"Do you know the real reason why he's pursuing Slatter?"

Andrea nodded. "So he finally told you?"

Resentment stabbed at Jenny's aching heart. "So you know about his mother, too. How long have you known?"

"Don told me on our honeymoon."

This only added insult to injury. "I suppose Colonel Hardy knows, too. I suppose the whole fort knows! Apparently I was the only one who *didn't* know. I didn't think you and I kept secrets from each other, Aunt Andrea. Especially when it affects one of us."

"Honey, I decided the issue was too private and should be resolved between you and him, without outside interference."

Andrea grasped her hand and held it between her own. "I wish there was something I could have said or done to convince him to remain. I've thought about it all night. Why do you think I drove out here so early this morning? I knew how you'd be feeling. I'm sorry, dear. So very sorry." Andrea began to sob.

Jenny's resentment dissipated, and she put her arms around her aunt.

"I'm sorry, Aunt Andrea. I guess I'm feeling so sorry for myself that I took my frustration out on you. I don't know how I'd have gotten along all these years without your help and guidance, and I need you more now than I ever did."

Andrea pulled a handkerchief out of her pocket and wiped her eyes. "I'd like to tell Mr. Rico Fraser a thing or two."

"I'm afraid it wouldn't do much good." Jenny tucked her arm through Andrea's. "Let's go inside and have a cup of coffee."

Once seated at the kitchen table, Jenny said, "Rico weaned me away from tea. He usually made the coffee in the morning. That's one of my best memories. Father would still be up in bed, and we'd sit here talking nonsense to each other." She shook her head and bit her bottom lip to keep from crying. "Total nonsense." Drawing in a deep breath, she said, "I could have kept him from leaving, you know."

"What do you mean? I don't believe Rico will ever rest until he has his revenge against Slatter."

"Nor do I. But I know he would have stayed if he knew I was carrying his child."

"His child!" Andrea could barely get the words out. "Are you sure?"

"I believe so," Jenny said. "My monthly has never been this late before."

"When do you expect . . . that is—"

Jenny smiled. "I can't say for certain. We've been intimate since the night of your wedding."

They sat in silence until Andrea asked, "Why didn't you tell Rico? You know he would have remained to do right by you."

"Which is the very reason I didn't tell him. I didn't want him to stay out of a sense of obligation. I wanted him to stay for *me*—because he loves *me*. But his happiness is more important to me than my own, so I let him leave."

Shaking her head, Andrea said sadly, "Oh, Jenny . . . did you ever think that it would have given him an *excuse* to remain? What makes you think he's happy now?"

Every moment took him farther and farther away from her. Bombarded with conflicting arguments, his conscience warred with the desires of his heart.

You vowed to track down the murderers of your mother. Would you forsake honor for love?

But you love Jenny and she loves you. Why deny yourself this chance for happiness?

Don Masters's words joined the internal struggle.

Is the vow to your dead mother at the height of your grief worth the cost of losing the woman who loves you?

There's not one thing you can do for her to change it.

Dammit! Dammit! Dammit! What should he do? Wasn't Don right? What of the living? He was breaking Jenny's heart. He was breaking his own.

No one in this world meant as much to him as

Jenny. And she made no secret of what he meant to her. What would his life become without her? She filled his every waking and sleeping hour.

He suddenly reined up, struck with the reality of the one person—the only person—whose answer he should have sought.

Would his mother have asked or expected him to seek vengeance in her name?

And he realized what her answer would have been.

She would have wanted him to seek happiness rather than the bitterness that had driven him for the past three years.

How could he have been such a blind fool? Such a pompous ass! Where was his faith . . . his trust in God to render justice? Consumed by his desire for revenge, he had presumed to take justice into his own hands rather than leave it for the law to resolve, as his mother would have wished him to do.

In doing so, he had dishonored the memory of the gentle, faithful, and forgiving woman she had been.

And he had done the same to Jenny: besmirched the beauty of her love due to his misguided guise of honor and integrity. Could she ever forgive him?

"Bucep, I've been a damn fool. I've got a different vow I'm planning to make, now, one that will take me the rest of my life to fulfill. I only hope she'll have me."

He wheeled the horse around and turned back to Jenny.

*   *   *

Jenny kissed Andrea good-bye and watched as she rode away, then walked over to the corral. Callie came over to her and Jenny petted the mare. "I bet you miss your boyfriend already, don't you, girl? I miss mine, too.

"Say, Callie, maybe your boyfriend left you a little Bucep behind so you won't forget him. Just like his master did to me," she said, unconsciously caressing her stomach. "I hope the baby's a boy, and that he has his daddy's dark hair and eyes. Those beautiful brown eyes—sometimes sad, sometimes devilish, and so tender at times that they seemed to touch my very soul."

Sighing, she went back to the house, which seemed more hollow and empty than ever. It had never felt like a home to her. Sometimes prison bars were invisible to the human eye—though not the heart.

Realizing she was once again sinking into self-pity, she began to censure herself. Hadn't she ignored the many warnings that Rico would one day ride away? Had she not declared she would have no regrets when he did?

She faced the reality that for a brief time she had known a great love—one that would linger in her heart the rest of her life. She'd been blessed with the promise of a child from that union. And now that the fairy tale had an unhappy ending, the time had come to pay the piper.

The walls suddenly seemed to close in on her, so she picked up a book and went out to the garden.

Within a short time, she began to feel the results of her sleepless night. Her eyes began to droop. As she began to drift into slumber, she suddenly sensed she was no longer alone, and opened her eyes.

Rico stood in her garden, his gaze fixed on her.

"I love you, Jenny, and I'm back to stay. Can you ever forgive me?"

For an instant Jenny felt a sense of absolute internal peace, and she thought she heard a woman's voice repeat what Rico had told her.

Whenever things look the darkest, look up, *Princesa,* for His help.

Smiling through her tears, Jenny rose slowly to her feet and walked into his open arms.

Later, after the man she loved more than life itself had made tender, soul-rendering love to her, Jenny told him she was carrying his child.

How could she once have believed he would look upon their child as an obligation? On the contrary, he was in awe.

And now, with the self-made yoke of obligation off his shoulders, Rico spoke freely of how much he had yearned for marriage and fatherhood.

"We'll marry right away, Princess, and go to California. By the time our child is born, we'll be living in our own house."

Jenny smiled. "Our *own* home."

Her heart felt as if it would burst right out of her chest—he had come back to her. No coercion. No sense of obligation. He had come back to her because he loved her, and her heart rejoiced.

Throughout the night, they spoke of their plans

for the future, their hopes for their unborn child. She wanted a son with his eyes; he wanted a daughter with her eyes, then agreed they would just have to have both.

He described California to her: Fraser Keep and the winery; how much she would love his cousins and how much they would love her.

And above all, they spoke of how much they loved each other.

Later, as Jenny lay drowsily on his chest, she remembered what had seemed like a celestial message to her in the garden. "Rico, have you ever heard the word preen-say-sah?"

"Yes, it's Spanish for Princess. Why?"

Jenny immediately recalled the beautiful, warm-eyed picture of his mother that she'd seen in his saddlebags.

Smiling, she cuddled closer to him, and with his arm wrapped around her, they slept.

It was almost noon when they awoke the following day. They decided to have lunch in town and then inform her father of their intention to wed.

They found him and Maude at a table in the Boots and Saddles. Frank took the news as Jenny expected. He complained about her selfishness and ungrateful-ness in running off to get married; that she was un-willing to repay her obligation to him for feeding her and keeping a roof over her head; how much it would cost him now to hire a housekeeper.

"I even closed my eyes to the two of you fornicating

in my home," Frank raved. "If you leave, daughter, don't expect to come back with your little bastard and find a welcome at the Double B."

"That's enough, Frank," Rico said. "I've listened to all I intend to, and I'm taking Jenny out of here. Your future grandchild was conceived in love, and there's no sin in God's eyes for that. We came here out of courtesy to inform you of our plan to wed. Nothing you do or say will change that.

"As for your accusation that we violated the sanctity of your home, you don't even *have* a home—it's merely a house. No love has ever existed there, either toward your daughter or your sister."

"That ain't so," Frank said. "There was love enough when Ellie was alive."

Ignoring the pitiful contradiction, Rico continued, "As for your reference to our unborn child, because you're Jenny's father—and for that reason *only*—I'll let it pass. But hear me well, Frank: don't *ever* speak to Jenny the way you just have, or call a child of ours a bastard again. Because I'll wipe the floor up with you."

The restrained anger in Rico's voice was far more threatening than all of Frank's bluster.

His tone considerably subdued, Frank said, "Since the two of you are set on getting married, I reckon I can't do much more than say what's on my mind."

"You could give us your blessing, Father. Be happy that you'll soon have a grandchild," Jenny said.

"I've said my piece, daughter."

Rico reached for Jenny's hand and drew her to her feet. "Let's get out of here, Jenny."

"Well, I haven't said mine!" Maude burst out. "Please sit down, Jenny. And you, too, Rico." She had risen and was standing with arms akimbo.

"For twenty years, Frank Burke, I've listened to you criticize your daughter for just being alive. It's time that gal has finally found someone who will face off with you and defend her. I didn't, and Andrea never did. But that's not to say we didn't love you, honey," Maude told Jenny. "Thank God this young man did. And if you don't wish them well, you stubborn old coot, I'll kick your ass out of here."

"Maudie, that ain't no way to talk to me," Frank protested.

"And that ain't no way for you to talk to them," She fired back. "So get on with it. I want to hear it from you."

Frank hung his head. "I reckon I spoke a little out of turn. When are you planning to get hitched?"

"On Saturday," Rico replied. "That will give Jenny time to get packed up and say her good-byes."

"Two days ain't much time to plan a wedding, honey," Maude said.

"I don't want any fancy wedding or reception, Maude. Rico and I thought we would just have a quiet dinner with Father and you, Andrea and Don."

"If you want a fancier wedding, daughter, I'll pay for it."

"I really don't, Father." Jenny slipped her hand into Rico's. "I just want us to get married."

Maude winked at Rico. "And get out of here as fast as you can. And since your father's made such a generous offer, I'll make you the best dinner the Boots and Saddles has ever turned out."

"We'd appreciate that, Maude," Rico said. "Now if you'll excuse us, I have to wire my family and give them the news, and we need to speak to Reverend Kirkland."

Rico kissed Maude on the cheek, and then extended his hand to Frank. "No hard feelings, Frank."

Frank slowly shook his hand. "No hard feelings, son."

"Whew!" Rico exclaimed once they were outside. "At least it didn't lead to bloodshed."

Jenny squeezed his hand and smiled up at him. "Have I told you lately how much I love you, Rico Fraser?"

"I'll never tire of hearing it, Princess."

25

The meeting with Reverend Kirkland went well, and their next stop was to break the news to Andrea.

She was ecstatic. Glowing with happiness, she hugged and kissed them both. "Oh, if only Don was here! He's been out on patrol and is due back tonight. I can hardly wait to tell him. And Saturday! Such short notice."

She took Jenny by the hand and they sat down at the table. "We've got a lot of planning to do, and not much time to do it in."

"If you'll excuse me, ladies, this is out of my realm. I have a wire to send, so I'll be back later."

As soon as Rico departed, Andrea said, "Before we discuss another thing, you must tell me: when did he come back?"

"Shortly after you left yesterday. He's given up searching for Slatter, and said he loved me too much to leave me."

"Oh, honey, I'm so happy, I could cry."

"Don't you dare or you'll have me crying, too! I've barely stopped since he's come back. I'm afraid I'm going to end up with puffy eyes on my wedding day."

"Now tell me how Frank reacted when you gave him the news."

Jenny shook her head. "You know Father. He was his usual negative self until my hero threatened him with bodily harm."

"He didn't!" Andrea exclaimed, laughing.

"But that's only the half of it—you should have heard Maude lay into him! Father was at a loss for words."

"My brother at a loss for words? Oh, I missed all the fun."

"Anyway, he and Rico ended up shaking hands. Father even offered to give us a fancy wedding and reception, but Rico and I had already decided upon a private wedding with only you and Don, Father and Maude."

"And that's about all we'll be able to arrange, in two days. So—which of your gowns do you have in mind?"

They planned the necessary details, and Andrea said she'd drive out the following day to help Jenny pack.

"I wish I could pack up my garden and take it with me," Jenny lamented.

"You can always plant another one, honey," Andrea said. "But a husband as handsome as yours would be hard to replace."

"And speaking of him, here he comes," Jenny said, her eyes gleaming with love. "I thought you were sending a telegram, not receiving one," she said when he entered and she saw the wire in his hand. "Who is it from?"

"Princess, you're not going to believe this. Remember me telling you that my family had planned a trip back to Virginia and I wasn't going because I was trailing Slatter and had no idea where I'd be at the time?"

Jenny nodded. "I remember."

"Well, guess what? They were all in town getting ready to board the train when they received my wire. They're going to stop here to attend our wedding!"

"Really! That's wonderful!" His enthusiasm was so infectious it spread to her. So what if a few more people than she had anticipated attended? "Will they be staying overnight?"

"Yes, according to Clay's telegram. They should arrive by tomorrow afternoon, and they'll be leaving the morning after the wedding."

"So how many will there be? I'll have to tell Maude, for the dinner."

"Counting children?" he asked.

"They have to eat too, and have a place to sleep." She arched a brow. "So how many altogether?"

Rico cleared his throat. "Ten adults, and eighteen children."

She heard Andrea's gasp above her own.

"But they don't want us to go to any extra work for their sake."

Jenny laughed. "Of course not. What's twenty-eight overnight guests?"

He hugged her and gave her a quick kiss. "You're a real jewel, my love. Oh, and one more thing, Princess."

"Yes?"

"How would you feel about a train trip to Virginia?"

The next morning, Jenny, Andrea, and Rico started cleaning up the ranch bunkhouse in anticipation of the Fraser family's arrival later that day.

"I pity the poor adults who'll have to stay in here with all those kids," Rico said. "Who's going to get any sleep?"

"At least the children can work off some of their energy outside. I can't imagine what it will be like for them cooped up on a train for—how many days before you reach Virginia?" Andrea asked.

Rico chuckled. "Six days."

"Six days!" both women exclaimed.

"I guess they're planning some overnight layovers. St. Louis for sure, before crossing the Mississippi."

"At least they'll only have two nights in here," Jenny said. "Rico and I can share my room, which leaves two bedrooms available in the house." Her chin started to quiver as she fought back her tears. "I wish you and Don were coming with us, Aunt Andrea."

"In truth, honey, I'm not. As a matter of fact, I wish

you and Rico were going alone. Our trip to St. Louis was so enjoyable because we were alone."

Jenny was dubious. "How could you be alone, surrounded by other people on the train?"

"They probably didn't even notice them. The romance sure has gone out of you," Rico teased.

"I'm going to remind you of that," she warned.

"Is that a threat or a promise?" Rico asked, grinning.

Jenny glanced shyly at Andrea. "I'll let you figure that out, Dan'l."

Andrea laughed. "Since you two are doing all this figuring, who do you *figure* will get the two spare bedrooms in the house?"

"The couple with the six-month-old baby should get one of them," Jenny said. "An infant would never sleep through the noise in here."

Rico nodded. "That's a good idea. And the men can cut cards for the other room."

When everything was scrubbed and all the bunks and cots had clean sheeting, the three of them looked around admiring their efforts.

"I think this should do just fine," Jenny declared. "At least they all will have a bed to stretch out in."

Andrea mounted her horse. "I have to freshen up, so I'll see you in town."

"If you see Father, tell him to join us when the train pulls in."

"I will, honey." She waved and rode away.

"We'd better clean ourselves up and get going too, or we'll be late, Rico."

Rico thought about the ten adults and eighteen children soon to invade the bunkhouse, and shook his head. "It will never be the same."

Hurrying back to the house, Jenny went directly to the bathroom, turned on the water, then pulled off her clothes. If she hurried, she'd have time to sponge herself off quickly and cool down.

She wasn't surprised when the bathroom door opened. Rico's hair was dripping, and he picked up one of the towels and dried it. "I already showered at the bunkhouse, so we have a little extra time. He grabbed another towel and held it open. " 'Come into my parlor, said the spider to the fly.' "

Jenny tried to look stern. "Rico Fraser, we do not have time for whatever you've got on your mind."

He wrapped the towel around her in the circle of his arms, then murmured huskily in her ear, "Do you realize that once we leave this house, we probably won't be alone for the next month?"

"That long? Oh, my!" She tried not to smile. "Perhaps it's a mistake to go to Virginia with your whole family on our *honeymoon*, Mr. Fraser."

He picked her up and carried her to her bedroom. Removing the towel, he lowered her to the bed.

He released his jeans and they dropped to the floor, then he stretched out on top of her.

"You're so beautiful, Princess."

Her heart had already started pounding from the feel of his flesh against her own.

Her finger toyed with his lips. "Why all the conversation," she asked teasingly. "I thought you were a man of action, with a quick draw."

He chuckled. "You are a lusty wench, lady."

" 'Lusty wench'? Is that a phrase you read in a novel?" she murmured breathlessly as he nibbled at her lips.

He silenced her with a drugging kiss, and she closed her eyes with a sigh of contentment when he covered her face and neck with quick, tender kisses.

A soft moan slipped past her lips when he slid a hand to her breast, then his tongue, and then his mouth, until he brought her to that point of no return—where each kiss, each touch, each whispered confession of love raised her excitement higher and higher, until there was no longer any restraint. Where ecstasy was the only purpose, and fulfillment the only goal.

They kissed and caressed each other's mouths and bodies with breathless mutterings of encouragement, sighs, and groans. Their lips remained joined when he rolled over onto his back. She straddled his hips, the bulge of his erection pressed against her, her breasts flattened against the damp hair of his chest.

He drew a hardened nipple into his heated mouth, then lifted her enough to enter her.

She began to contract against the erection that filled her and sucked in her breath under the wave of the exquisite sensation as her passion soared. Tantalizing shocks of pleasure spiraled through her.

Throwing back her head, she rode him in and out, reveling in the mind-shattering ecstasy as the lave of his tongue and mouth at her breasts increased with her tempo.

Then with a guttural growl that sent a thrilling shiver racing along her spine, he rolled her onto her back, still joined together, and his climax exploded with her own.

It took a while to catch her breath, then she whispered "I love you, Rico Fraser. My life began when you entered it, and it will end if I ever lose you."

Then she kissed him, slipped out of bed, and headed for the bathroom.

Rico's gaze followed the naked beauty of her rounded curves as she crossed the room. For a long moment he lay motionless, then murmured, "Yep, you're one lusty wench, Jennifer Burke. It's no wonder I love you. There's no halfway measures about anything you do. It's all or nothing at all. And I wouldn't want it any other way."

He got to his feet, pulled on his jeans, and hurried downstairs—back to the shower.

26

"Rico, I'm nervous enough for both of us, so will you stop pacing? I've never seen you so restless," Jenny said.

"I haven't seen any of my family since my mother's funeral three years ago. Since then Garth and Rory have had another son, Colt and Cassie had another son, and Jed and Caroline had two sons."

"Then Jed and Caroline win the blue ribbon. It seems sons run in the family," Jenny teased in an effort to relax him. "How many of the children are boys?"

"Let's see—Clay and Becky have five kids. Jake's about eight now, and they have six-year-old twins, Clint and Cody. Plus a set of four-year-old twins, Matt and Elizabeth."

"Hooray! Finally a girl. One out of five. Go on," Jenny said.

"Garth and Rory have two boys and a girl: Danny, Hope, and David."

"Looking better," she said. "The odds have narrowed to two to one."

"Colt and Cassie also have two boys and a girl: Jeb, Sam, and Peter. Sam is short for Samantha," Rico said.

"So the two-to-one odds are still holding up."

"Jed and Caroline have four children. Garrett should be thirteen now; Caroline had him long before she married Jed."

"So Garrett isn't a Fraser by birth."

"Interestingly enough, he is, but that's a story in itself. And since their marriage, Jed and Caroline have had Emily, Luke, and Mike. I've never seen Luke and Mike. Nor Garth's son David, who's only six months old."

"That adds up to fifteen children, which means there's three more."

"Well, then there's still Lissy and Steve. Lissy's the only sister among my cousins. She eloped with Steven Berg right after the war ended. She was the first of the Frasers to come west—other than my father, who was a forty-niner."

"So Lissy and Steve have three children?" Jenny said.

Rico nodded. "Two girls and a boy. Ted, Sarah, and Rachel."

"Hooray for Lissy and Steve! Two to one in favor of the girls. But it still ends up with two-to-one odds: twelve boys and six girls."

Rico kissed her on the tip of her nose. "Princess, you have a remarkable memory. Do you have any idea how long it took me to memorize all those names, ages, and who goes with who?"

"And we're going to get on a train with ten adults and eighteen children between the ages of six months and thirteen. You call that a honeymoon!"

"Jenny, the Frasers had this trip planned and arranged long before we even met. I couldn't commit myself to joining them until now. Trust me, you'll have the time of your life. This family is fun to be around."

"I'm sure they are, but I'm a stranger to them."

"Only until you're introduced. And as soon as we're married, they'll close around you like protective armor."

Jenny still had doubts. "Are you sure there's room for all of us on that train?"

"Actually, we'll have two private cars. One's a sleeper with compartments, and the other car is luxurious, according to Clay."

"And what about eating? How do you feed thirty people?"

"Whenever we want, we can go into the train's dining car. They also make stops where one can eat at Harvey restaurants, which are superb. The biggest problem will be keeping all those kids amused. But I think you'll enjoy the trip, especially the scenery and some of the cities we'll be passing through."

"You've convinced me, Dan'l," she said. "Using

two private cars must be very expensive. Just how successful is your family's winery?"

"It's really grown in the past couple years. They ship wine all over the United States, even to Mexico and South America. As for the expense of the private cars, Caroline's father is a friend of Leland Stanford."

"*The* Leland Stanford? President-of-the-Central-Pacific-and-one-of-the-Founders-of-the-Transcontinental-Railroad Leland Stanford?"

"That's right, Miss Burke." Rico chuckled. "It helps to have friends who own railroads. By the way, Caroline's father, Nathan Collins, will be one of our neighbors in California. Rory's father, Paddy O'Grady, lives at Fraser Keep too."

"Now my curiosity has been piqued. What about Becky's and Cassie's parents?"

"Becky was orphaned young, and Cassie's father has a ranch in New Mexico."

"What about mothers?"

"They're all dead, unfortunately."

"And everyone has their own home."

"Well, Pop O'Grady and Nathan Collins live together. The other families live in separate houses. The first thing we'll have to do when we move there is build our own house."

He had stopped pacing and had finally sat down and relaxed.

She said, "I'm still confused about something, though. I thought this compound where they live in California is called Fraser Keep, and you referred to the plantation in Virginia as Fraser Keep."

"Yes—Clay named it that when he came to California and became a vintner."

"With all the brothers in the west now, who lives on the Virginia plantation?"

"The eldest brother, Will, and his family. After the war he managed to make it profitable again and much of its greatness has been restored."

"So you've never met Cousin Will?"

"No, but I'm looking forward to it."

"And Clay came west and started a Fraser Keep in California. How did all your other cousins end up there?"

"Well, I mentioned that Lissy eloped with Steve, which resulted in Clay and Garth following her to bring her back. They met Becky in Independence. She needed a husband to be able to join the last wagon train leaving for California, so she got Clay drunk enough to marry her. But according to Garth, by the time they reached California they were in love. They went on to the Napa Valley and Clay became a vintner."

"What happened to Garth? Didn't he go with them?" Jenny asked.

"No, they split up and he went searching for gold—my father's mine, to be exact. The following year, after the plantation in Virginia had started to recover, Colt headed west to join Clay. He had always wanted to be a lawman, but after the war those positions weren't given to anyone who had fought for the Confederacy, so he figured he'd have a better chance out west. In New Mexico, the stage he was on was held up. He saved Cassie Braden's life and ended up in the

next town, where her father was the sheriff. Jethro offered him the job as his deputy, then sheriff when he
retired. Ultimately, Colt and Cassie moved to Jethro's
ranch."

"And what happened to Garth while all this was
happening?" Jenny asked. "Was he still out there
searching for gold?"

Rico couldn't help grinning. "That's when I entered
the picture. I was twenty years old then."

"You mean you had never met any of them before?"

"I never even knew I *had* cousins until they showed
up at the town where I was raised—*Tierra de Esperanza,* Land of Hope. They were in search of gold on
the *Monte del Diablo,* Mountain of the Devil."

"Sounds menacing," Jenny said.

"It was. Garth and Rory might have died there if
Clay and Colt hadn't shown up."

"And did Garth find your father's gold mine?"

"I think I'll save the rest of the story for the train
ride," he said.

"But you haven't told me about Jed and Caroline,"
Jenny said.

"Now that, too, is a fascinating story. They actually
knew one another in Virginia."

"But you said Jed isn't Garrett's father."

"Right. Jed was a sailor and spent most of his time
at sea. Nathan Collins had been his captain during
the war, when they ran the Yankee blockade to bring
food and supplies to the Confederacy. After the war,
Nathan inherited his brother's property and sawmill,

sailed to California, and then sold his ship. They ran into each other in San Francisco by accident a few years ago."

"Well, which one of the brothers *is* actually Garrett's father? I can't say I approve of the boy's real father not raising him."

"You'll change your mind when you hear the whole story. But I think I'll save that for—"

"The train ride," she said. "Darn you, Rico. You've whetted my curiosity, and now you make me wait for the answers."

At the sound of a distant train whistle, Rico jumped to his feet. "They're here!" he exclaimed joyously. He pulled her to her feet and they hurried outside.

The arrival of the two luxurious cars created a stir in Redemption. Since the town wasn't on the regular train route, they only saw boxcars or long freight cars on the trunk line.

When a horde of people started to disembark, Rico put a hand on Jenny's elbow and led her over. After the initial hugs and kisses, handshaking, and back-slapping, Rico began introducing Jenny. She tried to associate something with each adult, to be able to address them by name.

Merriment danced in the dark eyes of the man who held a small infant as he smiled at her and kissed her on the cheek.

"Hi, Jenny, I'm—"

"Garth," she said.

He laughed in amusement. "Uh-oh! Don't believe one word that Cousin Rico has told you about me."

"Oh—then that's not your six-month-old son in your arms?" she teased. Rico was right; to meet Garth was to like him. He exuded friendliness.

Garth slipped an arm around the petite blond woman with bright blue eyes beside him. "And this is my wife, Rory."

Rory Fraser hugged her warmly. "It's so wonderful to meet you, Jenny. You're as beautiful as Rico described you in his wire to the family."

If anyone was beautiful, it was the collection of women whose introductions followed. There wasn't a single thorn among the roses.

The easiest one to remember was Lissy Berg, the Fraser sister. She was the only woman with the Frasers' dark hair, and brown eyes. Cassie Fraser also had dark hair, but blue eyes. In addition to Rory Fraser, there were two more blond women: green-eyed Becky, and Caroline with deep blue eyes.

There was no possible way to identify the Fraser men. All were tall, dark, and incredibly handsome. The only distinguishing feature among any of them was Rico's olive coloring.

Determined to make an impression, Jenny quickly composed a light verse in her head to help her remember the women.

> *Rory has eyes of bright blue,*
> *While Becky's eyes are green.*

Caroline's eyes are deep blue,
And their hair a golden sheen.

Now Cassie's eyes are blue, too,
And Lissy's are Fraser brown.
But these two lovely ladies
Have a dark-haired crown.

Andrea and Don soon joined them, along with Frank and Maude, which necessitated another round of introductions. Fortunately, the men always introduced themselves with a handshake, and Jenny's little verse enabled her to quickly introduce each of the Fraser women.

With all the introductions completed, they said good-bye to Andrea and Don, and all piled into wagons and carriages and headed for the Double B.

Upon arriving at the ranch, the first thing settled was the sleeping arrangements. Because of their infant, Garth and Rory had one of the bedrooms, and Jed won the card cut for the other one. The men made quick work of moving in cots for their other children, including a cradle.

The other families quickly settled into the bunkhouse, and less than an hour later, all of the children six and under were put down for naps. As Jenny talked to the other five children, she again made up a rhyme to identify them.

*Lissy and Steve can be thankful to
   Heaven
For nine-year-old Ted, eight-year-
   old Sarah,
and Rachel who's seven.*

*Now Colt and Cassie have three
   children 'tis said.
This handsome lad is their seven-
   year-old Jeb.*

*And though Clay and Becky have
   four others to date,
This one I've just met is their eight-
   year-old Jake.*

Jenny was quite pleased with herself. She had already succeeded in identifying not only all his cousins, but also all of the women and seven of the eighteen children, along with their ages and who their parents were. And she was having fun doing it.

Seventeen down and eleven to go. You're doing great!

Frank took the men on a small tour of the Double B, and the six women relaxed in Jenny's garden with glasses of cool lemonade. As they chatted and laughed among themselves, Jenny decided that Rico was right; the Frasers were fun to be around. It would be difficult to dislike any of them, and they all made her feel that she was one of them, too.

Recalling Rico's reference to meeting his cousins

on the menacing Mountain of the Devil, Jenny persuaded Rory to describe the meeting in detail.

She couldn't have hoped for a better storyteller. Her eyes glowing with excitement, the vivacious blonde described their dangerous adventure and how close she and Garth had come to dying were it not for Rico's intervention.

"Rico told me that Clay and Colt saved your lives," Jenny said.

"Oh, they were very involved, too. But that's just like Rico, never taking credit for anything he does. Garth was down to his last bullet when Rico, Clay, and Colt rescued us."

"You met my Aunt Andrea at the station," Jenny said. "Rico saved her life and mine when we were kidnapped by Ben Slatter and his gang a few days ago."

"Ben Slatter! Rico's been trailing him for three years."

Jenny nodded. "I know."

"That evil man always made me feel as if I needed a bath," Caroline said.

"You knew Slatter?" Jenny asked.

"Yes. He was once our neighbor, and asked me to marry him after his wife died. He wasn't a wanted man at that time, but he was always a rough drunkard. Did Rico tell you Slatter and his gang tried to hang him? They beat him up so badly, he almost died."

"And when our husbands heard about it, they showed up and trashed the whole gang," Cassie added.

Rory looked sad. "I've always wondered if that gang raped and killed Aunt Elena out of revenge. But the mission and the town of Napa aren't anywhere near each other, so the men always thought it was an unfortunate coincidence."

There was so much more Jenny wanted to learn about Rico. "Did any of you know Rico's mother?" she asked.

Rory nodded and extended her left hand, adorned with a narrow gold band on the third finger. "This was her wedding ring. Rico's father, Henry Fraser, made it himself. She gave it to Garth for our wedding, and we were married at the mission by Father Chavez, Rico's uncle. I even wore her wedding gown. Aunt Elena was a gentle, compassionate woman with a heart as big as the son she raised." Tears rose to Rory's eyes. "When I think of what those vicious murderers did to her, it's no wonder Rico vowed to avenge her death."

Lissy slipped an arm around Rory's shoulders. "At least Rico had his revenge, honey."

Jenny's heart seemed to wedge in her throat. "I'm afraid we don't know for certain if he's dead."

All five of the women looked at her with shock. Becky was the first to speak. "You said Rico rescued you, so we assumed he killed Slatter."

"He did get two bullets into him, but Slatter escaped. Rico was unable to pursue him because Don Masters had been shot and Andrea had hurt her ankle seriously. So Rico had no choice but to get us back to the fort."

"So Slatter could still be around," Cassie said.

"There's been no sign of him since then, and no sightings other than a drunk who claimed he saw Slatter asleep under a tree."

Confused, Caroline spoke up. "But I heard Rico tell Jed that his search has ended."

"He gave up the search for my sake," Jenny confessed.

Rory lifted her head and smiled. "Rico must love you very much, Jenny," she said kindly. "And speaking for myself, thank you for bringing him back to us. None of us felt comfortable, knowing he was alone and pursuing that dangerous gang."

"We all feel the same, Jenny," Caroline said. "If it were one of our husbands, it would be unbearable. I'll never forget what Rico looked like after those animals got through with him."

"Well, I think we all should be grateful," Cassie added. "We not only have a wedding to celebrate, we'll have *all* our family together again. And speaking of family, when's your baby due?"

Jenny blushed. "So Rico told you."

"Honey, he didn't have to. That glow you have is from more than being a new bride," Becky said. "Believe me, we're all well acquainted with that glow. It shines over Fraser Keep like the sun."

"I'll say," Lissy spoke up. "Welcome to the family, darlin'."

They clinked their lemonade glasses together.

"The family," they toasted.

"God bless us," Becky declared. "Now, no more

Slatter talk. I want to see some smiles and hear some laughter or I'm going to start kicking some butts around here."

They all laughed and Cassie slipped an arm around Jenny's shoulder. "And honey, don't think she wouldn't."

27

The rest of the day passed swiftly, and before Jenny realized it, dusk had set in. The men built a fire and put a half dozen chickens on a spit. Jenny elected to roast potatoes—which had become her specialty—and the rest of the women cut up vegetables from the garden for a salad.

Andrea, Don, and Maude arrived with several large cakes, two apple pies, wine, and a keg of beer.

Over the course of the evening, Jenny memorized the names of six more children before they were put to bed. Her biggest surprise of the day was how much her father appeared to be enjoying himself, especially considering his outburst when he learned she was getting married. Apparently Maude had had a few additional words with him when they were alone.

She could tell he liked the Fraser men, even tolerated their children. And the women kept flattering him, which fed his ego. She watched with amusement as he now played ring-around-the-rosy with the children.

A sudden outburst of laughter came from Rico, who was at the fire with the other men. She smiled tenderly. She had never noticed before how easily laughter came to him. It was an infectious, warm sound and the laughter always carried to his eyes.

Glancing around at the people nearby, talking, laughing, and relaxing, Jenny realized what a contented day this had been.

Andrea, Don, and Maude were preparing to leave, so Jenny went over to their carriage to say good night.

Andrea hugged and kissed her. "Well, tomorrow is the big day."

"I'm so happy, Aunt Andrea. Tell me this isn't a dream I'll soon wake from."

"It does seem dreamlike," Andrea said. "Both of us finding love after all these years."

Jenny nodded. "It's strange, how so much happiness could come from such violence. Aunt Andrea, with both of us leaving him, do you think Father will get along?"

"I think he'll do just fine, honey."

"I'll see to that, Jenny," Maude said as she and Jenny shared a hug and kiss. "And we'll expect to see all of you at Boots and Saddles at nine o'clock."

"Come on, ladies, let's get going. We've got a long ride ahead of us," Don said.

Amid a barrage of waves and shouts of good-bye, the carriage moved away.

"I think I'll turn in," Rory said. "This has been a long day."

Cassie joined her. "I will, too. Those men can sit up and talk all night if they want to."

It wasn't much longer before Becky, Caroline, and Lissy did the same.

Jenny saw no reason to remain, either. Tomorrow was her wedding day, and the day after that they would be leaving for Virginia. She should take this opportunity to sleep while she had the chance.

Jenny awoke the following morning to what sounded like children's laughter. For several seconds she lay lazily trying to identify the sound. When she realized it *was* childish laughter, she bolted out of bed just as the clock in the hallway chimed seven. Good Lord! This was her wedding day, and they were expected in town in two hours! And the ride alone would take almost one hour.

Where was Rico?

She glanced back at the bed and saw he had not spent the night there. She went to the window, and saw that the men had begun harnessing up wagons and carriages.

Jenny hurriedly put on her robe, then grabbed fresh underclothes from a drawer. When she opened the door to rush to the bathroom, she nearly fell over the little girl sitting on the floor playing with a doll.

"I'm so sorry, Emily," she said apologetically to the four-year-old. "Did I hurt you, honey?"

"Mommy," the child shouted, and ran off crying in search of her mother.

Jenny dashed into the bathroom and locked the door, only to discover there was no hot water. Since there wasn't time to wait for the water to heat, she settled for a quick sponge bath.

By the time she returned to her room, there was still no sign of Rico. Had he already dressed for the wedding?

She had just finished putting on her gown when there was a tap on the door. She opened it to the smiling faces of Becky and Cassie, who entered with cheery good mornings.

"Good morning. Why didn't anyone wake me?"

"Your future husband insisted no one disturb you," Cassie said.

"And he's probably right," Becky added. "I doubt you'll get too much sleep for a while."

"Do either of you know where Rico is? Did he get any sleep last night?"

Becky shook her head. "I doubt it. Those men stayed up all night at the fire. I did see Rico in the barn shoeing his horse."

"Shoeing his horse! He should be dressing for the wedding." Jenny began to brush nervously at her hair. She needed Andrea at a time like this.

"You look like you could use a hand, Jenny," Cassie said. "Let me help. I'm pretty good with hair arrangements."

Relieved, she gave Cassie the brush.

While Cassie pulled Jenny's hair off her cheeks and

swept it up into a bun, Becky went outside and came back with several tiny blue and yellow flowers and strung them on a yellow ribbon. Cassie wove the ribbon around the bun and stepped back to admire the effect. "You look beautiful, honey."

Jenny and her handmaidens had just finished when Rico shouted up from below. "You all about ready up there?"

Becky leaned out the window. "I should ask you the same question, Rico Fraser."

"We're all set to go down here. I showered and dressed in the barn. So hurry up, we don't want to miss the wedding."

Joining Becky at the window, Cassie shouted back, "Very funny, Rico. We've been ready for hours, waiting for you. So start whistling 'Here Comes the Bride.' "

Maude Evans had risen at dawn to supervise the preparation of Boots and Saddles for the wedding. It was more than just the day of Jenny's wedding. She had always suspected that if his daughter and sister ever moved on with their own lives, Frank would turn to her. She had been right.

Despite knowing the man for thirty years, she had never expected the proposition he'd suggested last night and the steps he had already put in motion. If she agreed to his idea, it would change her life. And she wasn't sure if she really wanted to change it, no matter how much she loved that stubborn man. It was a tough decision to make, now that he'd put his cards on the table.

Oh, well, she had time to consider it. Right now she had this wedding to get through. As she added the final flower to the three-tiered wedding cake, Maude couldn't help smiling. Jenny and Rico getting married. If ever there was a match made in Heaven, it was those two. She had figured the same about Andrea and Don Masters, too.

She stepped back to assess the result. "You know, Bess, I think I missed my true calling in life."

"You mean you should have opened a pastry store?" asked the older woman, who had been Maude's kitchen assistant for the past twenty years.

"Yes. This cake is beautiful, if I do say so myself."

Maude left the kitchen to see how Bess's husband Ollie was doing in the other room. The bar was now lined with dishes for the wedding buffet following the ceremony. Checkered tablecloths covered all the tables, and colorful balloons were strung from the rafters and chandeliers, backs of chairs, or wherever Ollie had found a spot to tie one to.

Maude put her hands on her hips and shook her head. With her usual pragmatic approach to life, she said, "Maudie, there's just no making a silk purse out of a sow's ear. A saloon's still a saloon."

But even though no orchestra accompanied the entrance of the bride and groom, no music could ever have been sweeter than the song in their hearts. And after the families filed in and took seats at the tables, the grandest ballroom in the finest hotel could not have been filled with more love. There was hardly a dry eye in the room among those assembled to witness the wedding of Enrico Joseph Fraser and Jennifer Elizabeth Burke when Pastor Kirkland opened his Bible and began,

"Dearly Beloved, we are gathered here today . . ."

Jenny remembered only brief images of the ceremony: Rico standing tall beside her, the resonance of Pastor Kirkland's voice, a child's sudden laugh.

She must have responded to everything correctly, for suddenly, when asked for the ring, Rico slipped a gold chain around her neck. A tiny gold cross dangled from its narrow links.

Emotion swelled in her heart, as she recalled seeing the chain in his saddlebags, and realized it held great significance to him.

Once they had sworn their vows, and shared their first kiss as husband and wife, Rico gazed at his wife. She may not have been dressed in a fancy gown with a lacy veil, but no bride could be lovelier than his beloved Princess in the yellow gown she'd worn the first time he saw her—and fell in love with her.

And as Jenny looked up into the face of her husband for the first time, she thought that no groom could ever be more handsome or more heroic.

He was her hero, hers alone. His weapons were not the Colt on his hip or the thundering steed he rode, but rather a lopsided grin, the warmth of his chuckle, and the tenderness of his touch.

Her beloved.

Holding hands, the newlyweds turned to greet their well-wishers.

*   *   *

Later, Jenny had to admit to herself that she didn't feel any differently than she had before the ceremony. For no matter what she had once naively thought, or denied to the contrary, she had pledged herself to Rico Fraser from the first time he'd made love to her. No official wedding ceremony could ever make that love any more binding.

She was a Fraser now—a member of this throng who hugged and kissed her as she passed among them, accepting their wishes and love for a happy future. And the child she carried would be born a Fraser, the name she had come to love and respect.

Caroline came over to hug and kiss her. Then, with a poignant smile, she reached out and touched the chain.

"This belonged to Rico's mother. Slatter had taken it, and Rico had trailed them and faced them down in a barroom when Slatter tried to sell the chain for the price of a drink. That's the time they almost beat him to death."

Caroline shook her head in remembrance. "He was so feverish, the doctor didn't expect him to survive. In his delirium, Rico kept calling for the chain. When I found it and put it in his hand, he quieted.

"I believe it aided his recovery just as much as the medical attention. This was his most cherished possession, Jenny. He must love you so much to part with it." She threw her arms around Jenny, both of them teary-eyed.

Jed came over to them. "Ladies, ladies, I know it's

common to cry at weddings, but if the two of you keep this up we'll have to man the lifeboats."

"I just told Jenny the story behind the chain," Caroline said, dabbing at her eyes.

Jenny gently touched the chain at her neck. "And I'll treasure it the rest of my life. It means more to me than any ring ever could."

The meal that followed was delicious. By the time they returned to the Double B, the men, who had stayed up most of the previous night, were even more ready for a nap than the children.

Rico had just closed the bedroom door when Frank knocked and asked him and Jenny to join him in the library.

Rico noticed that Frank's hand was shaking when he poured him a drink and Jenny a glass of sherry. He then poured himself a drink and sat down. Hand in hand, Rico and Jenny sat on the couch and watched as Frank gulped his drink down, then got to his feet again and began to pace. Jenny glanced at Rico and shrugged, clearly perplexed.

"What I've got to say ain't easy to spit out," Frank finally began. "There ain't no way you get to be my age without making some mistakes along the way."

"I'm sure that's true of all of us, Father," Jenny said.

"Your mother, Jenny, was the most beautiful woman I'd ever seen. Do you know that you have her eyes and the same smile? You've got the same color of hair, too. And it bounces on your shoulders when you walk, just like hers did." He paused, clearly struggling with what he wanted to say.

"I was nearing thirty when she died. My heart was broken that night, and I wanted to die with her. Everything we had worked and struggled for in the past ten years suddenly seemed worthless, because she wouldn't be here to share in it."

Rico recognized the man's pain, for he'd felt the same sense of loss when his mother died, the utter heartache and helplessness. And he began to suspect what Frank was leading up to: a long overdue apology to his daughter.

"I cursed God that night, and turned my back on the gift He had given me to replace that loss—an infant daughter. And through the years, I turned into a bitter, selfish man who thought of no one's interests but his own. Jenny, I'm so sorry, and so ashamed, of how I've treated you all these years. No apology can erase those years, but I'd like to try and make the next twenty years better."

"I understand, Father," Jenny said softly.

"Seeing the love you and Rico have for each other made me remember that your mother and I knew such a love. There's been so much bitterness and self-pity in my heart, I'd forgotten just how good it felt to love and be loved that way."

Jenny looked at Rico, tears glistening in her eyes as he smiled at her.

"So I want you both to know that I'm very happy for you. These last couple days have made me see the love and happiness that's been missing in this house, the love and happiness that your mother would have wanted to remain.

"I want it, too. I want us to be a family. And nothing would please me more than if the two of you would stay and we give it a try. I know it could happen."

Rico saw the hesitation in Jenny's eyes, and he understood why.

"Sir, if you'll permit me, I'll speak for Jenny because I know what's in her heart. She's sought your love her whole life, and she won't reject it now, because she's a loving person who puts those she loves ahead of her own interests. No one knows that more than I." He squeezed her hand and smiled at her.

"But I also know that even a reconciliation between you is not the only happiness she's looking for. Jenny doesn't take to a life of ranching; nor do I. As generous as your offer of signing half of the Double B over to me was, neither of us would ever feel the Double B was our home, that we were the head of the household.

"You spoke of how you and Jenny's mother worked together to build the Double B, and Jenny and I need to do the same thing with a house of our own. We have to know that sense of pride and self-respect, that bond of achievement because we accomplished it together."

"You could build your own house right here on the Double B. There's plenty of room," Frank pleaded.

"It's deeper than that, Frank. Try to understand that Jenny doesn't have a love for the desert and open range. She yearns for lush, verdant countryside abundant with blooming flowers and forests. Fraser Keep in California can offer her that."

At the despondent look on Frank's face, Rico said, "And if you ever leave the Double B, you'd be welcome to join us. Just as Paddy O'Grady and Nathan Collins have done with their daughters."

Frank nodded. "Reckon I understand. Can't say I would have a couple days ago. But I understand now that Jenny's choices are just as important as mine. I want her to be happy."

"Thank you, Father." Jenny went over to him and they embraced.

Relieved that Jenny and Frank had finally made peace with each other, Rico said lightly, "It looks like you're just going to have to hire yourself a housekeeper, Frank. Now if you'll excuse me, I'm going to take a nap."

Jenny decided to go outside to see what the rest of the women were up to. To her surprise, there was no one in sight. They all must have decided to get out of the sun and rest.

She decided to water her garden and enjoy these few moments of peace and quiet.

What would become of her garden when she left the Double B? Maybe the housekeeper would take the time to care for it. The garden was so much easier to water since Rico had laid piping to it. All she had to do was turn on a valve right there to fill a bucket.

When she finished, Jenny turned to go back to the house, just as a figure staggered into the garden. She screamed in horror and dropped the bucket.

Bloodied, shirtless, and barefoot, his pants tattered, Ben Slatter stood there with a knife in his hand.

He leaped forward and held it to her throat.

28

At the sound of her scream, the men came running out of the bunkhouse.

Rico jumped to the bedroom window and saw no sign of Jenny, so he quickly pulled on his boots and grabbed his gun belt on his way out of the room. He encountered Jed and Garth at the top of the stairway.

"You heard the scream?" Garth asked.

Rico nodded and rushed down the stairway, followed by the two men. Caroline and Rory trailed behind their husbands.

Clay, Colt, and Steve were already outside, their stares fixed on Jenny and the man using her as a shield as he held a knife to her throat. Rico drew up abruptly when he recognized who it was.

"My God, it's Ben Slatter," Jed murmured behind him.

"Let her go, Slatter," Rico ordered.

"You gotta help me. They'll kill me."

The desperation in the man's voice alarmed Rico even more. The way he was holding Jenny, even an unintentional slip of his hand could harm her.

He fought his rising panic.

"None of these men will hurt you if you let her go, Slatter."

The killer's voice was high and shrill with terror. "I'm talking about the Indians! They've been torturing me but I escaped. You've got to help me. I'll let her go if you promise to help me."

"Let her go and we'll talk about it then."

At the mention of an Indian scare, the men and women had already begun to move their children into the house.

"All right, it's just you and me now, Slatter," Rico said. "Let her go, and no one will harm you."

"Why should I believe you? You're the bastard who shot me."

"You have my word."

Tension heightened when the men reappeared, now wearing gun belts or carrying rifles they had retrieved from where they'd been locked up away from the children.

"You want me to take him down, Rico?" asked Colt, who was the sharpshooter among them.

Slatter tightened his hold on Jenny. "I'm warning you fellas, if any of you try anything, this bitch is gonna die."

"My cousin Colt can shoot both your eyes out

before you can move, Slatter. So release my wife, and we'll give you a horse to get out of here."

"You give me your word you won't turn me over to them Indians? They'll torture me to death."

"You mean like you and your gang did to my mother? And to all the other women you raped and killed?" Rico's voice rose in rage.

"Okay, okay! Just get me a horse," Slatter cried frantically.

"Jed, go saddle up Bucep for him."

"But he's your . . ." Then Jed realized what Rico had in mind.

He went into the barn and emerged shortly with the saddled horse. "Here's your horse, Slatter. Now get the hell out of here."

Slatter shoved Jenny aside and climbed on the horse. When he tried to prod it to a gallop, it wouldn't budge. Rico whistled and the horse reared up on its hind legs. The move threw Slatter from the saddle, and he fell to the ground just as a band of Indians appeared.

"Oh my God, there must be two dozen of them," Jed murmured.

Rico already held Jenny in his arms. "Are you all right?"

"I am now," she said with a brave smile.

"Let's get you inside." He picked her up and hurried back to the house.

Blubbering like a child, Slatter lay on the ground. "Help me! Don't let them get me!" he cried as Rico passed by.

"What about Slatter?" she asked.

"I know what I would like to do, but I made you a promise. I won't break my word to you."

Inside, the rest of the men were closing the shutters and locking the doors, while the women were hustling the children to the safety of a hidden root cellar Frank had converted to a storage room. Frank was hauling out more rifles and ammunition.

Slatter began pounding on the door, begging to be let in. All eyes swung to Rico.

Clay said, "I know the man's an evil sonofabitch, but you're not going to hand him over to those Indians, are you?"

"Whose lives are more important? Slatter's, or the women and children?"

"Those Indians aren't wearing paint. I don't think this is a raid," Frank said. "Why don't we try to parley with them? Find out what this is all about."

"I was thinking the same thing," Rico said. "Let's go."

"I'll go with you," Colt said. "Kit Carson and I once parleyed with—"

"Cochise himself," his brothers finished in unison.

"Gentlemen, this is no time for petty sibling jealousy," Colt replied, restraining a grin, and ducking from the ball Garth threw at him that one of the children had dropped during the haste of concealing them. His grin dissolved when Cassie joined them.

"I figure eight gun hands are better than seven," she said.

"Cassie, get back into that cellar with our children, where you belong," Colt declared.

"Colt Fraser, you know I'm a good shot. I'm staying."

"Will you two refrain from family squabbles until you're alone?" Jed said. "Cassie, honey, please listen to him, or before we know it my thirteen-year-old son will be up here to lend a hand. Which will then result in his mother coming up, and before we know it, we'll have a chain reaction and this room will be full of women and children."

"Very well," Cassie said. She turned to her husband. "You're going out there, aren't you" she said solemnly.

Colt pulled her into his arms. "There's no risk, honey. We're going out under a flag of truce. The Indians will honor that." He kissed her lightly. "Now get back down with our kids. They're probably scared and need their mother."

"And their mother is scared, and needs their father," she said.

"Oh, no," Rico groaned, when Jenny appeared. "Cassie, take her with you."

"I've been sent as an emissary to find out what's going on up here," she said. "And to inform you, Cassie, that none of us can quiet Peter. He wants his mother."

"What did I tell you?" Colt said.

"Very well, I'm leaving. Just be careful out there."

"What do you mean by 'out there'?" she asked Cassie.

Frank chose that ill-timed moment to come into the room carrying a stick with a white pillowcase tied to it. "Okay, let's go."

Shocked, Jenny swung her gaze to Rico.

"Colt and your father are going out with me. We're just going out to parley," he said, as if reading her mind.

"And if the Indians don't choose to *just parley*, but feel action speaks louder than words, what then, Rico? Three against twenty-four sounds like pretty poor odds."

"Jenny, I've parleyed with the Apaches since I came here," Frank said. "Whether they agree or not, they do honor a flag of truce."

"Well, that's comforting to hear," she said, bereft. "I thought I could escape from the misery of this despicable place, but I guess that was naïve of me, wasn't it, Dan'l?"

He cupped her cheeks between his hands and smiled down at her. "Tomorrow, Princess. One more tomorrow." He kissed her then turned away. "Let's go." Removing his gun belt, he handed it to Clay. "Take care of this until I get back."

The three weaponless men stepped outside with a white cloth tied to a stick. Slatter staggered past them before they closed the door.

"We don't want to hear another word from your whining mouth or we're kicking your ass out of here," Clay warned. Slatter nodded, and crawled over to huddle in a corner.

Jenny walked over to him. "Mr. Slatter, I've lived in fear of you from the moment you entered my life, but I prevented my husband from carrying out his intentions to track you down and kill you. But as God is my witness if he is harmed out there, I'll kill you myself."

Cassie came over and put her arm around Jenny's shoulders. "Come on, honey, let's go and join the others. Leave this miserable piece of scum in his corner."

"How do you bear this, Cassie?"

"I learned how to a long time ago—every morning Colt pinned on that tin star and kissed me good-bye."

Tension mounted in the house as, rifles in hand, the other men moved out onto the porch, watching anxiously as three of the Indians dismounted and stepped forward to meet the approaching men.

In less than five minutes, the parley ended and the trio returned to the porch to confer with the others.

Wordlessly, Rico passed them and entered the house, headed straight for Slatter. Rico's hands curled into fists as he glared at the cowering outlaw.

"You rotten, murdering sonofabitch! I'd like to strangle you with my bare hands."

Clay walked over and put a restraining hand on Rico's arm. "Cool down and tell us what was said."

"They want Slatter. That's what was said." His anger still unchecked, he turned away.

Clay looked at Colt. "What happened?"

"The Indians said Slatter's been hiding in a cave right across the river, and he raped and killed the chief's fifteen-year-old daughter. So either we turn Slatter over to them or they'll attack the ranch and burn it to the ground."

"That would be suicide. They must have seen how much gun power we have here," Clay said.

"Dammit, I don't want to kill any of them in order to save this bastard's life," Jed said. "But I don't think my conscience would let me hand him over to be tortured to death."

Colt nodded. "Yeah, we've got a serious decision to make, and only a few minutes to do so."

"Conscience be damned!" Garth shouted in an outburst. "We have our wives and children to consider. There's no telling what might happen to them."

"All right," Clay said. "We've always gone with majority rule, so we'll have to decide this by a vote. Frank, do you—"

Suddenly he hesitated and lifted his head. "Did you just hear what I did?"

"Sounded like a bugle," Rico said. "And there it is again."

As they watched, the Indians on the knoll disappeared, just as a cavalry troop rode up led by Colonel Hardy.

"Glad to see you in one piece, Rico," Hardy said, dismounting. "When we saw the horse, I was afraid the worst had happened."

"Your arrival couldn't have been more timely, sir."

"What happened here?" the colonel asked as the men and their families began to pile out of the house.

Rico gathered Jenny in his arms as Frank related the incidents that preceded the cavalry's arrival. Then they turned Slatter over to the army.

"Good riddance, Slatter," Rico said as they led the man away.

Slatter's mouth curled into an evil sneer. "You and I ain't through, Fraser. You'll be seein' me again."

"Yeah—at your hanging," Rico said.

"Don't be so sure of that. I escaped from them once. I can do it again."

He climbed up onto a horse, and suddenly six arrows thudded into his chest, toppling him to the ground. All eyes swung to the nearby knoll in time to see six Indians wheel their horses and ride away.

"Mount up," Don shouted to the patrol.

"Hold up there, Captain Masters," Colonel Hardy said as he stared down at the body on the ground. He took the cigar out of his mouth and flicked the ashes away. "I don't recall seeing any paint on those Indians, Captain Masters. Did you?"

"Not a single streak, sir."

"Then I'd be inclined to say they obviously were not on the warpath."

"That would be my opinion also, sir."

"So it would appear that Mr. Slatter, here, has been the victim of a hunting accident. Does it appear the same to you, Captain Masters?"

"Yes, sir. It does," Don replied.

"And it would be regrettable to start an Indian war over an innocent accident."

Hardy stuck the cigar back into his mouth, and took several puffs. "Very regrettable indeed, Captain Masters. Tie the body to a horse and mount your troopers."

"Yes, sir." Don saluted and started to walk away.

"Oh, and Captain," Hardy said, "you might consider cutting some of those arrows out of him first. Six of them might be *too* big of an accident."

The colonel mounted his horse when the troop prepared to depart, and stopped where Rico and Jenny stood in front of the house.

"Rico, there's a reward out for this man, dead or alive. Under the circumstances, I'd say it belongs to you."

"Not me, sir. Divide it among your men." He slipped an arm around Jenny's shoulders and gazed down into the face of the woman he loved, who was smiling up at him.

"I've already gotten my reward."

Epilogue

Pandemonium reigned when the carriages and wagons full of Frasers and luggage arrived in Redemption to reboard the two private railroad cars awaiting them.

The men saw to the transfer of the luggage. The women rounded up the children to make certain all were accounted for, and after many kisses, hugs, and thanks, all boarded the cars except for Jenny and Rico, who hung back for a final good-bye.

Jenny and Andrea hugged and kissed, and Jenny promised to contact them as soon as she and Rico returned from Virginia.

Then Jenny kissed and said good-bye to Maude, who was wearing a new emerald ring on the third finger of her left hand.

When Jenny turned to her father, he handed her a sealed envelope.

"What is this?" she asked.

"One of them eastern cattle companies made me

an offer on the Double B. I've decided to sell it and give you and Andrea each a third of the sale, as well as thirds on the rest of my wealth. It should keep you sitting pretty for a long time. That envelope has all the information and legal papers. You can read them on the train."

"You sold the Double B! But Father, that ranch was your life!"

"Naw, I'm tired of ranching, girl. And Maude's selling the Boots and Saddles to Bess and Ollie. We decided we're gonna take it easy from now on. Rico, this money is as much yours as it is Jenny's. Lord knows you earned it. You said you wanted to go into business with your cousins. Well, you can afford to buy in now."

"That's very generous of you, sir—but we can't take your money."

"The hell you can't! You listen to me, boy. I wouldn't have a daughter now if it weren't for you. And I'd most likely be dead, too. I owe you a damn sight more, than this, so don't put no price on it.

"I've learned that money don't do me no good if I'm just gonna sit around and count it. I'm lucky my daughter and sister are alive and found the men they have. You and Don are fine husbands, and will be good fathers. Better than I was, that's for sure."

"I think we are all fortunate in the women we fell in love with. Including you," Rico said with a wink at Maude.

"You're right. It took me a long time to realize that. These are new beginnings for all of us: Jenny and you,

Andrea and Don, and Maude and me." He clasped her hand. "Maudie and me still have enough years ahead of us to enjoy a life together, so as soon as my crew returns and I get them squared away, we're gonna take a trip around the world. Figure that will keep us busy for a couple years."

"The first thing you should do is marry her, Father," Jenny said.

"She's considering it. I swear, a man shouldn't have to cope with two strong-willed women in one lifetime."

Rico slipped an arm around Jenny's shoulders. "At least I'm taking one of them off your hands, sir."

Frank flashed a rare grin. "Just like I said, Rico— you're a good man. I know you'll take good care of my daughter and my grandchild, and there ain't no price on that kind of peace of mind, either. I hope when we get back, we'll be welcome to visit."

"It will be a pleasure, sir."

The cars had been connected to a small engine that would pull them back to the main line, and the conductor tooted the whistle to depart.

Frank shook hands with Rico, then hugged and kissed Jenny. "I love you, daughter. Reckon I always have, though I was too stupid to know it, let alone show it."

Jenny kissed him again. "I love you, too, Father."

The whistle sounded again, and Jenny and Rico boarded the train.

Later that evening, after the private cars had been hooked up to the Union Pacific train now carrying them eastward, Jenny stood on the observation deck in the circle of her husband's arms.

She sighed in contentment. "I can't think of a time when I've ever been happier."

"I feel the same way," Rico said. "It's as if every care we've had in the world has been resolved."

"And whatever new problems come along, at least we'll be sharing them. Did you tell Clay we want to buy into Fraser Keep?"

"Yes, and he's already figured out some more ways to expand."

"You know what I'd like to do with some of the money Father gave us?"

"I know the first thing *I'm* going to do with some of it," Rico said. "Plant you a garden."

Jenny smiled. "With all different kinds of cacti?"

"Whatever you'd like. California is very green."

"It sounds lovely. And your cousins are wonderful. I feel as if I've known them all my life."

"That's how I felt about them when I first met them, too. So, what is it that you'd like to do with some of the money?"

"I had a long talk with Rory and Caroline earlier, and we'd like to build a school. There are enough children in the family alone to fill a couple of classrooms, and the other women feel there would be plenty of children from the surrounding area to make the project worthwhile."

"I think it's a great idea," Rico said. "Hmmm, so I married a future schoolmarm. It sounds kind of intimidating, Mrs. Fraser. That should keep me on my toes."

She turned in his arms and slid hers around his neck. "Like it or not, Dan'l, you're stuck now. As I reminded my father, the mistakes of our past can't be changed, but we have all our tomorrows."

"And Princess . . . our tomorrows are forever," he murmured as he lowered his head and kissed her.

The Frasers: Clay

Clay opened his eyes slowly, but the glare of sunlight caused him to snap them shut again. For a long moment he lay motionless. His head felt as if a horse had kicked him, and he couldn't raise it from the pillow. He didn't want to. He just wanted to lie there and die.

The previous night's events began to bombard his mind like a cannon fusillade. Dinner. Garth leaving. Rebecca Elliott calling him into her room. Good Lord! How much had he drunk? He could never remember a headache like this before.

He finally gave it another try, and this time he managed to keep his eyes open. "First things first," he murmured.

Raising his head, Clay realized there was another sleeping figure in the bed.

"Garth, wake up. We've got a lot to do."

He reached over to shake his brother awake, and

his hand encountered a shoulder considerably smaller and softer than his brother's. He shot to his feet, then groaned and grasped his head. His brain felt as if it were slamming from one side of his head to the other. The room finally stopped spinning enough for him to focus on the sleeping figure.

Garth didn't have long golden hair that fanned out on a pillow; Garth didn't have a lovely face with delicate features, and wide, sensual lips that tempted a man to cover them with his own. No, Garth didn't have any of that—but Rebecca Elliott did. He must have had a great time last night, but he couldn't remember a single moment, dammit.

He began to gather up his clothes. As he pulled on his socks, Clay realized the ring he'd bought for Ellie was gone. He had carried it throughout the whole war, and after he'd learned she'd married, he'd figured it would be a source of money if they ran out when they came west. For now they'd gotten jobs with the wagon train, but there was no telling what would happen after they caught up with Lissy.

Where in hell was the ring? Clay shook out his boot, then got down on his knees and crawled painfully around on the floor in search of it. But no luck.

Could the Elliott woman have taken it? If she thought she'd get a diamond ring for her services, she had another think coming. He riffled through her purse, then her suitcase, but there was no sign of the ring. Where in hell could she have hidden it?

He strode over to the bed and shook Rebecca's arm.

"Where is it? Give it to me *now*."

"Wh-What are you looking for?" Rebecca asked, startled awake by the abrupt move.

"The ring. Where did you hide the ring?"

She blinked and held up her left hand. "You mean this ring?"

Shocked, he stared at the band sparkling on her finger.

"You gave it to me." She sat up and slid out of the bed.

"I don't remember giving you the ring—or even getting in bed with you. But whatever we did, it wasn't worth the cost of that ring. So take it off," Clay demanded.

She looked good in that sheer nightgown, with her hair all tousled like a vixen. Damn good—but still, not worth-a-diamond-ring good.

Rebecca picked up a piece of paper on the dresser and handed it to him. "Maybe you should read this." She gathered up her clothes as he began to read the document. "I'm going to take a bath. We'll discuss this when I'm through."

As she left the room, Clay sat down on the edge of the bed, holding his aching head in his hands. The marriage license slipped through his fingers and fell to the floor.

Married! How could he have been so drunk that he'd married her? He racked his brain, but the last thing he vaguely remembered was her starting to undress him. How did it get from that to a marriage license?

The Lawman
Said "I Do"

Colt put the paper aside and stared out the window. The countryside was as wild and startling as the people who rode it. Erosion and extinct lava flows had carved out shallow canyons and craters around the narrow, mountainous trails, with stretches of colorful mesas abundant with forests, white-blossomed yucca, and deep-colored wildflowers. Trout streams, rivers, and cold-water lakes were everywhere.

Restless, he leaned back and reached for the newspaper again. The coach jostled and rocked like a cradle in a windstorm, which soon made reading too much of a challenge. Braden must have had a cast-iron stomach to keep that liquor down, with all the rocking going on.

As the hours wore on, Jeff Braden drank himself into a stupor. His sister had closed her eyes, but Colt could tell she wasn't sleeping.

Suddenly the blast of a gunshot broke the silence, and the driver pulled up sharply on the reins, sending a cloud of dust into the air. The woman was thrown forward and ended up in Colt's lap.

"I'm sorry," she gasped, her blue eyes wide with embarrassment. She quickly shifted over to her seat.

"No problem, Miss Braden. The pleasure was all mine."

Jostled awake, Jeff slurred, "What's going on?"

Five men with drawn pistols rode up to the stagecoach.

"Everybody out," one of the men ordered. "Get those hands up and grab some air."

Colt wasn't about to argue with a man holding a drawn pistol. "Just stay calm, Miss Braden," he advised.

She looked at him with contempt. "Practice what you preach, greenhorn." She raised her arms and climbed out.

Colt followed, and Jeff Braden staggered after him.

Gus, the driver, was out of the box and stood with raised arms. Buck, who had been riding shotgun, was lying on the ground, wounded.

"Get them gunbelts off."

The order came from one of the men who was still mounted: he appeared to be the leader.

There were five outlaws, and Colt figured he could only take out two before they took him down. That would probably get the Bradens killed, too. The fact that the outlaws hadn't shot the driver probably meant they didn't intend to shoot the passengers, either. He unbuckled his gunbelt and dropped it to the ground.

A couple of the outlaws tossed down a box from the top of the stage. As one of the other bandits shot off the lock, the piercing blare of a bugle sounded nearby. The sound was music to Colt's ears.

"Dammit!" the leader of the gang snarled. "Hurry up before that damn cavalry gets here."

One of the men stuffed the box's contents into a black bag, and the men all mounted.

To Colt's horror, Jeff Braden snatched up his gun.

"No, don't try it," Colt yelled, but Braden shot at the riders as they started to ride away.

Colt shoved the woman out of the line of fire and dove for his own gun as the outlaws fired back. He felt the sting of a bullet on his left shoulder but got off a shot, and the man holding the black bag fell from the saddle just as the cavalry arrived and thundered past in pursuit.

Blood oozed profusely from the wound to Colt's shoulder. Feeling woozy, he slumped down and leaned back against a tree. He pulled the bandanna from his neck and awkwardly tried to make a compress with his good hand. Cassie hurried over to help him while Gus went to the aid of Buck.

"Here, let me do that." She folded the bandanna into a thick pad and pressed it against his shoulder. "I'm going to have to take your shirt off."

"Why, Miss Braden, I'm shocked. You must control yourself; we've barely just met."

"Do you men ever have anything but sex on your

mind?" she grumbled in disgust. Quickly but gently, she slipped the shirt off him.

"You did that quite speedily. Have you had a lot of practice removing a man's shirt?"

"Yes, I have." His mocking look changed to surprise, and she grinned. "In case you haven't noticed, I wear men's shirts."

"Oh, I've noticed," he said. "And so appealingly that I can barely keep my eyes off . . . ah . . . it."

"So I've noticed," she countered as she studied the wound.

"Will I live, nurse?"

"Not if you don't hush up," she said. "Or I'll finish the job for that guy who tried to kill you."

Cassie pressed the bandanna against the open wound again. "Now, hold the compress tightly against it to stem the bleeding."

"I'm quite aware of what to do. I've been shot before."

"By a cuckolded husband, or some no-good, low-down Yankee, Fraser?"

"The latter, Miss Braden. But for now, can we cease refighting the war and get this over with before I bleed to death?"

His Boots Under Her Bed

Garth awoke the next morning and lay drowsily assembling the events of the previous night in his mind. As his head began to clear, the pieces of the puzzle took shape: leaving the Grotto, the attack, and his rescue by the woman. He'd had his fair share of close calls during the war, but shanghaied! God forbid. He'd *never* had a desire to sail a boat, much less go to sea for an extended time. The sea was more to his brother Jed's liking. During the war Jed had sailed on a privateer, running much-needed supplies through the Yankee ships blockading the Southern ports.

Garth had made a few necessary trips on the James River on a paddleboat or barge, but only when he couldn't persuade one of his brothers to do it for him.

Horseback was his love. He and his horse Boots got along just fine.

He sat up in bed with an urgent call from Nature to relieve himself of all that whiskey he'd drunk last night. Seeing no chamber pot, he unlocked the door and scanned the hallway, then hurried to the door marked PRIVY.

"Good morning," Rory greeted when he returned to the room. She continued to plump up the pillow on the bed.

"Good morning."

Why couldn't he remember making love to her? They must have shared her bed last night, but he hated to think he'd slept through it and missed the best opportunity he could ever hope for.

She sure was a pretty sight. Her blond hair was swept up to the top of her head and her face was scrubbed clean of the makeup she wore in the Grotto. Her plain homespun blue gown with a white collar added brightness to those blue eyes of hers. He'd woken up in the bed of a pretty woman more times than he could remember, but this one had to be about the best-looking one yet. He sat down on the edge of the bed and put on his boots.

"How are you feeling this morning?" she asked.

"Name's Garth Fraser, ma'am," he said.

"Yes, I know. Mine's Rory O'Grady."

He smiled at her. "It's a pleasure to meet you, Miss O'Grady. I'm beholden to you."

"That was some beating you took last night."

"Guess I'll survive. The message just hasn't reached my head yet."

Garth picked up his gun belt and strapped it on. "What did they hit me with?"

"It looked like a blackjack. I think all that whiskey you drank last night might be contributing to your misery, too, Mr. Fraser."

He winked at her. "You may be right. Call me Garth, Miss Rory O'Grady."

She felt a tug at her heart at the way his tongue curled around her name, and she smiled at him. He was an easy man to like. A real charmer, all right.

"So why did you do it, Miss O'Grady? You could have been hurt."

"I saw them following you and figured they were up to no good."

"Do you know anything about them?"

"About as much as you do. The big one's Bates and the other one is Skull. That's what they called each other last night."

"Did you ever see them before?"

"They came into the Grotto one night last week. Didn't speak to anyone. After a couple of drinks, they got up and left. Then they showed up again last night. Same thing. They just sat, not saying anything to anyone. When you came downstairs, they got up and followed you out. Rumor has it they shanghai strangers traveling alone."

"Guess it's more than a rumor," Garth said. "Why hasn't the sheriff arrested them?"

"The sheriff!" Rory scoffed. "He's as crooked as

they are, and probably in cahoots with them. I'm thinking Mo might be, too. But I don't think any of the girls are, because they're the ones who told me about Bates and Skull."

"Well, you saved me from a long sea trip, Miss Rory. I don't know when I can repay you, but you can be sure I will someday when I hit it big."

"Don't tell me you're a gambler, too. You men are all alike, always betting on winning that big pot."

"I'm not talking about gambling, Miss Rory. There's more than one kind of way to get rich."

She laughed. "Indeed. The *big* gold mine that's just awaiting for you to pick up the nuggets."

Garth chuckled. "Could be."

She gaped in shock. "It *is* that, isn't it? Holy sweet Mary! I sure had you pegged wrong, Garth Fraser. Figured you had something better under your hat than just a head good for smashing blackjacks over."

"Ah . . . about last night. Right now I only have a few dollars, but you're welcome to them."

" 'Tis a kindly offer, but why would I take your money?"

He glanced toward the bed. "You mean we didn't . . ."

She felt the heated flush of rising anger. "We certainly *didn't!*"

His smile of relief was just as irritating. "Then let me at least pay for the broken bottle of whiskey."

"You can be certain I'm doing just fine without your charity, Mr. Fraser."

He threw back his head in laughter. "You know,

Miss Rory O'Grady, I find it delightful how you slip in and out of a brogue whenever that pert little nose of yours gets out of joint."

Rory blushed and took a deep breath to regain control. She'd worked too hard to rid herself of the brogue to get careless now. Glancing up at him, she tried to ignore the effect his engaging grin had on her.

"The whiskey was put to a better use than it would have been here," she said. "Now if I were you, Mr. Fraser, I'd get out of town first thing this morning in case those two scoundrels are still around."

One Night with a Sweet-talking Man

The train whistle was blowing its final departure warning by the time Jed and Nathan arrived at the station. Jed could see that Caroline's displeasure increased when she saw that he accompanied her father.

"It's about time you got here, Father."

"I'm not a doddering old man, so mind your tongue, daughter."

"I apologize for delaying him, Miss Caroline," Jed interjected.

Garrett's wide grin at his beloved grandfather eased some of the tension. "Mama was worried that you'd miss the train, Granddad. You coming with us, Mr. Fraser?"

"Yes, then I'm continuing a bit further than you."

"Get on the train, Garrett," Caroline said.

Nathan patted the boy on the head and took his hand. "Come on, son."

They climbed on and just as Caroline followed up the steps, the train lurched forward and started to roll. She lost her balance and fell backward, but Jed caught her from the step below, preventing her from falling off as the train gained momentum. Their gazes locked for several seconds.

"Thank you, Mr. Fraser," she said breathlessly.

He'd always been powerless to resist a pair of beautiful eyes. "The pleasure was all mine. Do you know that your eyes deepen to purple when you're alarmed, Miss Caroline?"

She smiled slightly. "And what color would you say they are now, Mr. Fraser?"

"I'd say an exquisite azure, like the sky in summer."

Caroline Collins arched a curved brow. "Then if your theory holds true, Mr. Fraser, I guess that would indicate I'm no longer alarmed." She turned around and walked away.

His appreciative gaze followed the sway of her hips as she moved down the rocking train car. Caroline Collins intrigued him. She was as complicated as they come, and a hell of a beautiful female.

Garrett had sat by the window of one of the double seats facing each other. Nathan had taken the opposite seat, and Caroline sat next to her son.

"If you prefer not to ride backward I'll be glad to sit there, Miss Caroline," Jed said.

"Thank you, but that won't be necessary, Mr. Fraser."

"I think it's fun to ride backward," Garrett declared. "Don't you, Mr. Fraser?"

"Well, Garrett, I guess that if I had my druthers, I prefer seeing where I'm going, rather than where I've been."

"Hmmm." Garrett reflected for a long moment. "Mama, is that why you always tell me I never know if I'm coming or going?"

They all broke into laughter, and Caroline slipped her arm around his shoulders. "I wasn't just referring to train rides, sweetheart."

She leaned back and opened the book on her lap as Garrett returned to gazing out the window.

"What are you reading, Miss Caroline?" Jed asked.

"*A Tale of Two Cities* by Charles Dickens," she said.

"Are you enjoying it?"

"Very much so, Mr. Fraser. Have you read it?"

"Yes, several years ago. Do you enjoy reading, Miss Caroline?"

"I always have. Unfortunately, I have less opportunity to do so than I'd like." She shifted her gaze back to the page.

"Is your family expecting you, Jed?" Nathan asked.

"No. I thought I would surprise them."

"In a state this size, it's quite a coincidence we've settled so near to one another. Our home's in the Napa Valley, too."

"My brother Clay had hopes of becoming a vintner and was told the Napa Valley is a good region for growing grapes," Jed said.

"And has he succeeded?"

"Yes, very much so."

"I'm glad to hear it."

Soon the motion and the rhythmic clickety-clack of the rails had an effect on all of them. Caroline continued to read, Nathan slipped into deep thought, and Garrett slumped drowsily in his seat.

Jed was now free to ponder the riddle of Caroline. Everything about her was intriguing. It seemed incredible that a woman with her beauty wasn't married by now, especially with the shortage of women in the West. Even more, why hadn't she married the man who fathered her child?

As if sensing his gaze, she raised her eyes and for a moment they stared openly at each other. The expression in her gorgeous blue eyes remained enigmatic before she lowered them back to the page.

She made no attempt to disguise her dislike of him, but the reason for it was a mystery to him. Back in Virginia he had barely noticed the girl; he couldn't even remember ever speaking to her. He vaguely recalled that she was shy and rather bookish. He couldn't recollect seeing her at any cotillions or other social events.

"You said your family is not expecting you, Jed?"

Nathan's question jolted him out of his reverie. "Yes, sir."

"I understand that you're eager to see your family, but I wonder if you would consider joining us for dinner and spending the night at our home?"

"That's very thoughtful of you, sir, but I'd hate to inconvenience you."

"Not at all. In fact, there is a matter of deep concern that I wish to discuss with you, but I can't do it on this train."

"I understand. If it's that important to you, I would be delighted, sir."

He glanced at Caroline. Her book had fallen into her lap and she looked horrified.